Why couldn't he see her as a woman?

"I'm fine," she pointed out briskly. "I'm an adult. You don't have to feel responsible for me."

"I know I don't have to, but I do. Diane loved you," he said, staring at her intently. "She'd have done away with anyone who hurt you, and now I've done my best to hurt you. She'd want...she'd want me to take care of you." He drew a deep shuddering breath, his eyes glittering, his entire body taut with stress.

"Sarah, will you marry me?"

Dear Reader,

Linda Howard's work has long been an inspiration to readers, and her books have glittered like priceless diamonds in both the Silhouette **Special Edition** and Silhouette Intimate Moments lines. So it is with great pleasure that we welcome back *Sarah's Child*—a romance that represents the most treasured qualities of Silhouette **Special Edition,** a story that only gets deeper and richer with the years.

In Silhouette **Special Edition** novels, we're dedicated to bringing you the romance that you dream about— the type of stories that delight as well as bring a tear to the eye. And that's what Silhouette **Special Edition** novels are all about—special books by special authors for special readers!

The "Fashion A Whole New You" program has enabled us to present to you classic stories by authors whose work you've enjoyed throughout the years. Don't miss *Darling Enemy*—Diana Palmer's very first Silhouette Romance novel!—or the wonderful Annette Broadrick's *Bachelor Father,* an early Silhouette Desire. The Silhouette Intimate Moments winning contribution, *A Very Special Favor* by Kristin James, rounds out this special event.

I hope you enjoy this book, and all the others to come!

Sincerely,

Tara Gavin
Senior Editor

Linda Howard

SARAH'S CHILD

Silhouette Special Edition®

Published by Silhouette Books New York

America's Publisher of Contemporary Romance

SILHOUETTE BOOKS
300 E. 42nd St., New York, N.Y. 10017

SARAH'S CHILD © 1985 by Linda Howington
Originally published as a Silhouette Special Edition.

FASHION A WHOLE NEW YOU edition
published in September 1991.

ISBN: 0-373-15162-4

Printed in U.S.A.

Books by Linda Howard

LINDA HOWARD

says that, whether she's reading them or writing them, books have always been the ruling passion in her life. She cut her teeth on Margaret Mitchell and from then on continued to read widely and eagerly. In recent years her interest settled on romance fiction, since she candidly admits that she's "easily bored by murder, mayhem and politics." And after twenty-one years of penning stories for her own enjoyment, she finally worked up the courage to submit her own novel—and met with success! Happily, this Alabama author has been publishing steadily ever since.

A veteran of writers' conventions, autograph sessions and award ceremonies, she lives with her husband in Alabama. Her current writing project for Silhouette Intimate Moments is a sequel to IM #281, *Mackenzie's Mountain*. It's all about Joe "Breed" Mackenzie, and it should reach the stores sometime in 1992.

Silhouette Romance
DARLING ENEMY by Diana Palmer
Teddi Whitehall knew that rancher King Devereaux
was convinced she was nothing but a glamorous
playgirl. She also knew the truth wasn't going to
change his mind. So why did she feel so alive when
he was near?

Silhouette Desire
BACHELOR FATHER by Annette Broadrick
Tony Antonelli had broken Susan McCormick's
heart ten years ago, and every day their son was a
constant reminder of their shared night of passion.
Now Tony was back. Could two hearts ever mend
and beat as one again?

Silhouette Special Edition
SARAH'S CHILD by Linda Howard
Sarah had loved Rome Matthews for so long that
becoming his wife had made her world almost
complete. Only having his baby could have made her
happier. But Rome couldn't risk losing another
child—though the decision might cost him the
woman he loved....

Silhouette Intimate Moments
A VERY SPECIAL FAVOR by Kristin James
Adam Marshall's good deed for the month was to
initiate Emily, his shy secretary, into womanhood.
But when the wallflower became a perfect rose, his
cool detachment fled, and he began to lose his heart.

Chapter One

It was the end of a long week, and Sarah knew that she should go home, but just the thought of facing the broiling late August heat was enough to keep her sitting in her chair with the air-conditioning humming pleasantly overhead. She wasn't working; she'd swiveled the chair around and spent the last fifteen minutes simply staring out the window, too relaxed to really care that it was getting late. The sun had dipped low enough that the Dallas array of dazzling skyscrapers of glass and steel was outlined against a bronzed sky, which meant she'd missed the six o'clock news yet again. It was Friday evening; her boss, Mr. Graham, had left over an hour before. There was no reason why she shouldn't join the mass exodus on the streets below, yet she felt reluctant to go home. She'd taken such pains with her condominium; made it as homey and comfortable as she could, but lately the emptiness of it had been haunting her. She could fill it with music, rent any movie and watch it on the VCR, lose herself in reading and pretend that she was in any other country in the world, yet she would still be alone. Lately it was becoming a state of loneliness, rather than one of solitude.

Perhaps it was the weather, she thought tiredly. The summer had been hot and humid, wearing everyone down, but she knew inside that it wasn't the heat that was bothering her. It was the inevitable sensation of time slipping away, as summer died once more and became another autumn. It seemed that even in the fierce heat she could feel the chill of winter in her bones. It was more than the passing of another season: it was her own youth slipping away, inexorably draining from her grasp. The years had passed, and she'd devoted herself to her work, because there was nothing else, and now she realized that all the things she'd wanted had passed her by. She hadn't wanted riches, or material things. She'd wanted love, a husband and children, a home filled with laughter and security, the things she'd never had as a child. She'd stopped even dreaming about them, she realized, and that was the saddest thing of all. But then she'd never really had a chance: she'd fallen in love with the one man she couldn't have, and it appeared that she was one of those women who loved only once in their lifetime.

Her phone gave a muted ring, and a slight frown of puzzlement touched her brow as she reached for the receiver. Who would be calling the office at this hour?

"Sarah Harper," she said briskly.

"Sarah, this is Rome," a deep voice said by way of identification.

Her heart gave a jump and hung in her throat. She didn't need to hear his name to know who was on the other end of the line. She knew his voice as well as she knew her own, and the clipped accent that hadn't softened despite years in the south would always give him away. But she swallowed the lump, straightened her spine, and pretended this was just another business call. "Yes, Mr. Matthews?"

He made an impatient sound. "Damn it, don't call me that! It's all right in the office, but this...this isn't business."

Sarah swallowed again, but she couldn't say anything. Had she conjured him up? Had thinking about him produced this call? After all, it had been months since he'd said anything to her other than a polite "good morning" whenever he came into the office to talk to Mr. Graham.

"Sarah?" He was really impatient now, and his rising ire was revealed in the way he barked her name.

"Yes. I'm still here," she managed.

"I'm selling the house," he said abruptly. "I'm boxing up Diane's things...and the boys'.... I'm going to give them all to the Salvation Army. But I found a box of things that Diane had kept from high school, stuff that the two of you did together, pictures, and I thought you'd like to go through it. If you want any of it, you can have it. If not..."

He didn't finish the sentence, but she knew. If not, then he'd burn it. He'd take all of those memories and destroy them. She winced inside at the thought of going through the box and reliving the years she'd grown up with Diane, because the loss still hurt, but neither could she let him burn Diane's mementos. Perhaps she couldn't go through the box yet, but she'd keep it, and in later years she'd be able to take the things out and remember without too much pain, with only sadness and nostalgia.

"Yes," she said hoarsely, forcing the word out. "Yes, I want it."

"I'm about to leave now, to go to the house and finish packing. You can get the box anytime tonight."

"I'll be there. Thank you," she whispered, and he hung up, leaving her with the phone still pressed to her ear and the dial tone buzzing.

Her hand was shaking as she replaced the receiver, and suddenly she noticed that she was no longer sitting. At some point during the conversation, tension had propelled her to her feet. Quickly she leaned down to get her purse from the lower drawer of the desk, then locked the desk and turned out the lights, locking the door behind her as she left.

It wasn't only her hand that was shaking; her entire body was quivering. Talking with Rome always did that to her. Even after years of training herself not to think about him, of not allowing herself to even dream about him, just hearing his voice had the power to reduce her to jelly. Working for the same company was bad enough; she'd even transferred to a different department so she wouldn't see him as often, but that had eventually backfired on her: He'd been promoted steadily through the ranks and was now one of the corporate vice presidents. Her position as secretary to the senior vice president threw her constantly into contact with him; the only salvation she'd had was that his attitude toward her was strictly business, and she'd forced herself to treat him in the same manner.

What else could she do, when she'd been foolish enough to fall in love with her best friend's husband?

Even though the shadowed multilevel parking deck was at least ten degrees cooler than the street, the heat still slapped her in the face as she walked quickly to her car, a late model, low-slung Datsun 280-ZX. The car was, she feared, an example of her growing tendency to collect *things* to replace the emptiness at home. All her life she'd sworn to avoid the cold hollowness of her parents' home, yet as she grew older she tried harder and harder to fill the empty places with *things*. The car was gorgeous, and it got her where she was going faster than she needed to be there; she enjoyed driving it, she liked it, but she hadn't needed it. The car she'd traded in had been a good car, and it hadn't been that old.

Rather than drive straight to the house where Rome and Diane had lived, in one of the posher Dallas neighborhoods, Sarah deliberately drove to a restaurant and wiled away an hour and a half, picking at her seafood while all of her instincts screamed at her to hurry, to see Rome as soon as she could. But some part of her was reluctant to enter the house where he'd lived with Diane, where she and Diane had laughed and played with the babies. She hadn't been inside it in two years...yes, it had been almost two years since the accident.

When her watch told her it was eight o'clock, she paid her tab and drove slowly, carefully, to the house. Her heart was pounding again, and she felt a little sick to her stomach. Her palms were damp; she clutched the steering wheel more securely to make certain it didn't slip in her grip.

How did she look? She hadn't checked her appearance. Her lipstick had worn off surely, but she didn't bother to replace it. With one hand she felt to see if any strands of hair had escaped from the severe twist she wore while working, but it still felt reasonably tidy, so she sighed and forgot about it.

Rome's dark blue Mercedes was in the driveway, so she parked behind it and got out, walking slowly up the sidewalk to mount the five shallow steps and press her finger to the doorbell. The grass had been kept mowed, she noticed, and the shrubbery was trimmed. The house didn't look empty, but it was. Heartbreakingly empty.

After a moment, Rome opened the door and stepped aside to let her enter. After a brief glance at him, Sarah felt as if she'd been punched in the stomach. She hadn't expected him to be wearing a three-piece business suit, but somehow she'd forgotten how powerfully he was built, how impossibly virile he looked in tight jeans. He wore track shoes, no socks, an old pair of jeans, and a white T-shirt that clung to his muscled torso, and he looked absolutely beautiful to her.

He glanced down at her, taking in the trim business suit she still wore. "You haven't been home yet?" he asked.

"No. I stopped to eat dinner, but I haven't gone home." It was uncomfortably warm in the house; he'd opened some windows but hadn't turned on the central air-conditioning. She pulled off her light linen jacket and started to hang it in the closet as she'd always done when visiting Diane, then caught herself and instead simply tossed it over the stairway railing. As he led the way upstairs she loosened the collar of her white tailored silk blouse and rolled the sleeves up to her elbows.

Rome paused before the doorway to the bedroom he'd shared with Diane, and his dark eyes were shadowed, his mouth grim, as he looked at the closed door. "It's in there," he said briefly. "In the closet. I'll be in the boys' bedroom packing their things. Take your time looking through the stuff."

Sarah waited until he'd gone into the other bedroom before she slowly opened the door and entered Diane's bedroom, turning on the light and standing for a moment looking around. Everything had been left as it had been the day of the accident. The book she'd been reading was still lying on the bedside table. Her nightgown was tossed across the foot of the bed. Rome hadn't spent a night here since Diane had died.

Sarah pulled the box out of the closet and sat down on the floor to go through the contents, tears blurring her vision as she picked up the first photograph of her and Diane together. God, if it hurt her this much to lose a friend, how did Rome feel? He'd lost his wife and two sons.

She and Diane had always been best friends, all the way through school. Diane had been a human dynamo, laughing and chattering, propelling the quieter Sarah along the way. Her blue eyes had sparkled, her honey-brown curls had bounced, and she'd infected everyone who came into contact with her with the enthusiasm for life that brightened every day for her. Oh, the plans she'd made! She was never going to marry. She was going to be a famous fashion designer and travel all over the world. Sarah's dreams had been only of a real family, one with love in it. Somewhere along the way their plans had been switched. Diane had fallen in love with a tall dark-eyed young rising executive who worked for the same company where Sarah had gotten a job, and from that moment on Sarah had known that her dream would never come true. Diane considered a glamorous career as a fashion designer well lost when she could have Rome Matthews, when she could give birth to his two adoring and adorable sons and bask in his love. Sarah quietly devoted herself to the job that was her only solace.

She'd tried not to love Rome, but she'd discovered that emotions weren't easily controlled. If she hadn't loved him before he met Diane, she might have kept her feelings from growing into anything serious, but she'd been his from the first. From the moment she'd met him, she'd known, deep inside that he would be more to her than just a colleague. It was his eyes, she thought; they were so deep and dark, eyes with a burning inner intensity. Roman Caldwell Matthews was no lightweight. He had drive and ambition, coupled with a lightning intelligence that had carried him through the ranks of middle management like a meteor. Oh, he wasn't handsome: his face had a rough-hewn, slightly battered look to it; his cheekbones were too high and sharp; his blade of a nose had been broken once; and his jaw was as solid as a piece of granite. He was a man who would reach out and grasp life, and shape it the way he wanted. He'd been friendly enough to her, but Sarah knew she was too pale and quiet to interest a man with his forceful personality.

Still, the summer when she'd invited Diane to the company picnic she hadn't expected him to take one look at Diane's vibrant beauty and claim her for his own. But it had happened, and Diane and Rome had married five months later. Three months after their first anniversary Justin had been born, and two years later Shane. Two beautiful little boys, with their mother's looks and their father's determination, and Sarah had loved them because they were Rome's children.

She'd remained as close to Diane as before, but she'd always been careful not to infringe on the time Rome spent with his family. He traveled a great deal, and Sarah limited her visits to the days he was out of town. She couldn't say just why, but she sensed that Rome disapproved of her close friendship with Diane, though to her knowledge he'd never said anything. Perhaps it was that he simply didn't like her, though she'd never done anything to earn it. She'd tried to stay out of his way, and she'd never, never told Diane anything about how she felt. There was no point in it; it would only have distressed Diane, and hurt their friendship.

Sarah had dated, and still did, but only casually. It wouldn't have been fair to some other man to encourage a closer relationship when there was no way she'd be able to return any love offered to her. Everyone who asked, teasingly, when she was going to marry, had received the same reply: She loved her work too much to wash dirty socks for some man. It had been a lighthearted, stock answer, and it had served the purpose of protecting her vulnerable heart, but it had been a lie. She'd never wanted a career, but it was all she had left, so she'd given it her best. The charade had fooled everyone but herself.

Rome had been devoted to Diane and the boys. The freeway accident, almost two years before, had almost destroyed him. It *had* destroyed the laughter in

him, the fierce-burning fire in his eyes. Diane had been
driving the boys to school, and a drunk weaving his
way home in the early-morning traffic had crossed out
of his lane and hit them head-on. If he hadn't been
killed immediately, Sarah felt that Rome would have
choked the man with his bare hands, he'd been so insane with grief when he'd been told. Justin had been
killed on impact; Shane had died two days later. Two
weeks after the accident Diane had died without ever
regaining consciousness or knowing that her sons were
gone. During those two weeks, Sarah had spent as
much time as she could at her friend's bedside, holding the limp hand and trying to will her to live, but
fearing that Diane wouldn't want to wake up from her
death sleep. Rome had been a permanent fixture on
the other side of the bed, holding the hand that bore
his ring, his face gray and drawn, locked inside himself. Diane had been his only hope, his only remain-
ing bit of sunshine, and her frail light had flickered
and gone out, leaving him in darkness.

Gently Sarah went through all of the snapshots,
seeing herself and Diane in various stages of their
childhood and adolescence, mixed in with photographs of the boys as babies, toddlers, and rowdy little boys. Rome was in some of those pictures, romping
with the boys, washing the car, mowing the grass,
doing all of the normal things that fathers and husbands do. Sarah lingered over a picture of him lying on
his back in the grass, wearing only a brief pair of
denim shorts, holding Justin dangling over his head.
His strong brown arms were steady as he held the toddler up, and it was evident that the child felt secure in
his father's hands. Justin had been shrieking with
laughter. On the grass beside them, Shane had been

trying to climb to his baby feet, and one tiny plump hand had clutched the hair on Rome's chest in an effort to pull himself up.

"See anything you want?"

The question startled her, and she jumped, dropping the picture back into the box. She realized that he was asking in general and hadn't noticed her staring at his picture with sick longing, but her shadowy green eyes were wide and wary as she scrambled to her feet, smoothing her skirt.

"Yes. I'll take the box. There are a lot of pictures in here of Diane and the boys...if you don't—"

"Take them," he said curtly, walking into the room. He stopped in the middle of the floor and stood looking around, as if he'd never been there before, but his eyes were bleak, and his mouth looked as if it would never smile again. He did sometimes smile, Sarah realized, after a fashion, but it was merely a polite movement of his lips rather than an expression of humor. Certainly the smile never reached his eyes and lit the dark fires that had once smoldered there.

He jammed his hands into his pockets, as if he had to do something to keep them from knotting into fists. His shoulders were tense, braced against the impact of memories that this room must bring to him. He'd slept in that bed with Diane, made love to her, wrestled with the boys on early Saturday mornings when they came running in to wake him up. Quickly Sarah leaned down to pick up the box, turning her gaze away from him to keep from witnessing his anguish.

The anguish was as much in her as it was in him. She loved him enough to wish Diane back for him, so he could smile again. He would always be Diane's anyway, because her death hadn't stopped his love for her. He was still grieving for her, still hurting from her loss.

"I'm finished in the boys' room," he said remotely. "Everything's packed up. I...I—" Suddenly his voice broke, and Sarah's heart broke with it. He drew a ragged breath, his chest heaving with the effort it took to control himself.

Suddenly his face twisted with rage, and he whirled to slam his fist against the dresser, rattling the bottles of perfume and cosmetics that still littered the top. "Dammit, it was such a waste!" He cursed violently, then groped for the dresser as his body sagged under the weight of his anger and grief. He'd never known defeat until his family had been taken from him. Death was final, permanent, striking without warning and destroying the life he'd built for himself.

"In some ways, losing the boys was worse than losing Diane," he said in a muffled tone. "They were so young; they hadn't had a chance at life. They never knew what it was like to play high-school sports, or go to college, or kiss their girlfriends for the first time. They hadn't made love, or seen their own children born. They never had a chance."

Sarah clutched the box to her breast. "Justin kissed his girlfriend," she said shakily, a tiny smile breaking through in spite of the pain. "Her name was Jennifer. There were four Jennifers in his class, but he told me very firmly that his Jennifer was the 'pretty one.' He kissed her right on the mouth and asked her to marry him, but she got scared and ran away. He told me that he 'spected she just wasn't ready for marriage yet, but he'd keep his eye on her. That's practically verbatim," she added, laughing a little. She'd imitated Justin's way of talking, drawling and tough for a seven-year-old, and Rome's mouth twitched. He glanced at her, and suddenly his dark brown-black eyes were dancing with golden lights. He made a choking sound, then he was laughing, throwing back his dark head on the deep healthy sound.

"My God, he was a tough little nut," he chuckled. "Poor Jennifer wouldn't have had a chance."

Neither had poor Sarah. Justin had received all of his tough charm straight from his father.

Her heart jolted at his laugh, the first genuine laugh she'd heard from him in two years. He hadn't talked about the boys, or Diane, since the accident. He'd bottled up all of his memories with the pain, as if he had to keep them locked away in order for him to function on even a basic level.

She shifted, still clutching the box. "These pictures...if you ever want any of them, they're yours."

"Thanks." He shrugged his wide shoulders, as if trying to ease the tension in them. "This is rougher than I thought it would be. It's still...almost more than I can handle."

Sarah ducked her head, unable to answer or look at him without crying. This was so traumatic for her that she was beginning to doubt her ability to get through it, but she couldn't do anything to make it any harder for him. If he started to cry, she'd probably die on the spot. Part of the agony she'd felt after the accident had been for Rome, knowing how he was suffering. She hadn't even been able to put her arms around him at any of the services; he'd held himself stiffly erect, his face utterly white and withdrawn, sealed off by his grief from everyone around him. Rome had been alone, unable to share his pain.

When she looked up again, Rome was sitting on the bed where he'd slept with Diane, her silk nightgown in his strong hands. His head was bent, and he pulled the silk through his fingers over and over again.

"Rome—" She stopped, not knowing what to say to him. What *could* she say?

"I still wake up at night and reach for her," he said in a rough tone. "This is the nightgown she wore the last night we spent together, the last time I made love to her. I can't get used to her not being there. It's an empty pain that won't go away, no matter how many women I take."

Sarah gasped, her Nile-green eyes widening and becoming shuttered; he glanced up, his eyes bitter. "Does that shock you, Sarah? That I've had other women? I was faithful to Diane for eight years, never even kissing another woman, though sometimes when I was on a trip I'd lie awake all night, wanting a woman so much that I hurt all over. But no one else would do; it had to be her. So I'd wait until I came home; then we wouldn't sleep that entire night."

Sarah's throat tightened, and she retreated from him as an unexpectedly savage pain slashed at her. She didn't want to hear this. She'd always tried not to think of him in bed with Diane, trying not to envy her friend, eternally striving to keep jealousy from ruining their friendship. She'd succeeded while Diane was alive, but now Rome's words were tearing at her, forcing images into her head that she didn't want to see. She turned away from him, her face averted as she tried to avoid hearing his words. The bed squeaked as he left it; then suddenly his hands were gripping her arms with a hard grip, jerking her around to face him. His face was white and full of rage, a muscle jerking in his temple. "What's wrong, Saint Sarah? Are you so buried in that mental convent of yours that you can't stand hearing about normal people who enjoy the sinful activity of sex?" He was snarling at her, and Sarah was frozen in his grasp, stunned by the anger that had erupted in him. Dimly she realized that he wasn't angry at her as much as he was angry at the fate that had taken his wife from him and left him with only emptiness in his arms, but still, Rome in a temper was a man to fear.

He shook her, as if he wanted to punish her for being a warm, living woman, when Diane was forever gone. "I still can't sleep with another woman," he rasped in a voice harsh with pain. "I don't mean sex. I had sex with another woman only two months after Diane died, and I hated myself for it the next morning...hell, as soon as it was finished! It felt as if I'd been unfaithful to her, and I felt so guilty that I went back to my hotel room and threw up. I didn't even particularly enjoy it, but I did it again the next night, so I'd feel guilty again. I tried to make myself suffer, to make myself pay for being alive when she was dead. There've been a lot of women since then; every time I...need sex, there's always a woman who's willing to lie down with me. I need sex and I've been taking it, but I can't sleep with them. When it's over, I have to leave. In my mind, I'm still Diane's husband, and I can't sleep with any woman but her."

Sarah felt suffocated, suspended in time by his hard grip on her arms, his hot breath on her cheek, and his enraged face so close to hers. She wrenched away from him, her hands tightened into fists. She couldn't hear about his intimacies with another woman, with any number of other women. She gave Rome a wild, desperate look, but he didn't notice. With a groan, he sank to his knees on the floor, burying his face in his hands, and his shoulders shook.

There wasn't enough oxygen in the room; she gasped at it, feeling her restricted lungs strain in an effort to drag enough air into her body. Her senses whirled, as if she might faint, but she didn't. Somehow she found herself on her knees beside him, and she put her arms around him as she had longed to do so many times. Instantly his strong arms locked around her, holding her in a grip that threatened to crack all of her ribs. He buried his face against her soft breasts and cried, harsh sobs that tore out of his body in great shudders. Sarah held him, stroking his hair, letting him cry; he was entitled to it, and he'd gone for too long without letting someone else share in his grief. Her own face was wet, but she didn't notice the hot tears that blurred her vision. All that mattered was him, and she rocked him gently back and forth, with no words, but only her presence to shield him from the bitter loneliness that had turned his heart into a winter land of desolation.

Gradually he quieted, and he moved closer to her, his hands moving up her back. She felt the deep breaths he was taking as they expanded his chest, then the warmth of the expelled air on her breasts. Her nipples tightened in automatic, shameful response, hidden beneath her silk shirt and lacy bra, and she clenched her fingers in his hair in a movement that was beyond her control.

He lifted his head, his eyes still damp, and the darkness of his pupils had become so total that there was no brown in them at all. He stared at her, then reached out and tenderly wiped the moisture from her cheeks with his thumb. "Sarah," he said on a whispering sigh, and touched his mouth to hers.

She went still, all breath suspended in her body, as thousands of her prayers were answered in that light touch of his lips. Her hands moved to his shoulders, the nails digging into the layers of muscle that corded his frame. It was just a simple kiss of thanks, but the bottom dropped out of her stomach and the blood rushed from her head, so intense was the pleasure that assailed her. She sank against him, her soft body melding to his from shoulder to thigh, as they knelt there on the floor. Automatically he supported her, his hard arms around the female curves of her body, holding her to him.

He drew back and looked at her again, and now the expression in his eyes had sharpened to a look of glittering awareness. He was too much of a man not to recognize her feminine response. His gaze dropped to her tremulous, generous mouth, her lips softly parted, and instinct drove him to dip his head to drink from her sweetness again. This time there was nothing light about the touch of his lips; it was a kiss that was man-hungry and fiercely demanding. She gasped, and he thrust his tongue into her mouth with masculine need and command, an intimate kiss that almost shattered her with delight, and she whimpered softly into his mouth. His arms cradled her to him, his body controlling hers as he took her down to the floor.

Her senses reeled; it was so like the few forbidden dreams she'd had that she forgot where they were, forgot everything but the man who leaned over her, his mouth hot and tasting of passion. Her digging nails telegraphed her response to him, her body warming and arching to his, seeking the intoxicating heaviness of his weight.

There was no sense of time or location, nothing but the spiraling physical need that had flamed between them, unexpected and out of control. She felt his hands on her body, touching her breasts, dipping down beneath her skirt to rub her thighs and stroke intimately between them, wringing a wordless cry of need from her lips. No word of protest surfaced in her mind. She let him do as he wanted, mindless of everything but the delight his knowledgeable hands were bringing to her. He knew women, and his expertise made her wild. She offered her slim body for his delectation with no conscious thought of anything except how sweetly, hotly satisfying it was to be in his arms, to know his kisses and his caresses.

He surged to his feet, lifting her in his arms, her slight weight no trouble at all for his powerful muscles. In a few swift steps he was at the bed, lowering her onto it, coming down to join her with a low growl on his lips as he pulled her under him, spreading her legs with his and settling himself against her in a movement as natural and as basic as breathing.

Sarah clung to him, dizzy with the need he was arousing in her, her mouth tender and fervent under his. She'd loved him for so long, and at the moment she felt as if all of her wishes on falling stars were coming true. She was willing to let him do anything with her, and she knew what he wanted. She could feel the virile hardness of his body as he pressed against her. The layers of clothing between them were too much, unbearable barriers that kept their fevered flesh apart.

Then suddenly heaven ended. He stiffened on top of her, then rolled away and sat up on the edge of the bed, bending over to drop his head in his hands. "Damn you," he said thickly, his voice full of disgust. "You're supposed to be her friend, but you're rolling with *her* husband, in *her* bed."

Dazed, Sarah sat up and straightened her clothing, pushing her hair out of her eyes. She heard the accusation in his voice and found that she couldn't get angry with him; she understood how guilty he was feeling, and how emotionally vulnerable he was after the emotional storm he'd just experienced. "I was her best friend," she said shakily.

"You're not acting like it!"

She slid off the bed, standing on wobbly legs. "We're both upset," she said to his bent head, and her voice was wobbly too. "We both went a little out of control. I loved Diane like a sister, and I miss her too." She began to retreat, unable to stand there any longer, feeling as if she'd borne all she could for one night, and her tongue was out of control, babbling without her choosing the words she'd say. "There's no need to feel guilty about it; there wasn't anything really sexual about it. It was just that we were both so upset—"

He shot off the bed, his face wrathful. "Nothing sexual, hell! I was between your legs! Another minute, and we'd have been having sex! What would you have called it then? Would we have been 'comforting' each other? My God, you wouldn't know sex if it bit you on the leg! You're too much of an iceberg to know anything about men, or what they want!"

Sarah spun around, her face white, her green eyes stricken. Her generous mouth trembled. "I don't deserve that," she whispered, and bolted for the door, flying down the stairs before he realized that she was leaving. With a roar, he started after her.

"Sarah!" he yelled furiously, reaching the front door just as she turned the ignition key and started her little red fireball of a car, jerking it into gear and reversing out of the drive with the squeal of rubber on pavement. He stood in the doorway, watching the red glow of the taillights until they disappeared around the corner; then he slammed the door shut and cursed violently for several minutes. He noticed that she'd left the jacket to her suit, and he picked it up. *Damn!* How could he have said that to her? She was right; she hadn't deserved it. He'd lashed out at her because of his own guilt, not just over what had happened that night, but over the years he'd spent looking at her and wanting to take her to bed, even though she was Diane's best friend.

Rome stared at the linen jacket in his hands, and his mouth tightened. Didn't Sarah realize what a challenge she was to men? She was so cool and pale and distant, so complete unto herself. She was devoted to her career, and she made it pretty plain that she didn't need a man for anything beyond casual companionship. It had been rumored for years that she'd been the mistress of the chairman of the board, but Diane hadn't thought so, and he trusted Diane's judgment. Instead Diane thought that Sarah must have had a love affair that had gone sour, but as she'd said more than once, Sarah was deep and kept a lot of things to herself.

He remembered the first time he'd wanted Sarah; it had been at his own wedding. He'd been impatient to leave with Diane, and then he'd seen Sarah, standing a little alone as she so often seemed to be, her white-blonde hair twisted up on top of her head, her pale face wearing a polite mask. Was she never hot or mussed, he had wondered. Never fidgety? He'd thought of how she'd look if he'd had her in bed with him, that pale hair tangled by the wildness of their passion, her mouth red and swollen from his kisses, her slim body dewy with perspiration. His own body had suddenly become taut, swollen with need, and he'd had to turn away to disguise his condition. How he'd resented her, because even at his wedding to Diane, he'd been lusting after Sarah.

The years hadn't changed the situation. She was always aloof, cool to him, and she never stayed around if he came home while she was visiting Diane. He loved Diane and was faithful to her, totally satisfied with her in bed, but there always remained, in the back of his mind, the knowledge that he wanted Sarah. If she'd given him the come-on, would he have remained faithful to Diane? He wanted to think so, but he couldn't be certain; look what had happened the first time he'd kissed Sarah! He'd been ready to take her right then, on the floor, but he'd had a moment's concern for her soft skin and he'd lifted her to the bed, a break in his concentration that had eventually stopped him. But she hadn't been cool and reserved in his arms; she'd been warm and responsive, and her legs had parted for him without hesitation. Her cheeks had been flushed, and a few fine tendrils of hair had escaped their confinement to curl enticingly around her temples.

That was how he wanted her: with that neat, aloof image of hers shattered. He'd come home early from a trip once, and she'd been in the pool with Diane and the boys. She'd been laughing and frolicking like a child herself, her long hair loosened for once and floating around her like a fairy cloud. He'd changed into his own swimsuit and gone out to join them, and as soon as he'd appeared, Sarah had stopped laughing. She'd been very casual about it, but she'd made her excuses to Diane, hauling herself out of the water, and swiftly dried off before pulling on a ragged pair of denim shorts that only accentuated her long lovely legs. The sight of her in a pale yellow bikini had so aroused him that he'd had to take a fast dive into the water, and when he surfaced, she was already walking swiftly away.

A man couldn't have asked for a better wife than Diane, or a more loving one. But as much as he loved her, as much as he still ached for her, he still wanted Sarah. It wasn't a question of love at all; the finer emotions didn't enter into it. His attraction to her was purely physical. He'd lashed out at her because, with her, sex would be more of a betrayal than it had been with those other nameless, faceless women. They'd been only bodies, without personality. But he knew Sarah, and he couldn't wipe her identity out of his mind. He wanted sex with *her;* he wanted to watch her when she went wild beneath him, he wanted to hear her call his name during the throes of passion. And she was Diane's best friend.

Hours later Sarah curled numbly in bed, her tears finally exhausted, but she couldn't sleep. She felt battered, her insides torn apart with hurt. When the phone rang, she was tempted to ignore it, because no matter who it was, she didn't feel like talking to them. But any call at two o'clock in the morning could be an emergency, and finally she reached over to lift the receiver. When she said hello, she winced at the sound of her own voice, which was still thick with the tears she'd shed.

"Sarah, I didn't mean—"

"I don't want to talk to you," she interrupted, the sound of that deep voice shredding the fragile control she'd gained over her emotions, and she began to weep again. The soft sobs were evident in her voice despite her efforts to hide them. "I may not know anything about men, but you don't know anything about *me!* I don't want to talk to you anymore, do you hear?"

"God, you're crying." He groaned softly, a harsh, masculine sound that filled her with equal portions of pain and longing.

"I said I don't want to talk to you!"

He somehow divined her intentions and said "Don't hang up on me!" in sudden wrath, but she did anyway, then buried her face in the pillow and cried until her eyes were dry and burning.

"You don't know anything at all about me," she said aloud into the darkness.

Chapter Two

It was a good thing the next day was Saturday, because after a horrible night spent alternately crying and staring at the ceiling, Sarah slept late and rose still feeling tired, her eyes heavy-lidded, her movements slow. She forced herself to do her routine chores, then that afternoon flopped down on the sofa, too tired and uninterested to tackle anything else. She needed to shop for groceries, but simply couldn't face the hassle. A quick mental inventory of her cabinets reassured her that she wouldn't starve, at least not for a couple of days.

The doorbell rang, and she got up, answering the summons without thinking. As soon as she opened the door and looked up into Rome's dark face, a feeling of despair settled on her shoulders. Why couldn't he have waited until Monday? She'd have recovered by then and wouldn't be at such a terrible disadvantage.

She didn't even have the comfort of being properly dressed. Her long hair was loose and hanging down her back; her jeans were old, tight, and faded; and the oversize jersey she wore probably revealed the fact that she was braless. She fought the urge to cross her arms protectively over her chest, even when his eyes dropped to survey her from her feet, clad in blue socks, all the way up to her face, which was bare of even a trace of makeup.

"Ask me in," he commanded, his voice even deeper than usual.

She didn't extend a verbal invitation; she couldn't. Instead she stepped back and opened the door, and he moved past her into the room. He was dressed casually, in well-cut tan slacks and a blue pullover shirt, but he still made her feel like something found in the city dump. "Have a seat," she invited, finally controlling her voice enough to speak. He sat down on the sofa, and she seated herself across from him in an oversize armchair, unable to make polite chitchat, just waiting for him to break the tension by speaking.

Rome wasn't aware of any tension; he had been taken too much by surprise by her appearance, and he was having difficulty dealing with this startling new aspect of her character. He'd expected her to be dressed in heels, sleek black pants, and a silk blouse, her coldness firmly in place as a barrier between them. Instead she looked very young, very relaxed, and very sexy in those comfortable old clothes. She had the sleek, aristocratic grace of form and carriage that made it possible for her to wear anything, even an old football jersey, with casual elegance. He knew that she and Diane had been the same age, so that made her thirty-three, but there was a freshness about her bare face that took at least ten years off her age. This was how he'd often imagined seeing her, or at least a variation on the theme. The remote poise he'd expected was gone, and he realized that he had her at a disadvantage. With relish, he looked her over again, his eyes lingering on the obvious freedom of her breasts beneath the jersey, and to his surprise and intensified desire, a warm blush heated her cheeks.

"I'm sorry about last night," he said abruptly. "At least, about what I said. I'm not sorry I kissed you, or that I almost went to bed with you."

Sarah looked away, unable to meet his intense gaze. "I understand. We were both—"

"Upset. I know." He gave her a crooked little smile as he interrupted her. "But upset or not, I kissed you the second time because I wanted to kiss you. I'd like to see you, take you out to dinner, if you can forgive me for what I said."

Sarah wet her lips. Part of her wanted to jump at the opportunity, any opportunity, to spend time with him, but the other part of her was cautious, afraid of being hurt. "I don't think it would be a good idea," she finally said, choking the words out of her dry throat. "Diane . . . Diane would always be in my mind."

His eyes went black as pain assailed him. "And in mine. But I can't lie down and die with her; I have to keep living. I'm attracted to you, and I'll tell you up front that I always have been." He ran an agitated hand through his dark hair, disturbing the lock that usually fell over his forehead. "Hell, I don't know," he burst out in confusion, "but last night, for the first time, I could talk about them. You knew them, and you understand. It's all been dammed up inside me, and I can talk about it with you. Please, Sarah, you were Diane's friend. Now be my friend.''

She sucked in her breath, staring painfully at him. What irony, that the man she'd loved for years should come to her begging for her friendship, because he felt he could talk to her about his dead wife. For the first time she resented Diane, resented the hold Diane had on Rome that hadn't loosened even in death. But how could she say no to him, when he was staring at her with desperation tightening his features? How could she say no to him regardless of what he asked her? It was the raw truth that she couldn't deny him anything.

''All right,'' she whispered.

He sat there for a moment; then her words sank in and he closed his eyes in relief. What if she'd refused? In a way he couldn't understand, it had become vital to him that she not freeze him out. She was his last link to Diane, and more than that, the night before he'd finally broken the ice that surrounded her and found that she wasn't cold at all. He wanted to do that again. The thought of bringing her to passion interfered with his breathing and made his loins grow heavy.

To take his mind off his growing desire, he looked around the condo and was again surprised. There was no glass or chrome, only comfortable textures and soothing colors. Her furniture was all sturdy and overstuffed, inviting to a tired body. He wanted to stretch out on her sofa, which was long enough to accommodate his long legs, and watch a baseball game on television while idly munching on freshly popped, salty popcorn, with a can of frosty beer in his hand. The room was that soothing, that comfortable. This was where she let her hair down, literally, he thought, surveying with pleasure the pale tumble of her hair. When she pulled it back into the tight, severe twist she wore at work, she subdued all hint of curl, but now he could see that her hair wasn't weed-straight. The weight of it pulled most of the curl out, but the ends had a tendency to form frothy, bouncy curls. She was so blonde, it was startling.

"I like this room," he said, his eyes on her.

Sarah looked nervously around, aware of how much of herself was revealed in the atmosphere she'd created for her private lair. Here she'd made a home that gave her the warmth and security she craved and had lacked all her life. She'd grown up in a home that had provided physical comfort, but left her out in the cold when it came to love. The house had been immaculate, and "done" to perfection by a hideously expensive interior decorator, but the coldness of it had made Sarah shiver, and she'd invented excuses, even as a child, to escape it. The coldness had reflected the hostility of the man and woman who lived there, each of them so bitter at being trapped in a loveless marriage that there had been no warmth or laughter for the child who, though innocent, had been the chain that held them together. When they finally divorced, only a few weeks after Sarah had entered college, it had been a relief for all three of them. Never close to her parents, since then Sarah had drifted even farther from them. Her mother had remarried and lived in Bermuda; her father had also remarried, moved to Seattle, and was now, at fifty-seven, the doting father of a six-year-old son.

The only example of warm home-life Sarah had known was that provided by Diane, first with Diane's parents, then with the home she'd made with Rome.

Diane had had the gift of love, a warm outpouring of affection that had drawn people to her. With Diane, Sarah had laughed and teased, and done all of the normal things that a teenage girl did. But now Diane was gone. At least, Sarah thought painfully, Diane had died without ever knowing that her best friend was in love with her husband.

Suddenly she collected her manners and scrambled to her feet. "I'm sorry. Would you like something to drink?"

A cold beer, he thought. And salty popcorn. He'd bet anything he had that Sarah wasn't a beer drinker, but he could picture her curled by his side, sipping on a soft drink and delving her hand into the bowl for popcorn. She wouldn't talk during the game either, but during the commercials he'd tip her head back and kiss her slowly, tasting the salt on her lips. By the time the game ended, he'd be so wild for her, he'd take her there on the sofa, or maybe on the carpet in front of the television.

Sarah shifted uneasily, wondering why he was watching her so intently. She put a hand to her cheek, thinking that she could dash into her bedroom and do a fast cosmetic job on her face. Anything would be an improvement over nothing.

"I don't suppose you have beer?" he asked softly, not taking his eyes from her.

Despite herself, she chuckled at the question. She'd never bought beer in her life; all she knew about it was the catchy jingles on television. "No, you're out of luck. Your choice is limited to a soft drink, water, tea or milk."

His eyebrows rose at that. "No spirits?"

"I'm not much of a drinker. My metabolism can't handle it. I found out in college that I'm the world's cheapest drunk."

When she smiled, her face took on an animation that made him catch his breath. He shifted uncomfortably. *Damn!* Everything she did made him think of sex.

"I think I'll pass on a drink, unless you're inviting me to dinner?" His eyebrows rose in question.

Sarah sank back into her chair, unnerved by the speed with which he presumed on their newly formed friendship. How could she invite him to dinner? It was already late in the afternoon, and she hadn't bought groceries. The most nutritious meal she could offer him would be peanut butter sandwiches, and Rome didn't look like a peanut butter man. What did he like to eat? Frantically she tried to call to mind the type of meals Diane had prepared, but Diane had been such a total disaster as a cook that her efforts had been limited to the simple things she could prepare without too much risk, and which reflected necessity rather than anyone's preference. Sarah was an excellent cook, but there was a limit to what could be done with a partial loaf of bread and a jar of peanut butter.

Finally she turned up her palms helplessly. "My cupboards aren't bare, but they're the next thing to it. I can invite you to dinner, but it will be a late one, because I'll have to go shopping first."

Her candor delighted him, and he laughed, a genuine laugh that made his dark eyes dance with light. Sarah caught her breath. He certainly wasn't handsome, but when he laughed, Rome Matthews could charm the birds out of the trees. That dark velvet laugh made her spine tingle, and she thought of lying in bed with him in the darkness, after making love. They'd talk, and his voice would wash over her, the rumbling tones making her feel secure and protected.

"Why don't I take you out to dinner instead?" he offered, and suddenly Sarah knew that he'd planned that all along, but had decided to tease her first.

"All right," she accepted softly. "What do you have in mind?"

"Steak. If we can't find the world's biggest steak in Texas, then it can't be found. I haven't had lunch," he confessed.

Because he was so hungry, they had an early dinner. Sarah sat across from him and chewed her steak without really tasting it, her mind on Rome and every nuance of his expression, every word he uttered. She felt bemused by the turn of events; she simply couldn't believe she was eating dinner with him, making normal conversation, as if the abrupt, searing moments in his arms the night before had never happened. She'd been out to dinner hundreds of times before, but always with men who had never ruffled her layers of indifference. She wasn't indifferent at all with Rome: she felt bare, exposed, though it was an inner vulnerability that wasn't revealed by her calm expression. Her nerves were quivering, and her heartbeat was accelerated.

Still, she managed to make normal conversation, and it was inevitable that the talk should turn to their work. Sarah's boss, Mr. Graham, the senior vice president, nominally outranked Rome, but it was no secret that when Mr. Edwards, the chairman of the board, retired, Henry Graham wouldn't be the one who advanced to the chair. Rome was young, but he was a brilliant corporate strategist, and he understood every phase of the company. Sarah thought he was perfectly suited for such a high position of authority; he had the forceful personality, the intelligence, the charisma, needed to handle the job. In the years she'd known him, she'd only seen him lose his temper once while at work, and that display had sent people scurrying for cover. He had a temper, but it was usually under iron control. That made it doubly surprising that he'd lost his temper with her the night before, with so little provocation.

At first Rome was a little stiff, as if wary of saying too much to her, but as the hours wore on he relaxed with her, leaning forward over the table in interest, his gaze fixed intently on her face. Sarah didn't generally volunteer her opinions, but she was unusually observant, and her years of concentration on her job had given her a lot of insight into the hidden mechanisms of office politics, and the capabilities and weaknesses of the people they worked with. With Rome, her usual guards were gone, wiped completely out of her consciousness. She simply responded to him on all levels, too happy just being with him to think of protecting herself. Her face, usually so remote and shuttered, became alive under the glow of his attention, and her Nile-green eyes lost their shadows to sparkle at him beguilingly.

The conversation didn't lapse when he drove her home, and they were so intent that, when he stopped the car in front of her condo, they sat in the car like teenagers reluctant to end a date, rather than going inside for coffee to finish the evening. The streetlights illuminated the interior of the car with silvery light, washing away all shades of color except for the darkness of his hair and eyes and the pale sheen of her hair.

She was ethereal in the artificial moonlight projected by the streetlights, her low voice gentle in the darkness.

Rome suddenly reached out and took her hand. "I've enjoyed this. It seems like forever since I've been able to talk to a woman. I haven't had a relationship with a woman since Diane died. I don't mean sex," he explained calmly. "I'm talking about being able to be friends with a woman, to talk to her and enjoy her company, to relax with her. I think I've missed that the most. Tonight . . . well, it's felt good. Thank you."

Sarah turned her hand in his and squeezed his fingers lightly. "That's what friends are for."

He walked with her up to her apartment. Sarah unlocked the door and opened it, reaching inside to turn on the light before she turned to face Rome again. Her smile was gently sad, for she hated to see the night end. It had been, for all its lack of drama, one of the best times of her life. "Good night. It's been fun." More than fun. It had been heavenly.

"Good night." But he didn't leave. Instead he stood in the doorway, soberly regarding her. He lifted his hand and stroked her cheek with his forefinger, then slid his hand around to cup her chin in his palm. He leaned toward her, and Sarah went weak with anticipation, her eyes widening as fevered delight shot through her. He was going to kiss her again. Lightly his mouth touched hers, his lips moving with tender expertise over her parted, breathless mouth. His warm taste filled her, and Sarah's lashes fluttered, then slowly closed. With a zephyr of a sigh she swayed into his arms; he needed no more encouragement than that. Locking his arms around her, he pulled her up against his chest and gradually deepened the kiss, as if he were wary of going too fast for her, giving her time to accept or reject each new move.

There was no question of her rejecting him. It wasn't in Sarah's makeup to say no to Rome in any way. She felt the heat of his body burning her through the layers of their clothing, and the warmth was a beacon that drew her closer. She wound her arms around his neck and eagerly accepted the more intimate intrusion of his tongue. A naked, wanting heat began building in her, and she wanted to be closer to him, to mold herself against him so tightly that his flesh would be hers.

His hands moved restlessly over her back, wanting to seek richer ground but restricted by the tight control he kept on himself and the situation. Sensing her safety with him, Sarah kissed him with undisguised hunger, not caring that he might look beyond the obvious explanation for her behavior and arrive at the correct conclusion that her attraction to him went beyond sex. But sex with him would be so good, she thought giddily, clinging to him. His experience was obvious in the firm but gentle way he touched her, the leisure with which he approached every caress. If he'd taken her into the bedroom right then, she'd have followed him without a murmur of protest.

But he lifted his mouth from hers, though he sighed and rested his forehead against hers for a moment before reaching up and disentangling her arms from about his neck, then setting her away from him. "Now it really is good night. I'm going to be in bad shape if this goes on much longer, so I'm stopping it here. I'll see you Monday morning, at work."

Quickly Sarah reached for her composure, drawing it about her like a garment, and she tried to disguise the raggedness of her breathing. Her body felt betrayed, but he was right: it had to stop there, or it wouldn't stop at all. "Yes. Good night," she breathed, before stepping into her apartment and quietly closing the door.

Rome went to his car, but sat in it for a long time before starting it and driving away. No, she wasn't cold at all, despite the way she looked and that ice-queen manner she used. He hadn't wanted to leave her; all his senses had been clamoring for the comfort to be found in her soft, warm body, but to his surprise, he'd found that he couldn't take her as casually as he'd taken the other women who'd been with him the last two years. She was Diane's friend, and Diane had loved her; his conscience wouldn't allow him to treat her as a sexual convenience. Besides, he really had enjoyed having dinner with her. She had a surprisingly keen sense of humor, and when she relaxed, she was really lovely, with her eyes sparkling and her soft mouth curved into a smile.

And when she kissed him, she'd kissed him as if she meant it. The unquestioning response she'd given him had almost driven him beyond the boundaries of his control. The feel of her soft hips pressing into him was enough to make him forget everything but the warm female body in his arms. Far from diminishing on closer acquaintance, the physical interest he'd felt in her for years was intensifying every time he saw her. He'd seen her long white-gold hair in a shimmering halo around her shoulders, and now he wanted to see it spread across a pillow as she lay waiting for him, her slim, graceful body bare, her mouth swollen and pouty from his kisses. A possessive surge made him grind his teeth, and he thought of the cold shower he'd have to take before he'd be able to sleep. If he'd stayed with her, he'd be relaxed and sleepy by now, all of his tensions drained out of him.

But she wasn't just any woman. He couldn't use her and then toss her aside. Apart from the fact that they had to work together, he wanted more from her than that. A one-night stand wouldn't do it with her; he wanted to unlock all her secrets, thrill time and time again to the sweet, hot way she melted against him. He thought of having an affair with her, and was surprised to suddenly find himself wondering if an affair would be enough to satisfy him. He wanted to know everything about her; he wanted to completely shatter her cool control and learn all the things that he could do to give her pleasure. He was adrift, and he needed Sarah right then more than he could comprehend, in all ways.

It was more than just physical, he realized abruptly. He could talk with her; she was intelligent, amusing, but there was the added bonus that he didn't *have* to talk to her, because she had a quality of serenity that made silence possible. Whenever he looked into the shadows of her exotic green eyes, he had the feeling she understood everything, without words.

But she was a dedicated career woman; she'd made it pretty clear over the years that she did just fine on her own, thank you, without a man making demands on her time. She'd probably reject out of hand any hint of seriousness from him, so he had to keep it light, casual, let her become accustomed to being in his company. He had doubts, though, about his ability to keep it light whenever she turned into his arms and answered his kisses so ardently. He wanted to throw her across a bed and kiss her from her head to her feet, feast his senses on the sleek womanliness of her body. But what would she say?

Maybe she wouldn't reject an offer of an affair. She was, after all, a modern, adult woman; if her response to him was anything to go by, she was willing to have sex with him, but he knew from working with her that she kept her personal life strictly separated from her business life. That would be one strike against him, but he thought he could eventually convince her. He'd take it slowly with her, not rushing her, letting her lower all those defenses of hers. He couldn't say why, but he sensed that she was wary with him, deep inside where he couldn't see. Perhaps she was wary with all men. Diane had wondered aloud sometimes if Sarah hadn't had a married lover and been burned pretty badly by him.

There was a well-camouflaged vulnerability about her, and he wondered what fool had been stupid enough to have all that pale glory in his bed and let her slip away from him.

Sarah hadn't expected to hear from Rome again that weekend, so when she answered the phone the next afternoon and heard his voice, a thrill of pleasure sang through her. Before she could do more than say hello, however, he cut across her greeting.

"Sarah, Henry's had a heart attack, a bad one."

Shocked, Sarah almost dropped the phone, and she tightened her grip on it. Her boss hadn't seemed the sort to be struck by heart trouble. He was a small man, wiry to the point of thinness, and very active. He was an avid golfer, jogged every day, and in Sarah's memory had never indulged in any of the excesses people were warned against. He wasn't the dynamic man that

Rome was, but Sarah was fond of him. "Will he live?" she finally asked quietly, going straight to the most important question.

"It's touch and go. His wife called me; I'm at the hospital now." Someone in the background said something to him, and Rome said, "Hang on a minute." He covered the receiver with his hand, reducing his words to a muffled jumble of sounds. Then he came back to her, his voice brisk. "He took some reports home with him this weekend that we'll need Monday morning. Can you go over to his house and pick them up? The housekeeper will let you in."

"Yes, of course," she agreed automatically. "Which reports do you need?"

"The Sterne financial statement, and the projected growth pattern. Look, go through his briefcase and pull out whatever you think we'll need. I'll see you in the morning."

"But what hospital is he in—?" Sarah began, only to be cut off by a click. Well, there wasn't anything she could do now anyway. She'd find out more the next morning, and perhaps then there would be a more definite prognosis than "touch and go." Distressed by her boss's sudden illness, she quickly combed her hair, then drove over to his house. As instructed, the housekeeper let her in, and the tiny little woman told Sarah the details. Mr. Graham had seemed fine that morning, and had played nine holes of golf. After lunch, he'd complained of pains in his left arm, then abruptly collapsed.

"It can come at any time," the housekeeper said solemnly, shaking her head. "You just never know."

"No, you never do," Sarah agreed.

It was the next morning, when she was called to an unusual meeting in Mr. Edwards's office, before Sarah realized that Mr. Graham's heart attack could drastically affect her own job. Rome was present too, his dark eyes concerned as he watched her.

Sarah darted a quick glance at him, quivering as she thought of the way he'd kissed her, then just as quickly looked away. She couldn't meet the intensity of his gaze and keep her mind on her job, and that was distressing. No matter how much pressure she'd been under, she'd always been able to perform her duties; it was upsetting to realize that Rome could throw her off balance with just one look.

"Sarah, sit down, please," Mr. Edwards invited, his shrewd eyes kind as he watched her. Sarah had always gotten along with Mr. Edwards, but he'd never before asked her to attend a meeting. She sat down and calmly folded her hands in her lap.

"Henry won't be back," Mr. Edwards said gently. "I've talked to his doctor personally. If he takes it easy, avoids stress, and doesn't have another attack, he may live a number of years, but he won't be able to work. He's going to take an early retirement. Rome is being promoted to senior vice president."

Again Sarah risked a quick glance at Rome, to find him still watching her with that unnerving intensity. He leaned forward in his chair and offered, "I can't hire you as my secretary. Kali has been my secretary for years, and of course she'll move up with me."

That wasn't a surprise. Sarah gave him a gentle smile that ripped through his insides, causing his fist to clench suddenly. She hadn't expected to be his secretary; it would never have worked anyway. She simply couldn't have worked so closely with him, every day. It had been bad enough just seeing him occasionally. "Yes, of course. Am I being fired?"

"Good lord, no!" Mr. Edwards said, startled. "No, don't think that at all. But we wanted to give you a choice. I'm bringing a man in from Montreal to replace Rome, and his secretary doesn't want to relocate. If you want the job, it's yours, and he's agreeable. If you'd rather transfer to some other department, just say so. You've done an outstanding job for Spencer-Nyle over the years; the choice of jobs is yours."

Sarah thought of transferring, but she really liked the intense atmosphere of the executive offices, where decisions were made that affected thousands of people. The challenge kept her interested, and though she was in proximity to Rome, the fast pace of her work tended to keep her mind off him during the day.

"I'd like to be his secretary," she finally answered gravely. "What's his name?"

"Maxwell Conroy. He's been directing our Montreal office very competently. I believe he's English."

"Yes," Rome confirmed. Probably Rome had already pulled Maxwell Conroy's personnel file from the computer and memorized every word of it.

"Good," Mr. Edwards said heartily, rising to his feet and signaling that they were dismissed. Rome followed Sarah out the door, but didn't return to his own office. He was close behind her as she went into her office, and he closed the door behind them. Feeling absurdly nervous, Sarah moved away from him and sought refuge behind her desk.

"I want you to know," he murmured, leaning over the desk and bringing his face close to hers, "I want you for my secretary...badly...but my common sense tells me that I'd never get any work done. I'd be the stereotypical boss who chases his secretary around the desk, so for the sake of the company, I suppose I'll have to keep Kali."

Sarah stared at him, losing herself in the dark wells of his eyes. "I understand," she whispered.

"Do you?" He straightened, his smile quizzical as he looked down at her. "I'm not so certain that I do. Maybe you can explain it. Will you go out to dinner with me tonight?"

She normally didn't make dates during the week, as she never knew when she would have to work late, but when Rome asked her, her usual caution flew out the window. "Yes, please." She couldn't hide the pleasure in her eyes, and he stared at her for a moment before he leaned down once again and kissed her once, hard.

"I'll pick you up at eight. How does Chinese sound?"

"Wonderful. I love Chinese."

Her hands shook after he'd gone when she tried to get through her routine paperwork. This was beginning to look like a serious relationship, and there was no way she could back off from it, no way she even wanted to. She thought of Diane, and her eyes closed briefly. She would have died in Diane's place, if she could have, but no one had been given a choice. Rome was free now, physically and legally if not emotionally, and whatever chance she had with him, Sarah meant to take it.

If he didn't have a business dinner scheduled, Rome took her out every night that week. Sarah didn't question her good fortune; she simply enjoyed every

moment she had with him. Reminding herself that
he'd asked only to be friends, she tried not to say anything or make any gestures that he could interpret as
being flirtatious, though sometimes that hardly
seemed to matter. When he kissed her good night, his
light kiss would linger, as if he were inexorably drawn
to the soft warmth of her mouth, and soon she'd be
locked in his arms as they kissed with all the pent-up
fervor of teenagers. But there was no more than that;
he always drew away before any deeper intimacy developed between them, and Sarah took that to mean
that he didn't intend any serious relationship to grow
between them. He seemed content with things as they
were; he had companionship and lively conversation
from her, as well as the comfort of shared interests.
She wanted more; she wanted everything he had to
give, but perhaps he *was* giving her all he had. She
knew that Diane was never far from his mind, and
whenever they talked about her, as they inevitably did,
his expression would grow bleak.

A week after Mr. Graham's heart attack, Maxwell
Conroy flew in from Montreal. He was a tall, lean
Englishman with a precise British upper-class accent,
a cap of golden hair, and the liveliest, most wickedly
dancing blue-green eyes Sarah had ever seen. He was
more than handsome; he had an ageless, aristocratic
beauty to him that held women bemused, staring at
him helplessly. If Sarah had been able to see anyone
but Rome, she would probably have fallen in love with
Maxwell Conroy on sight, but as it was, he received
only her usual polite, slightly remote smile.

He wasted no time. The first time Sarah was alone
with him he asked her out to dinner.

She looked up at him with startled, wide eyes. There was no way of mistaking his intentions, not with those luminous eyes so plainly telegraphing his thoughts. She bit her lip; how could she refuse him without making things difficult between them at work? She didn't want to commit herself, though, because Rome could ask her out at any time. "I don't think that would be a good idea," she finally refused, keeping her voice gentle. "We have to work together, and you know that although there aren't any actual company rules against employees dating, it's generally discouraged within the same department."

"I also know that as long as people are discreet it's generally ignored."

She drew a deep breath. "I'm seeing someone else."

"Would he mind?" Maxwell asked promptly, and Sarah gave a low chuckle.

"Probably not," she admitted, her laugh fading into an echo of pain that was revealed in the way the soft green of her eyes grew misty with shadows.

"Then he's a fool," Maxwell said under his breath, his eyes on her sleek, pale knot of hair. "If you should decide to give someone else a chance, do let me know."

"Yes." For a moment, she met his warm, piercing gaze. "I will."

In all truth, she was more attracted to Maxwell than she'd been to any other man in her life, except for Rome. She'd liked Maxwell on sight, and in a curious way she felt relaxed with him, for she sensed that he recognized the boundaries she'd set and would respect them until she gave him permission to go beyond them.

That afternoon Rome and Maxwell lingered in the hallway, finishing a discussion before leaving for the day. Sarah locked up the office and murmured a good night to them as she walked past, carefully not letting her glance linger on Rome.

Maxwell turned so he could watch her walk down the hallway, his brilliant eyes narrowed with interest. Rome's dark gaze sharpened, and he too turned to watch Sarah, noting the grace with which she walked, the way her skirt moved fluidly about her lovely legs. He didn't like the way Maxwell was looking at her, like a cat lovingly surveying the canary it was about to have for lunch, and a slow curl of anger began in his stomach.

"She's a very pretty woman," he commented, probing for a response, and every nerve in his body waited for Maxwell's answer.

Maxwell shot him an incredulous look. "Pretty? She's bloody beautiful. She's so subtle, so understated, that you have to really look to see how pure and classic her face is."

Rome had seen her face glowing with pleasure, her lips swollen from his kisses and begging for more. He was proceeding at an excruciatingly slow pace, waiting for a signal from her that she was feeling the frustration of ending their evenings with only kisses. Yes, she liked his kisses, but there was still an aloofness to her that he hadn't been able to break, and no matter how torridly she kissed him, she didn't invite him further. He was beginning to feel desperate, his body aching for release. He'd been devoting his evenings to her, so there'd been no casual meeting with any other woman to relieve his sexual urges. He hadn't come up against such a mental stone wall since he'd been a randy teenager, determinedly trying to seduce his virginal girlfriend every Friday night in the backseat of his car.

But if Sarah ever lost her self-control enough to give in to passion, it would be with him. He'd be damned if he'd let Maxwell see her with that cool reserve melted into primitive heat and longing. Her desire would be his, and his alone.

"I've noticed how she looks," he said evenly, but his tone signaled a warning to the other man. Maxwell looked at him sharply, then sighed.

"So, you've beaten me to her, have you?"

"I've known her for years," Rome replied obliquely.

That elicited a snort from Maxwell. "I've known my mother's housekeeper for years too, but I don't warn men away from her."

Rome laughed, something that had become easier during this past week. Despite himself, he liked Maxwell. Max might pursue Sarah relentlessly, but he'd never be sneaky about it; he'd simply take his chances. That made no difference to Rome's determination to have her all to himself, but he relaxed, his eyes meeting Max's with complete masculine understanding.

Max shrugged with an elegant movement of his lean shoulders. "I'll be waiting in the wings, if you should fail."

"I'm reassured," Rome said sardonically.

Max smiled at him wryly. "Don't be."

Chapter Three

The cocktail party to welcome Max to the Dallas headquarters was overflowing with people anxious to be seen by and talk with the upper echelon of Spencer-Nyle. Rome, Mr. Edwards, and Max were the center of attention, as they were the triumvirate that controlled billions of dollars and thousands of jobs. Mr. Edwards, a lean, quiet man whose shrewdness and corporate savvy had kept him at the top for fifteen years, had hand-chosen his lieutenants and been well-rewarded for his trust in them. Rome was being groomed for the chairmanship, which he would certainly attain when Mr. Edwards retired. Watching the ambitious young executives swarm around him, Sarah realized that it was common knowledge, up and down the ranks, that Rome was Mr. Edwards's chosen successor. Max, on the other hand, was an unknown, but

already there was an ease between him and his supe-
riors that told everyone he was on the inside.

Tired of being pumped for information about Max,
Sarah developed the strategy of staying on the move.
It took a well-planned schedule to move in, take up a
handful of peanuts or dip a stalk of celery into the
cheese dip, then waltz on without pausing long enough
to give anyone an opening. She clutched her single
drink of the evening in her hand, taking tiny sips and
trying to eat enough to absorb the alcohol before it
could go to her head. Earlier, a quick foray into the
tiny kitchen, where the caterers were frantically trying
to keep pace with the appetites of the guests, had produced a small glass of milk, which she had slugged
back with all the delicacy of a stevedore downing his
first frosty beer after working all day in hundred-
degree heat.

"You're gobbling peanuts like you've been on a
starvation diet," Rome said in her ear, startling her.
He took the cocktail from her hand and replaced it
with a tall glass filled with a pale amber liquid and ice
cubes. "There. Drink this instead. Ginger ale." He
winked at her, and finished the cocktail for her.

"I've already raided the refrigerator for milk," she
laughed, her eyes twinkling up at him. "Did you think
I was in danger of falling on my face before the party
was over?"

He regarded her somberly, noting that there was no
hint of the usual sadness in her eyes that night.
Whether it was the small amount of alcohol she'd
drunk that made her laugh so gaily, or whether something had happened to make her happy, he didn't
know, but it didn't matter. Since it was as much a
business occasion as a social one, he hadn't brought

her to the party, but he fully intended to visit her when it was over. From the way she was looking at him now, she might be relaxing those invisible restraints that had kept her from responding to him more fully.

"No, you'd never do anything as disgraceful as getting drunk," he finally said in answer to her question. "You're too much the perfect secretary. You already have Max eating out of your hand."

"Max is a dear," Sarah responded warmly, looking around for his tall, graceful figure and missing the way Rome's eyes darkened to a stormy black. "I was fond of Mr. Graham, but I'll admit that I enjoy working with Max more. Max keeps things hopping."

Introducing Max into the conversation had been a mistake. Rome moved instinctively, placing himself between Sarah and the rest of the room, blocking her view of Max.

"Do you mind if I come over tonight?" he asked, but there was a harsh note in his voice that commanded rather than asked, and Sarah eyed him warily.

"If you like. I wasn't going to stay much longer anyway. Have you had dinner, or is this all you've had too?" With a wave of her hand, she indicated the colorful but unfulfilling array of dips, snacks, and fresh vegetables that she'd been raiding all evening.

Rome had a healthy appetite. "I'm starving," he admitted. "Do you want to go out for a late dinner?"

"No, I think I'd rather stay home," she said, after considering the invitation for a moment. "I have some chicken left over from yesterday; how do you feel about chicken sandwiches?"

"I'd trade all that rabbit food for just one chicken sandwich." His mood lightening, he grinned at her, and Sarah smiled in return. He was more relaxed with her now than he'd ever been before, and she was blooming under his attention. Perhaps he was beginning to think of her as something other than a friend; the hope of it made her radiant, and the glow of her face beckoned more than one glance from the other men in the room.

Suddenly Max was at Rome's elbow, his smile tender as he looked at Sarah.

"You really should be by my side," he said lightly, noting how well the apricot color of her dress suited her creamy complexion. "After all, I'm still totally lost without you. Without you to point me in the right direction these last few days, I'd have made a perfect idiot of myself."

He'd already stretched his hand out for Sarah when Rome forestalled him by extending his own arm, blocking the gesture. Something hard and frightening was in his dark face as he looked at Max. "I've already warned you once," he said with soft, purring menace. "Sarah is off-limits to you."

"Rome!" Shocked, taken completely off guard, Sarah gasped his name, dismay filling her. How could he behave like this at a business function?

"She isn't wearing your ring," Max pointed out calmly, not turning a hair. "You'll have to take your chances."

White with distress at the way a casual, light-hearted conversation had turned so abruptly into barely restrained male aggression, Sarah stepped back from both of them. "Stop it!" she ordered, her voice shaking so much that it was barely above a whisper. "Don't either of you dare say another word!"

Rome's nostrils flared and he moved swiftly, his hard arm passing around Sarah's slender waist. "I'm taking Sarah home," he said deliberately, his hard fingers biting into her soft flesh. His words were loud enough to be heard, and several people turned to look at them. "She doesn't feel well. Make our excuses, Max; see you in the office."

Sarah knew that she was pale enough to give credence to his lie, and he hustled her out of the suite before anyone could approach. The arm around her waist had lifted her almost off her feet; he was effectively carrying her. "Rome, stop it," she protested, trying to wriggle away from him and walk under her own power.

He swore softly under his breath and adjusted his grip on her, leaning down to slide his other arm under her knees and lift her completely into his arms. Sarah caught her breath as the swift motion made her head whirl dizzily, and she clutched at his shoulders. The elevators were down a long corridor, and they passed a man in a white dinner jacket who stared after them with great interest.

"You're making a scene," she whispered. "What's wrong with you?" She was too startled to even be angry, but she felt as if she were groping her way through a fog, because she failed completely to understand his motives.

He jabbed the down button with his elbow, then bent his head and kissed her with such deliberate intimacy that she curled in his arms, her mouth opening for his tongue. He could have been standing in the middle of the street for all she thought about their location. When he kissed her like that, every thought left her head, leaving her preoccupied only with the slow burning pleasure he gave her with just a kiss.

An electric ding signaled the arrival of the elevator. Still carrying her, Rome stepped into it; they were the only occupants, and she stared at him in bewilderment. His expression was clearly revealed under the bright artificial lights, but she was still unable to decipher it.

"You can put me down now," she ventured softly. "Were you intending to carry me through the lobby of the hotel?"

"This is Texas," he replied with a hint of wryness. "No one would be surprised, though for form's sake I suppose I should throw you over my shoulder." But he let her down, though he kept his arm firmly anchored around her waist.

"What was that all about?" she asked as the doors slid open and they stepped out into the vast ultramodern lobby, overwhelming with its glass and greenery.

"It's called staking a claim."

She considered that in silence for a moment. She wasn't coy, nor did she believe in dissembling; she wasn't going to simper and pretend she didn't understand. On an instinctive level, though, she was a little alarmed by the swiftness with which he'd moved. She darted a quick nervous glance at him, one that he intercepted and read, and his mouth tightened fractionally. Looking at him, with his hard face set in determined lines, she knew that she'd been cut from the herd the way a stallion would isolate the mare he'd chosen. The thought made her mouth go dry, and her knees feel weak. Perhaps he wasn't a native Texan, but he knew just how to go about it. The move Max had made on her had awakened a possessive streak in Rome, and instinctively he'd snatched her away from the other man; now he was determined to finalize his possession.

"My car is here," she said, making a motion with her hand as if to halt him.

"Forget about it." He didn't even glance down at her as they stepped out onto the sidewalk, where the warm night breezes fanned his face. "I'll bring you back for it in the morning."

"I'd feel better if I drove it home." She spoke firmly, and he sensed her decision, realizing immediately that the car gave her a feeling of independence that she needed, after the way he'd high-handedly whisked her away from the party. He didn't want her out of his sight for a minute, but he was afraid that if he pushed too hard, he'd run the risk of making her retreat back behind her cool mask. He was close, too close, to breaking her reserve for him to let his impatience ruin things now. Having her was becoming an obsession with him; shattering her control was a goal that occupied more and more of his time and thoughts.

"All right," he agreed, deciding to use the time alone during the drive to her apartment to cool himself down. He was feeling violent and caged, and he needed to ease himself with the soft magic of a woman's flesh. Sarah's flesh. She was the only specific woman he'd wanted since Diane's death, and he wanted her so violently that he almost resented her for getting to him the way she had.

She was so pale and composed and sure of herself, like an ice-queen. Would she be that cool and controlled in bed, or would those shadowy green eyes blaze with animal need? He imagined her beneath him, writhing in the throes of desire he'd awakened in her, with wild cries tearing up from the depths of her slender body as he drove into her again and again and again. . . .

He stopped his fantasy, sweat breaking out on his forehead as he watched the graceful swaying of her body as she walked away from him. He went to his own car and waited until her little red car passed him; then he pulled out behind her and followed closely on the drive to her apartment.

Sarah already had the door unlocked when he arrived, and she glanced at him warily as he entered behind her. His dark eyes still held that dangerous look, with a hunger in them that she understood but couldn't measure. She wanted him—she'd always wanted him—but at the same time she didn't want to be a one-night stand for him, a fast coupling for the purpose of easing him, forgotten as soon as it was finished. Spontaneously she tried to slow him down.

"Would you like coffee?" she invited, dropping her small purse on the sofa and moving away from him to the kitchen.

"No." His refusal was flat.

"I think I'll have something to eat, just to be on the safe side," she called over her shoulder. "How about one of those chicken sandwi—"

Without warning, he seized her from behind, his hard hands locking on her waist and pulling her back against him. His head bent, and his hot breath blew over the curve of her neck, lightly touching her sensitive skin and awakening all her nerve endings. She shivered a little, but didn't try to pull away; instead she pressed back against the virile contours of his body.

"I don't want a sandwich," he muttered, nipping at her neck with his teeth, then soothing the slight sting with butterfly strokes from the tip of his tongue. Sarah's eyes closed in ecstasy, and she let her head fall back against his shoulder, baring the vulnerable curve of her throat to him.

His breathing was becoming hard and fast, rasping in her ear, and the way he moved against her buttocks vividly demonstrated his arousal. His right hand shifted from her waist, sliding boldly upward to rub and cup her breasts, his touch burning her through her dress.

"I want to break Max's jaw when he looks at you as if he wants to do this." There was a roughness to his voice that she hadn't heard before, the guttural tone of fierce desire. His hands were all over her, stroking her as if to stake his claim as he'd told her he would do, and she leaned against him, her eyes closed, shaking a little as waves of pleasure assaulted her, each one stronger than the one before. With a harsh, impatient sound, he quickly tugged down the zipper of her dress and dropped the garment to her hips, then dispersed with her bra, freeing her breasts to his hands and gaze.

Sarah moaned softly as he cupped both of her breasts in his palms, kneading her soft flesh and gently pinching at her pink nipples. "You're so beautiful," he groaned and the rough desire in his voice made her feel beautiful. She loved the way the mounds of her breasts filled his palms, hardening and thrusting out to seek his touch.

Abruptly he turned her in his arms, holding her so tightly against him that her ribs ached, while he kissed her with blatant hunger. With his tongue, he told her what he wanted to do, and the symbolism was unmistakable. Sarah gasped under his mouth, seeking air to feed her starving lungs. "Rome...please!" But she didn't know if she begged for mercy, or for more of the primal pleasure he was giving her. Her body was growing heavy and liquid, and a deep inner throbbing made her move restlessly against him.

"Yes," he said against her throat, interpreting her plea as he chose. He bent her over his arm to give himself access to her tempting breasts, and she gave a thin cry when his hot mouth closed over her nipple, sucking it strongly into his mouth. Blackness swirled over her, a warm, velvet blackness that blocked out any reservations she might have had about belonging to him. She dissolved into a purely physical animal, instinctively seeking more of the pleasure he offered her. Her hands roamed his body as his had roamed hers, impatiently brushing away the layers of cloth that separated her from his hard muscled flesh. He trembled wildly at her intimate touch and pleaded with her for more.

At some point, they dropped to the floor, the plush carpet soft under her back. Too impatient to undress her completely, he lifted her skirt out of the way and stripped her panty hose down her legs. Sarah reached for him, her expression rapt, lost in the passion he'd aroused in her, and he caught his breath sharply. "Easy, easy," he said hoarsely, not wanting it to end too quickly, and knowing he was perilously close to satisfaction. He wanted to make certain she was satisfied too; he wanted to see her face at the peak of her pleasure. He held back, twisting his body away from her inciting hands, while he stroked and petted her, bestowing fleeting, intimate caresses on her that had her arching for more.

Sarah cried out at the tension that was building in her, the sensation that was as frightening as it was pleasurable, as if she might explode into a thousand little pieces. His warm hand, his devilishly dancing fingers, were doing things to her that were destroying her control, her sense of self. "Let go, let go," he cajoled in a rough whisper against her ear, and she did, crying out unintelligible sounds of passion fulfilled, her hands clutching at him as her body writhed in the glory that consumed her.

Just as she began the downward slide into peace and relaxation, he pinned her to the floor with his weight, adjusted himself between her thighs, and thrust into her with one powerful deliberate movement. Sarah was unable to hold back the sharp single cry that tore from her throat, and her body jolted in shock. But she reached up to wind her arms around his neck, clinging to him, as she offered him the comfort of her loving body. He groaned thickly against her throat and lost all control, taking her swiftly, a little roughly, and somehow, despite her discomfort, lighting again that small spark of desire in her. It was over before that spark could grow into the inferno that would consume her; with a cry from between his clenched teeth, he reached his own pleasure.

The upheaval of her senses left Sarah dazed; she lay on the carpet after he'd rolled from her, her body feeling buffeted, shocked, and quite unlike her own. Alien sensations were still sending their wild messages to her brain, and she labored in a benumbed manner to sort out and understand them. She might have lain there and even gone to sleep if his angry, tightly controlled voice hadn't jerked her to full awareness.

"Damn it, Sarah, you could've warned me!"

Still a little disoriented, she sat up with movements that weren't quite coordinated, frowning in a faint, quizzical manner as she fumbled with her dress, pulling it up over her shoulders again and pushing at the skirt until it once again covered her legs. "I...what?" she mumbled in confusion; then she sighed in sudden weariness and lifted her hand to cover her eyes.

He swore, a basic Anglo-Saxon word that blasted against her sensitized skin, making her flinch slightly. She couldn't grasp why he was angry; was it because of Diane? She gave him a sudden haunted look that stopped him in his tracks, as if her eyes briefly lost their veil and let him see the pain that ravaged her daily. Then she looked away, and tried to gather her trembling legs beneath her to stand up.

He said something violent under his breath; then he crossed the room in three quick strides to lean down and swing her bodily into his arms, straightening without any sign of strain. "What did you expect?" he snapped, taking her to the bedroom and placing her on the bed. "Keeping me in the dark was a damned stupid thing to do!" Despite his anger, his hands were gentle as he undressed her.

Sarah lay quietly as he cared for her. Finally she'd understood the reason for his anger. Her inexperience wasn't what he'd expected. She only wanted to know if he'd been disappointed, or if he was angry because he'd been caught off balance. When he'd dressed her in a nightgown and propped her up on the pillows, he sat down on the bed beside her, the light from the single lamp throwing harsh shadows across his roughly etched face. He drew a deep breath, as if reaching for control.

A rather inappropriate hint of humor made a smile tug at her lips. She fought it, knowing that he wasn't in a humorous mood, but it spread anyway. Her soft mouth curved in a tender smile, and she teased gently, "Having sex hasn't turned me into an invalid. I could've undressed myself."

He glared at her, then saw the tenderness in her smile that invited him to share the moment with her. Realizing that he'd been treating her like someone who'd been wounded, he lost the hard edge of his temper, then found himself feeling sheepish. He fought off the feeling, keeping his expression grim. "Then you're luckier than you deserve to be. I could've hurt you, really hurt you. Damn it all, you should have told me it was your first time!"

"I'm sorry," she apologized gravely. "I didn't know the procedure."

For a moment he looked as if he would explode, pure fury burning in the dark depths of his eyes. But he was a man who controlled his temper, and he exerted that control now, refraining from even speaking until he trusted himself again. He finally thrust his hand roughly through his tousled hair, ruffling it even more. "You're thirty-three years old. Why in *hell* would you still be a virgin?"

He sounded totally baffled, as if it were beyond his comprehension. Sarah shifted in embarrassment, fully realizing what an anachronism she was. If she'd been born even one generation earlier, she wouldn't have been so obsolete; chastity would have been expected of her until she married. But instead she was a not-so-modern woman locked into a more progressive society. It wasn't that she lacked the normal curiosity and desires, or that she was a prude; her deeply ingrained need for security had kept her from risking her "all," as it were, in any relationship that would be too casual and transient to satisfy her instincts. Then she'd met Rome, and that had stopped cold any other man's chances with her, but Rome had also been off-limits. If she couldn't have him, she hadn't wanted anyone else; it was that simple, and totally impossible to explain to him.

She didn't even try to answer; she just looked at him, with the shadows once more gathering to dim the light that had been in her eyes.

Suddenly Rome quivered as if he'd been struck, staring down at her with an expression of torment on his face. What would Diane say, if she knew he'd just seduced her best friend? Pain clawed at his insides, pain and guilt, as he suddenly realized that the physical act of release he'd sought with other women, which had meant an act of physical betrayal, had been nothing compared to the way he'd just betrayed Diane with Sarah. Sarah hadn't been just a faceless body to him. He'd been aware of her every moment; he'd wanted her for the qualities and characteristics that made her peculiarly herself. Not only that, the pleasure he'd had with her had been shattering, totally wiping out the memories that usually plagued him after sex, memories of making love with his wife, of lying in the darkness with her afterward and talking their hearts out. He hadn't thought of Diane at all; Sarah had filled his mind and his senses, which was the greatest betrayal of all.

He had to move away from her. He surged to his feet and paced restlessly across the room, once again thrusting his fingers through his hair. Why did she have to lie there and look at him with those mysterious eyes? He couldn't even begin to understand her. He'd thought that if he could take her, reduce her to the common status of all the women who'd lain beneath him during the past two years, then she would lose her mystery and he'd no longer feel so obsessed by her, but that hadn't happened. Instead she'd revealed a secret that made her even more mysterious, and now she'd retreated again into her private self, too distant for him to reach.

It was, abruptly, more than he could stand. He felt suffocated, and he glared at her in anger at the panic that was consuming him. "Hell," he uttered in complete disgust. "Look, are you all right?"

Sarah lifted a slim eyebrow. "I'm fine." She sounded cool and in perfect control, as usual.

"I've got to get out of here," he muttered. "I'm sorry; I know I'm acting like a bastard, but I can't—" He stopped, shaking his head in bafflement. "I'll call you tomorrow."

He was at the door before Sarah found her voice again. "There's no need. I really am all right."

The look he gave her was almost violent; then he was gone, and a few seconds later she heard the door slam. Immediately she got out of bed and went to lock it, then crawled back into bed, wincing as her body protested the movement.

So, already the fragile companionship that had been growing between them was shattered, by a swift, consuming act of lust. That was all it had been for him, though she'd gone into his arms with love. She knew that it was much too soon in their relationship for it to be able to support the stress of lovemaking. He'd taken her, and she'd seen the anger, the guilt, in his eyes when he'd looked at her. Because she was so acutely sensitive to him, she'd known that he was thinking about Diane and regretting the wanton moments on the carpet.

Sarah didn't cry; she'd hoped, but the dream had been so brief that she hadn't really let herself start believing in it yet. He was gone, but then she'd never had him, not in any way that counted. She hadn't had his trust, or his love. His interest in her hadn't made sense anyway.

What now? Could she really go on working for the same company as he did, seeing him every day? Or had she finally reached the stage where she couldn't take any more, when she'd have to be cowardly in the interests of her own sanity? After all, she'd been brave for more years than she cared to remember, and bravery had gotten her nothing but a constant ache in her heart and an empty apartment. She was thirty-three, after all; she was already past the prime age for marrying and having children, and the love that she'd always craved had eluded her. The total summation of her life was that she had a nice apartment, a snazzy car, and had wasted her life by loving her best friend's husband. Time, and life, were passing her by, slipping away from her outstretched arms without even pausing to look at her.

Midnight was the time for making plans for the future, when the past had proved barren. She lay there, forcing herself to be logical and deliberate, even when it hurt. In her own best interests, she'd have to find another job. She'd never get over Rome if she saw him every day. She would begin looking for a suitable job Monday morning, and she didn't think it would be that difficult; she'd made a lot of friends and contacts during her years with Spencer-Nyle, when she'd worked so hard to develop a career that she'd never really wanted. Diane had been the ambitious one, making stupendous plans that she'd chucked the instant after meeting Rome. All Sarah had ever wanted was someone to love, a husband who looked at her with devotion, children to love and raise as best she could, and a home to provide a warm haven from the rest of the world. The man who loved her wouldn't be Rome, she realized anew, and the pain struck her as strong and fresh as it had from the first.

What good would leaving Spencer-Nyle do her if she kept mooning over a man she couldn't have? It was time—past time—for her to forget about Rome and start looking for someone who would love her in return. Max's lean, intelligent face swam into her view, and she caught her breath. Max?

She wouldn't use him. He deserved better than that. But the fact remained that she'd been more attracted to Max than she'd ever been to any man other than Rome. If he asked her out again, she'd accept. After all, she would be leaving the company, so there wouldn't be the dangers inherent in a boss-secretary relationship.

She could even grow to love him. Perhaps she'd never love him with the depth or fierceness that she loved Rome, but there were different types of love in the world, all of them precious. She'd no longer reject any of them.

Her brave new plans were never given a chance to work. The strident sound of the doorbell jerked her awake before seven o'clock the next morning, and she stumbled out of bed, then had to find a robe to drag on before answering the door.

Leaning against the door tiredly, stretching muscles that ached, she called cautiously, "Who is it?"

"Rome."

Sarah stiffened against the door, suddenly alarmed. How could she get over him if he kept coming back into her life? She didn't want to be hurt any more. She hadn't let herself think about the way he'd taken her because she couldn't handle that yet, couldn't begin to accept that he'd had her, then walked away. Diane had come between them, and she always would be between them.

"Sarah," he commanded in a low voice when she didn't open the door. "We have to talk. Let me in."

Biting her lip, knowing that there had to be a postmortem, she unlocked the door and opened it, stepping away as he entered the apartment. Quickly she looked at him, then averted her eyes. "Coffee?"

"Yes, and plenty of it. I haven't slept."

He looked it. He'd changed clothes, into jeans and a red polo shirt that looked fantastic with his olive complexion, but the lines on his face were harsher than ever, and dark circles lay under his eyes. He was somber, even grim. He followed her into the kitchen and while she put on the coffee he leaned his hip against the tall kitchen stool, one booted foot hooked on the bottom rail of the stool, the other leg stretched out before him. He watched her closely, wondering how she could look so unruffled even though it was plain he'd gotten her out of bed. Except for the thick pale tangle of her hair, she was as remote as an alabaster statue, cool and lovely to look at but not inviting to the touch.

"I want you," he said suddenly, startling her, and her eyes widened.

"I'd planned to have you," he continued, gauging every nuance of her expression, noting her reactions. "Last night didn't get out of hand; I'd intended to have you from the moment I hustled you out of that party. I was going to take you, then forget about you. But it didn't work that way," he said softly.

Sarah stared at the coffee maker as if the slow drip of the coffee into the glass pot fascinated her. "I'd say that everything went according to plan," she forced herself to say lightly. "I don't have anything to compare it to, but it seems to me now that as far as seductions go it was highly successful. I didn't even think of saying no."

"That's when things started to go wrong. You were a virgin, and I couldn't forget about you. I jeopardized you by my lack of control—"

Sarah's head jerked up, as the thought of pregnancy occurred to her for the first time. She stared at him for a long moment, counting in her head, then relaxed against the cabinet. "I should be safe from that," she muttered. "It's the wrong time."

"Thank God," he sighed, closing his eyes. "I couldn't have stood that. I have enough on my conscience as it is."

"I'm an adult," she pointed out briskly, thrusting alarm away from her. "You don't have to feel responsible for me."

"I know I don't have to, but I do. Diane loved you," he said, staring at her intently. "She'd have done away with anyone who hurt you, and now I've done my best to hurt you. She'd want…she'd want me to take care of you," He drew in a deep shuddering breath, his eyes glittering, his entire body taut with stress.

"Sarah, will you marry me?"

Chapter Four

Sarah stared at him. As marriage proposals went, that one was fairly insulting, so much so that for a long moment she couldn't even react. She loved him, but this was a bit much. So he thought she'd marry him to ease his guilty conscience? Was she such a desperate case that he thought she'd jump at the chance? Worse, was he right? Trembling inside, she didn't know if she'd have the strength to turn him down, even knowing that he'd asked her for the worst possible reason.

To give herself time, she turned to get two coffee mugs down from the cabinet, keeping her back turned to him while she concentrated on regulating her breathing, carefully easing her senses back onto an even keel. Turning one smooth ceramic mug in her fingers, she finally managed one normal word. "Why?"

Rome's skin had an ashen hue beneath the olive tint, and she knew that it hadn't been easy for him to ask her. How could it be, when he still waited, in his heart, for Diane?

Like any good businessman, he began by outlining the advantages of a merger. "I think we could have a good marriage. We're both career people; we'd each understand the pressures the other was under, the demands that cut into the time we'd normally have together. We get along better now than we ever have, and the trips I have to take would give us breathing space away from each other. I know you're used to being independent, and having time to yourself," he said cautiously, watching her in an effort to guess her reception to his proposal, but it was like searching for expressions on the smooth, cool face of a china doll. "We'd know how to stay out of each other's way."

The coffee was finished. Sarah dumped the grounds, then poured the steaming deliciously scented brew into the mugs. Handing one to him, she leaned against the counter and blew gently on the coffee to cool it. "If we need so much time apart, why bother to get married?" she finally asked. "Why not just keep on the way we've been?"

His dark face softened as he looked at the pale tumble of hair that curled itself like living arms around her shoulders. "Sarah, if you were a woman who could accept a casual affair, you wouldn't have been a virgin last night."

Shivering, Sarah reminded herself that he was a good chess player. He knew how to defend and attack, and how to slide in under a weak argument. No, she wasn't a woman to sleep around, because she'd never been able to see any man but him. Couldn't he see the obvious? A woman who'd been a virgin for so long, despite the normal opportunities to change that condition, could have had only one reason for going without question into his arms the night before.

"It was good last night," he said softly, his words winding themselves around her heart like a vine, tugging her close to him, bending her to his will. "You felt so good that I went a little crazy, but I could still feel the way you softened inside. If I could have waited, would you have gone a little crazy for me? Was it beginning to feel good to you?"

He slid off the stool, coming closer to her, his dark velvet voice seducing her all over again. Standing before her, he drank his coffee, watching her all the while over the rim of the mug.

Sarah sipped the coffee too, holding it on her tongue so the tart taste of it could delight her taste buds. She could feel the heat climbing in her face, and she cursed her pale complexion that made even the faintest of blushes instantly apparent. "Yes, I liked it," she finally admitted jerkily.

"I'd be a good husband. Faithful, hardworking, loyal, just like Fido the Wonder Dog, or whatever the mutt's name was." She glanced up quickly and saw the amusement sparkling in the depths of his eyes, golden now as his mood lightened. "I like being domesticated," he continued, his clipped accent slowing as he thought out his words. "I like the stability of it, the companionship, someone to drink coffee with on rainy mornings and cold winter nights. It's raining now; isn't this nice?" He cupped the ball of her shoulder in his palm, his fingers kneading the delicate joint; then he deliberately slid his hand inside the collar of her robe, his fingers gliding under the edge of her nightgown to fondle the cool sweetly swelling curves of her breasts.

Sarah held herself perfectly still, her body quivering inside from the run of pleasure. He wasn't being fair; how could she think clearly when her body, superbly fashioned by nature to respond to the touch of the man she loved, was demanding all her attention? Intellect was a fine thing, but Rome was fast teaching her how little her mind could control her body's natural desire.

Rome watched her closely, seeing the soft mists of passion cloud the cool directness of her eyes. Her lashes drifted down, her lids growing heavier, and her breath was coming faster between her softly parted lips. His own heartbeat was picking up speed as he felt her breasts growing warm beneath his touch, the enchanting woman smell of her rising to his nostrils and telling him, without him even thinking of it, that she was his for the taking. Before it was too late, he drew his hand back, but the need to touch her drove him to reach for her again, clasping her slim waist and pulling her to him. Her coffee sloshed dangerously close to the rim, and he rescued both of them, setting his own mug down, then taking hers and placing it beside the other one.

Then she was securely in his arms, her soft body nestled against his, adjusting herself without thought to the hard contours of his muscular frame, and that adjustment made both of them gasp.

"You see?" he muttered shakily, burying his face against the slippery silk of her hair. "We're good together. Damned good."

Sarah laced her arms around his back, feeling the dampness of his shirt where he'd sprinted through the rain. The fresh smell of rain and the coming autumn mingled with his own vital male scent, luring her, and she rubbed her nose into the hollow of his shoulder. What kind of marriage would she have with him, heaven or hell? Would she be content with what he could give her, or would she slowly shrivel inside, dying because she wanted all of him and his heart would always be Diane's? At that moment, standing there in the kitchen with their arms locked around each other, she felt that she could ask nothing more of heaven, but when the daily grind of life wore her down, would she need more from him?

Slowly his big hands moved up her back, finding and stroking each separate rib and vertebra. "Say yes, baby," he cajoled huskily, the first endearment he'd ever used with her, and she melted inside, going weak. "I want you; I've always wanted you, all those years when you were giving me that delicate cold shoulder. There was no way I was going to jeopardize my marriage to Diane by going after you; I loved her too much. But I've always wanted you, and Diane isn't between us anymore. I think ... I think she'd like the idea of us taking care of each other."

Her face hidden in his shoulder, Sarah closed her eyes in pain. When he spoke of Diane, every word was a sword that cut into her heart. How could she ever be strong enough to live with the knowledge that she'd never replace Diane in his affections? But even as she writhed inside in pain, Rome lifted her even more tightly against him, and his action sent all her thoughts into confusion. Gently shifting their positions, he leaned back against the cabinets and spread his legs to support Sarah's weight, pulling her intimately against him and holding her tightly to his chest.

"If I'm going to have you, then I'll have to marry you." Catching her jaw in his fingers, he gently forced her to lift her head so he could see her face. "You're just not the type of woman who could handle anything less. I'm offering you a commitment, a legal relationship with all the rights that grants you. I'll be faithful to you; I prefer a commitment with one woman to a thousand one-night stands with women whose names I can't even remember. We know each other; we know what to expect. And we're friends; we can talk to each other about the office, about a hundred things that we have in common. We'd have a partnership that a lot of people would envy."

He had it all worked out, all the logical reasons why a marriage between them would work. Their home would be an extension of the office, with sex as the icing on the cake. She could just see them, tidily putting folders into their respective briefcases, then falling on each other with feral desire, office decorum shattered under the fierce need to blend their bodies together in the ancient ritual that ensured the survival of the species.

Abruptly his hands tightened on her, and she could feel him tensing against her body. "Before you make up your mind, there's something you should know." A harsh note, barely revealed, told her how much he didn't want to say what he was thinking, but in a negotiation, the negatives were always weighed, as well as the positives, and he was treating this like a business merger.

"I don't want children," he said harshly. "Ever. After losing Justin and Shane, I can't bear being around children. If you want children, then I'll back off now, because I can't give them to you." Pain twisted his features; then he controlled himself, and an expression of bleak resignation settled in place. "I just can't get over..." His voice trailed off, and she felt his shoulders draw up, as if bracing themselves under a burden that showed no signs of lifting.

Sarah swallowed, wondering how many marriage proposals were followed by a bluntly honest statement from the prospective groom on why the woman shouldn't marry him. How many women would want to marry a man who offered companionship instead of love, a man who didn't want a family, a man who would be gone on frequent trips? And she remembered what he'd said the night he'd packed up all the boys' things—that he hadn't been able to sleep in the same bed with a woman since Diane's death. She wouldn't even be able to share the nights with him! A woman would have to be crazy to accept such a proposal, Sarah thought. Crazy in love.

She stepped back from him and looked at his hard dark face, the face that had lived in her dreams for years. She thought only briefly of her dream of raising a houseful of children, his children, then gently told her dream goodbye. Those children lived, after all, only in her dreams, while Rome was very real, and if she turned him down now, heaven might slip forever out of her grasp. So he didn't love her; he cared for her, respected her, enough to want to make their relationship legal. Miracles *did* sometimes happen, and as long as they lived, there was always the chance that he would grow to love her. But even if he never offered her his heart, he was offering her all that he could. She might turn him down, out of pride, but pride wouldn't replace the living warmth of the man. Pride wouldn't make love to her with the swift hard passion he'd shown her the night before. With a woman's intuitive wisdom, she knew that, so long as he desired her so strongly, she had a chance of warming his wintry heart again.

"Yes," she said calmly. "Now what?"

Her brief matter-of-fact acceptance didn't shift him off balance—his only reaction was a deep intake of breath that swelled his chest—then he pulled her against him again. "What I'd like to do is strip you naked and take you on the nearest flat surface I can find—"

Sarah interrupted, groaning. "The floor again," she protested teasingly.

"Or the table. Or the cabinet top." The powerful reaction of his body told her that, while his words were teasing, his body was serious. Sarah held her breath, wondering if her already stiff muscles could survive an amorous encounter on the hard tile of the kitchen floor. Clasped against him as she was, she couldn't see his face, or she'd have cried out at the passion etched on his features.

Rome held her tightly to him, wanting to absorb her into his flesh. The relief that had flooded through him at her casual acceptance of his proposal was so great that he'd felt almost faint; then he'd been seized by the primeval desire to finalize their bargain in the most basic way possible. He wanted to brand her as his; feel again the softness of her body beneath him. He'd planned his proposal very carefully, couching it in the most logical terms he could present, letting her know he wouldn't disrupt her carefully ordered world. The idea of marrying her had come to him during the night, and he really did feel that Diane would approve of his marrying Sarah. More than that, he liked the idea of her having his name and being in his bed every night. The fiercely possessive streak in him wanted to mark her off-limits to every other man, especially before that damned Max Conroy could work his potent charm on her. But until she'd looked at him after he'd asked her to marry him and very calmly said "Why?" he hadn't realized how desperately he needed her to say yes. Her affirmative answer, finally given, and in such an offhand manner that he was shaken by how little enthusiasm she had for the idea, had lifted a weight from him that he hadn't even known was there until it was gone and he felt his freedom from its restrictions. Lord, how he wanted her!

He rubbed his beard-roughened chin against her temple and reluctantly shifted her away from him. "We can wait," he said, wanting to embroil her in plans before she had a chance to have second thoughts. "We have to plan everything, and make arrangements."

"We have to make breakfast," she added, taking her cue from him and keeping everything light and practical. "Unless you've already eaten?"

"No, I hadn't even thought about it. I didn't realize I was hungry until you mentioned it, but damned if I'm not starving."

She smiled a little, thinking that he'd just revealed that he'd been suffering from an attack of nerves, though she wasn't going to drive herself mad trying to decide whether he'd been afraid she'd turn him down or afraid she'd accept.

"Let me comb my hair; then I'll make the biggest breakfast you ever saw."

"While you're combing your hair, *I'll* start on the biggest breakfast we ever saw," he amended. "Do you want the works?"

She nodded, feeling happier than she ever had before, and her appetite seemed to have increased in response. Though normally a light eater, she felt hungry enough to put away a man-size breakfast. "I like my eggs over medium," she informed him on her way out.

"I'll expect you back before then. It doesn't take that long to comb your hair!"

"How do you know?" she retorted smugly. "You've never seen me."

His low chuckle followed her as she went to the bedroom. When the door was closed behind her, she sat down on the bed and clasped her hands on her knees, every muscle in her body quivering in delight. She couldn't believe it. After she'd torn herself to pieces over him for years, he'd walked in the door and asked her to marry him. His reasons were logical, but that didn't matter. To a starving woman, half a loaf was better than no bread at all. She thought of the mornings they would share, cooking breakfast together, lingering over a last cup of coffee, and her heart felt so full of happiness that she had trouble dragging oxygen into her chest. A marriage opened up a whole new world of intimacy. Not just sexual intimacy, but the tiny things like sharing the bathroom mirror when they were in a rush to get ready for work, trading sections of the newspaper on Sunday mornings, having someone to rub the strain from her neck and shoulders after a hard day.

Suddenly she didn't want to be away from him a moment longer than necessary. She splashed cold water over her face, combed her hair and pulled it back with a clasp on each side, and swiftly changed into jeans and an oversize white shirt. She rolled the sleeves up as she returned to the kitchen.

The bacon was frying when she entered the room, and she sniffed in deep appreciation. Rome was rummaging in her cabinets, and he emerged with a box of instant pancake mix. "Pancakes *and* eggs," he announced. "Silver-dollar pancakes."

She shrugged and went along with him, not certain that her appetite was healthy enough for pancakes as well, but his probably was. While he was mixing the batter, she set the table, poured the orange juice, and got out the eggs.

"We'll have to find a new apartment," he said casually. "Neither of ours is large enough to hold all our things."

"Ummm." Thinking to spare him the necessity of spelling out to her that he wouldn't be sleeping with her, she said casually, "I'd like to have a three-bedroom apartment, if we can find one at a reasonable price. It would be nice to have an extra bedroom in case anyone came to visit."

He went curiously still, but his back was to her and she couldn't see his expression. To let him know that she wasn't going to dwell on the subject, she said just as casually, "I'll have to quit my job."

His head jerked around, his dark eyes incredulous.

"Well, I will." She smiled at him. "I can't work at Spencer-Nyle if I'm going to be married to you. It's unprofessional, and I don't think it would work very well, even if Mr. Edwards agreed."

His jaw set grimly. "I didn't think of that. I can't ask you to quit your job for me. I know how much it means to you—"

"You don't know anything," she interrupted. "I was thinking of quitting anyway." It was time Rome Matthews began learning a little about the woman he planned to marry, and the first lesson was to begin breaking it to him, gradually, that she wasn't a dedicated, high-powered businesswoman who got the greatest satisfaction of her life from her job. "It's just a job," she said deliberately. "I like it, and I've done my best at it because I don't believe in only half doing something, not because I'm devoted to it. I'd begun thinking of quitting, as I said. After last night, I didn't see how I could go on working with you."

He gave her a disbelieving look. "You'd quit just because we had sex?"

"I didn't think I could keep things professional between us at work."

"Look, I could arrange something—"

"No," she said mildly, not giving him time to finish. "I'm not planning to sit on my rear and let you support me, if that's what you're worried about. I've worked too hard to settle into a routine of soap operas, and I wouldn't have anything else to occupy my time. I'll get another job."

"That's not it," he growled angrily. "I'm well able to support you even if you wanted to sit on your rear for three lifetimes. I just hate the thought of you giving up your job because of me."

"It's the only reasonable thing to do. I'm not *that* attached to it, and you're an executive; I'm not."

"You'll look for another secretarial job?"

"I don't know." Thoughtfully she broke an egg into the skillet. "I have some money saved up; I might go into some sort of business for myself. I could open a dress shop, like every lady of leisure with money and time on her hands does.'' She grinned at the thought.

He shook his head. ''Whatever you want, as long as it's what *you* really want. If you want to stay at Spencer-Nyle, I'll throw my weight around.''

''I really think I'll be happier out of the office routine. I've done it for a long time now, and I'm ready for a change.''

After a moment, he chuckled wickedly. ''This is really going to drive Max crazy.''

''Rome!'' Laughing helplessly at him, she shook her head. ''What a fiendish thought! Did you ask me to marry you just so you could force Max to get a new secretary?''

''No, but it serves him right.''

''Don't you like him?''

He lifted his eyebrows. ''I like him a lot. He's a hell of an executive. But liking him at work, and liking the way he looks at you are two different things.''

Sarah decided that she really owed Max a big favor if his interest had sparked the possessiveness in Rome that had resulted in last night. As she finished cooking the eggs, she stole glances at Rome, and a thrill went through her every time. They worked so well together, it could have been the hundredth breakfast they'd shared instead of the first. She only hoped that this first breakfast was an indication of how smoothly their married life would go. She wouldn't push him, but she hoped, with every fiber of her being, that she could teach him how to love again.

Telling Max, that Monday morning, wasn't the easiest thing she'd ever done. He was at first disbelieving, then outraged, as he realized that she was turning in her notice.

"The bloody barbarian did this deliberately," he fumed, pacing up and down the office, so angry that his vivid eyes were glittering. Temper radiated from him like electricity. "He knew you'd quit and leave me totally lost."

"Thank you," Sarah said dryly. "I can't tell you how much it reassures me to think that Rome asked me to marry him solely to upset your routine."

Max halted in his pacing, staring at her, and his eyes softened. "I need a good hard kick in the rear," he finally admitted ruefully. "Ignore me, darling. My nose is out of joint because he's already won the race, and I was left standing at the starting post. It's so damned embarrassing."

Sarah laughed, because the image of Max's mooning over her was so ludicrous. He was sophisticated down to his fingertips, and every woman in the building would give her eyeteeth for a chance with him...every woman but herself. He watched her as she laughed, her face lit by the inner glow that riveted him every time he saw it. As if drawn by her gentle warmth, he moved closer to her, a little sad because that glow wasn't for him, and she'd never grace his life as he'd so often imagined her.

"If he ever makes you unhappy, you know where I am," he murmured, stroking her satin cheek with his forefinger. "Be careful, darling. Beneath that controlled corporate image the man's a wolf on the prowl, and you're just an innocent lamb. Don't let him have you for lunch."

Max didn't state the obvious, that Rome didn't love her, but she knew that the thought was in his mind. He was observant enough to know that Rome's actions sprang from libido, not from emotion.

"You do know what you're doing?" he worried.

"Yes, of course I do. I've loved him for a long time."

"Does he know?"

She shook her head.

"Then, don't tell him. Make him work for it; he'll appreciate it more." A shrewd look entered his eyes. "Why do I have a feeling that the lamb is going to get the best of the wolf?"

"I don't know, but I hope you're right," she said shakily. "You don't know how much I hope so!"

"Just remember: If it doesn't work out, cut your losses. I'll be here if you need me. I have a fantasy," he mused. "It's a very simple one. I fantasize that I take you back to England with me, marry you in the stone relic of a church where my family has shackled themselves for more generations than I can count, and get you with child. Providing heirs would be my favorite occupation."

Sarah laughed again, blushing, and part of her wished it could have been Max. Her love would have been safe with him. But instead she'd given her heart to a man burdened by the past, a man who wanted her body and her companionship, but not the wealth of love inside her.

"May I kiss you?" he asked, sliding his hand from her cheek to cup it around her chin, lifting it so he could look her full in the face. "Just once, and I promise to never ask you again... as long as you're with Rome."

Looking into those wickedly dancing turquoise eyes, Sarah knew he didn't have a chaste good-bye kiss in

mind. He wanted to kiss her with passion, with all the
heat of his superb male body. She knew very well that
Max wasn't in love with her, but she knew, as he did,
that had things worked out differently he could have
been the one she married. Only the timing of their
initial meeting had prevented it. Knowing that she
could have loved him if she hadn't loved Rome first
and forever blinded herself to other men made her feel
a little sad and a little happy at the same time. "Yes,
as a good-bye kiss," she said, and rose a little on tiptoe to offer her mouth to him.

At the same moment that his mouth touched hers,
Sarah heard the door open. She knew that Max heard
it too, but he didn't pull away. With the devilishness
of his personality, he instead drew her closer even
when she stiffened reflexively against him, wrapping
his arms around her and locking her tightly to the hard
warmth of his body. He kissed her deeply, his tongue
dancing across hers, taking his time about it and savoring the taste and feel of her. Every nerve in her
body jingled, telling Sarah that it was Rome who'd
entered, but she found herself totally helpless in Max's
embrace; beneath that slender, elegant frame were
steel muscles. At last he lifted his mouth, and she
gasped for breath, hanging in his arms, and he looked
straight across the room into Rome's narrowed dark
eyes, a brilliant smile lighting his face. "Do you have
any objections?" he asked mildly.

Rome crossed the office to them and gently took
Sarah out of Max's embrace. Pulling her into the
strong safety of his arms, he cradled her against him.
"Not this once," he said smoothly. "Not as good-bye.
But that was your one free ride, and I'm giving you

that only because you've lost. If there's a next time, you'll have to pay.''

''Fair enough.'' Max grinned and held out his hand to Rome. ''Congratulations.''

They shook hands, grinning like idiots, and Sarah rolled her eyes. She'd been expecting bloodshed, at the least, but instead they were the best of buddies. Men! Who understood them?

''I'm stealing her for a long lunch hour today,'' Rome said. ''We have a lot to do: blood tests, license, apartment-hunting. I'll be free at twelve-thirty. Can you make it by then?'' he asked Sarah, glancing down at her.

Sarah had already made plans of her own, and she shook her head. ''I can't. I have an appointment at one.''

Max rocked back on his heels, looking extraordinarily pleased at hearing Sarah already balking at Rome's directions. Rome ran his office with ball-bearing precision, and his cold, cutting sarcasm was known throughout the far-flung divisions of the Spencer-Nyle corporation. Only Anson Edwards was above Rome's infamous bullying, but then Anson Edwards was legendary for his own scathing temper when faced with incompetence and stupidity. Max waited with pleasure for Rome's reaction to the way Sarah had refused his request.

But if he'd expected the hobnail boot to come down, he was disappointed. Rome lifted an eyebrow in silent inquiry, then said, ''We'll make it tomorrow, then.''

Rome had to use his iron will to keep from demanding of her just where she was going, but he remembered the arguments he'd used to convince her to marry him. They would have to respect each other's need for time alone. Sarah was still very much the aloof, rather solitary woman he'd always known her to be. She'd agreed to marry him, but only after he'd carefully pointed out the plusses for both of them. He'd have to be careful to give her the personal space she needed, the mental and physical privacy she was accustomed to. He could live with that, as long as she came willingly into his arms and gave him the hot, sweet comfort of her body, though it seemed he wasn't even going to get that the way he'd thought. She'd made it pretty plain to him that she expected her own bedroom, and he'd had to grind his teeth to keep from telling her plainly that she'd be sleeping in his bed. He hadn't wanted to sleep with any woman since Diane, until he'd held Sarah in his arms. She was so elusive. He wanted...he *needed*... the dark hours spent with her, when even the simple act of lying beside each other in slumber created bonds that would hold her to him. But not yet; he had to move so carefully with her, not panic her into backing out of the marriage.

Pushing his characteristic possessiveness aside, he walked her back to her office, and his critical eye noted that Max's kiss hadn't brought the delicate apricot tint to her face that she wore whenever *he* made love to her. Leaning over her desk, he gave her a quick hard kiss, as much to watch that entrancing rise of color as to taste the sweetness of her mouth. "Tonight? We can go through the newspapers and mark those apartments that look suitable."

Pleased, Sarah smiled at him. "Would seven be all right? That will give me time to have some sort of meal almost finished."

"Forget about cooking. I'll bring something over."

Watching him walk out of the office, Sarah had to pinch herself to be certain she wasn't dreaming. They were really going to be married.

He'd made love to her the night before, and the thought of it made her heart leap into her throat. If the first time had been unbridled passion, the second had been a lesson in the rewards of self-control. It had all begun so casually, while they were watching the evening news on television. During a commercial, he'd tilted her face up to kiss her, and the kiss had lingered, become many kisses. Soon she was lying naked on the sofa, and he had patiently, carefully guided her to full satisfaction, lingering at each plateau and savoring her response, making her as hungry for him as he was for her. He'd also taken care of the protective measures, which had prompted Sarah's call first thing that morning to her doctor, which was why she had an appointment at one o'clock.

It was two thirty when she finally got back to the office, a packet of pills in her purse and her head ringing with Dr. Easterwood's warnings and advice. At the age of thirty-three, she was becoming almost too old for taking birth control pills to be safe. Dr. Easterwood had prescribed the lowest dosage available, with the stern warning that she wanted to see Sarah every six months, and that two years was the maximum length she'd give Sarah before an alternative method would have to be decided on.

Max came out of his office when he heard her enter, a slight frown marring his classic brow. "Are you all right? You were gone longer than I expected."

"I'm fine. I had a doctor's appointment, and you know how it is: you never get in at the time of your appointment."

"Rome has already called twice," he informed her impishly.

She worked with a smile on her face and an inner happiness that was based on the attitude Rome was exhibiting. Love or not, the way he was acting told her that he cared, and she would take whatever she could get. He wasn't showing the often impatient possessiveness with which he'd demanded Diane's time, but Sarah didn't expect that he'd feel that way with her even if he did eventually come to love her. Diane had been beautiful, vibrant, a live wire who caught everyone's attention the moment she walked through the door. Sarah felt that too often she herself resembled a white mouse more than she did anything else. Vivid makeup made her look like a clown, while sparing makeup just tended to be more of the same. She'd found a compromise, over the years, that kept her from blending completely into the background, but her coloring was so fair that she'd never be able to use the kind of dramatic makeup that would draw all eyes to her immediately. She'd like to make Rome sit up and take notice whenever she walked into a room, but somehow she felt that that role was beyond her.

That night, after they'd eaten the sweet-and-sour chicken he'd brought, they spread the newspapers on the table and went over the ads for apartments for rent, with Rome circling the ones he thought might be suitable. Sarah carefully kept herself from thumbing through the columns of houses for sale, knowing that he'd never agree to buying a house. The suburban routine would remind him too strongly of the family he'd lost, and the playing children would drive him insane.

He tapped his pen on one ad that he thought particularly likely, and Sarah leaned over to read it. Her hair, loosened from its knot, swung forward over his tanned forearm, and he went very still. Not noticing, she read the ad, pursing her lips as she considered it.

"It sounds good. Roomy enough, but it'll probably cost the Earth—" As she spoke she turned her head to look up at him. He moved swiftly, and her words were broken off with a gasp as he turned her and pulled her onto his lap, his mouth coming down to stifle the rest of what she'd been saying, cradling her on his left arm while his right hand moved boldly over her body, searching out all of the erotic places that he knew would reward him for his diligence.

Sarah made a soft sound in her throat, sinking against him. His powerful body made her feel surrounded, utterly secure, and she had the thought that she didn't need a homey, comfortable apartment to make her feel safe as long as he held her in his arms. The strength that he kept under control when he was handling her was evident in the steely sinews of his thighs, the rock hardness of his chest. She sought the warm solid contours of his flesh beneath his shirt, sliding her hands beneath the fabric to clench her fingers on him. He nibbled at her mouth, finally releasing it; then he tilted her head back and kissed his way down her throat. "So what if it costs the Earth?" he muttered. "We'll look at it tomorrow."

"Hmmm," she agreed dreamily, no longer interested in apartments.

He unbuttoned her shirt and pressed a kiss to the top swell of her breast, above the lacy edge of her bra. "That damned Max! He knew I was watching."

"Yes." She opened her eyes and smiled at him, her eyes misty with pleasure. "He's a devil."

"He's lucky you weren't kissing him back." He returned her smile, but his tone was feral, his dark eyes narrowed. "Then I wouldn't have been so civilized."

As it had been, he hadn't liked it—he hadn't liked the idea of Max's kisses lingering on her mouth. He wanted only his taste on her lips, so he'd kissed away Max's touch. He kissed her again, for good measure, then reluctantly buttoned her blouse and hoisted her back to her own chair. "We'd better not push our luck," he grunted. "I came over straight from the office, and I don't have anything with me."

Sarah cleared her throat. "About that... my appointment today was with a doctor. I got a prescription for birth control pills."

He leaned back, draping his arm over the back of his chair while he looked at her searchingly, alerted by the hesitancy in her manner that she'd tried very hard not to reveal. His craggy black brows lowered. "Is it all right for you to take them?"

"She's letting me try them, but only if I go back for regular checkups," she admitted on a sigh. "She gave me two years, maximum, before I have to switch to something else."

"If it's dangerous, don't take them." He reached out and took her hand, tracing his thumb over the soft skin on the back of her hand. "I've been thinking about having surgery. It's safe, and permanent."

Sarah shied away from that solution. Its permanency was the one big drawback, for her. Sometime in the future Rome could change his mind about not wanting anymore children, even if this marriage with her didn't work out. She was so acutely aware that he didn't love her that she had to allow for the possibility of him falling in love with another woman, and perhaps that woman would want his children. Perhaps he would want her to have his children. Feeling herself shatter inside at the thought, she pulled away from him before she revealed too much about how she felt. Instead, averting her face, she said in a stifled voice, "We can talk about that later, if the pills don't work out."

Puzzled, he stared at her, running the words they'd just said through his mind again and trying to decide what he'd said that had made her withdraw from him and put on that frosty face he so detested. She'd been so relaxed and natural with him lately, forgetting to guard her actions, and he'd become used to her smiles, her gentle teasing. Now she was Miss Ice-Queen again. She'd begun getting edgy when she'd first mentioned the pills. She wasn't telling him something, and he knew it. He'd thought, when he'd first made love to her, that he'd discovered the reason for her reserve, but now he was seeing it spring up again, and he knew that Sarah had other secrets hidden behind the green shadows of her eyes. He would have liked to delve inside her mind and find out how her mind worked, why she hid so much of herself. He wanted to know her; he wanted all of her secrets laid out where he could see them. The way she withdrew from him triggered in him a primal, violent response to pursue and subdue, an instinct bequeathed from the age when men lived in caves and wore animal skins, and chose their woman by force.

"One of these days," he said in a soft voice, deadly in its intent, "I'm going to find out what makes you tick."

Sarah looked up at him with panic running just below the controlled surface image she presented to him. If he did, if he found out that she loved him, what would he do? Would he accept it, or would he promptly bow out of a marriage that was more than he wanted?

Chapter Five

They were married three weeks later on a Friday evening, after work, by a judge who'd agreed to perform the ceremony in his chambers. To her complete surprise, Max was one of the witnesses, and he winked at her as she and Rome took their places before the judge. About fifteen friends from work stood behind them in the small chamber, their feet shuffling about and their discreet whispering providing a rustling background to the ceremony. Sarah had worked out her two weeks notice and had spent the last week driving herself into the ground trying to get their apartment ready and everything that they weren't going to use either sold or put into storage.

The apartment that they'd finally taken had seemed much too expensive to Sarah, but Rome had overridden her objections to it. It was a big roomy condo, as big as a medium-size house. It had seven rooms, and a large terrace-balcony where they could barbecue and lie in the sun, and where she could put her multitude of plants. It also had a gas fireplace in the living-room, which she suspected was what had sold Rome on the apartment. He'd looked at the fireplace with an expression of almost fiendish satisfaction, and she'd had to admit to a few shivers of anticipation herself when she thought of the coming winter and the nights they would spend in front of the flames.

The best thing about the apartment to her way of thinking was the building manager, who lived on the bottom floor. Marcie Taliferro was a thirty-two-year-old divorcée, a free-lance writer as well as building manager, and she had the most fantastic fifteen-year-old son Sarah had ever seen. Derek Taliferro already stood six feet tall, and was a hard and lean hundred and seventy pounds, and not only was he shaving every other day, he really needed to, which was mind-boggling. His voice was a smooth, deep baritone, and he had inherited his father's classic Italian looks, from the dark curls on his head to his imperious Roman nose. He worked after school at a small grocery store and helped his mother around the condo, as well as being at the top of his class in school. Rome had yet to meet Derek the Wonder, as even Marcie called him, with a little awe in her voice as if she couldn't believe she'd really mothered that perfect specimen. Derek was saving his money to go to college, but from what Marcie had said, he'd still be a long way short, and unless he was lucky enough to get a scholarship, he was going to have a long, hard haul getting through college. Sarah didn't know if Rome had any strings to pull with any colleges, but if there was ever a kid who deserved a break, it was Derek Taliferro.

Marcie was a friendly, commonsense type of person; a little short, a little plump, but the plumpness was mostly muscle. She had red hair, and freckles dashed across her nose, but she lacked the temper that was usually associated with red hair. She tackled every job with a casual manner that made it seem much easier than it really was; she'd helped Sarah move their furniture in and arrange it, since Rome had left that Monday morning on a business trip and hadn't returned until Thursday night.

Sarah eyed him covertly as the judge ran through the ceremony. He was dressed in a dark blue suit, with an impeccable pale blue pinstripe shirt, a discreet tie of navy and burgundy silk, and a burgundy silk handkerchief peeking out of his breast pocket, the splash of color looking smashing with his dark coloring. Suddenly she found it a little difficult to breathe, and her heart began racing in anticipation of the night to come. They'd found the opportunity to make love only three times, as a spate of trips had taken him away several times, and her own natural functions had displayed the world's worst timing. She wanted him, and her body felt weak and warm.

He was tense, his arm rigid where her fingers lay lightly in the crook of his elbow. His deep voice was strained, and his hand shook when he slipped the plain gold band on her finger. As soon as the ring was on, Sarah closed her fingers into a fist, as if she could anchor it to her flesh. Then he was brushing her lips with a light kiss, and it was over. He drew back, his hand locking with hers, and he gave her a smile that merely twitched at the corners of his mouth, then faded.

Everyone came up to shake their hands and congratulate them. Max was the last of all; he shook Rome's hand, then framed Sarah's face in his palms and said softly, "My word, you're lovely! Are you so happy, then?"

"Yes, of course," she whispered, and lifted her face for his kiss, his mouth barely touching hers in the lightest of caresses.

"Damn it, Max," Rome said impatiently. "Why does it seem that you kiss her more than I do?"

"Maybe I'm just smarter than you are," Max returned, grinning.

Sarah clung to Rome's hand, wondering if he thought she looked good. Several people other than Max had commented on her glowing looks, and she knew that it was due as much to the new makeup job she had as it was to her happiness. She'd gone to a hairstyling and makeup salon, and the makeup artist had showed her some new delicate translucent shades that gave her color without being too harsh. Her eyes were made up only slightly darker than usual, but that small difference was a gigantic one. Her Egyptian eyes were more exotic, her lashes feathered, while shadows and secrets lurked in the green depths. Apricot color dusted her cheekbones, and her mouth had a soft, lush quality to it. That wasn't lipstick; that was the way she felt. Beneath the pale rose silk dress she wore, her body was quivering, aching, needing him.

But not yet. Reservations had been made at a swank restaurant, and everyone went along. Lobster and champagne seemed the perfect feast, but Sarah was so nervous that she scarcely noted the snow-white meat of the lobster or the sparkling champagne that slipped down her throat. She wasn't aware that she was getting tipsy until she turned her head to say something to Rome and the room suddenly dipped. She blinked, surprised.

For the first time that entire evening Rome grinned, his dark face lighting as his teeth flashed whitely. "Were two glasses of champagne too much for you?"

"You let me drink *two* glasses?" she asked weakly, clinging to the edge of the table. "Rome, I wasn't joking about my alcohol tolerance. I won't be able to walk out of here!"

"We were just married; everyone will think it's romantic if I carry you out," he said calmly.

"Not if I'm waving the tablecloth like a flag and singing Highland ballads at the top of my lungs," she predicted darkly.

He chuckled but moved the champagne glass away from her plate and signaled the waiter. Shortly thereafter a glass of milk appeared by her side, and she sipped it gratefully. Everyone at the table groaned and predicted dire results from the mixing of champagne and milk, but Sarah knew a lifesaver when she saw one, and she wasn't about to turn it down. Even with the milk slowing the rate at which the alcohol was absorbed into her bloodstream, she knew she wouldn't be steady on her feet when they left the restaurant.

She wasn't; Rome's arm was clamped around her waist like a vise as he helped her to his car. He settled her in the seat and walked around to get behind the wheel, calling out good-byes and acknowledgments to all the best wishes their friends were giving them. After he closed the car door, he sat for a moment, fiddling with the key ring in his hand. Finally he put the key in the ignition and turned to look at Sarah, who was lying back in the seat with her eyes half-closed and an intriguing smile on her lips. The streetlight caught her eyes, making them sparkle like moon dust. She was so soft and feminine, and her subtle perfume rose to his nostrils, tempting him to search it out all along her satiny skin. She was his wife now, a legally intimate partner... his *wife!*

He almost groaned aloud, thinking of another wedding, and Diane's radiant face as she came down the aisle to him, the hunger in the kiss he'd given her at the end of the ceremony. His wife! Diane had been his wife, and he'd never thought another woman would occupy that position, bear that title. Until the ceremony had begun, he hadn't had any doubts about this second marriage, but when the familiar, haunting words reached his ears, he'd broken out in a cold sweat. He didn't, couldn't, regret marrying Sarah, but suddenly the memory of Diane was haunting him. Diane was gone from him now, really gone. He couldn't call her his wife now, because by the grace of the laws of Texas and the United States, and his own determination, the woman at his side was now his wife.

Sarah Matthews. He said the name in his mind, imprinting it there. Sarah Matthews, his wife. Pale, elegant Sarah, always so distant, but now she was his. He knew that no other woman should be in his mind tonight, but he couldn't stop thinking about Diane, couldn't stop comparing her to Sarah. Diane had been so much more forceful than Sarah, capable of standing up to him and arguing with him toe-to-toe, chin-to-chin, then kissing him with all the fervor of her fiery nature. She'd glowed with color, her skin taking on the gold of the sun, her head full of bright gold-brown curls, her eyes as blue as the midsummer sky. Diane had been the sun, warm, shining, while Sarah was the moon, pale and cold and aloof. Sarah... what was it about her that made her so mysterious? Her veiled, shadowy eyes? Had he ever wanted anyone before the way he wanted Sarah? Her mysteries only lured him on, making him want to solve them.

But when he walked Sarah to their new apartment, on this first night they'd both be spending there, he knew he couldn't make love to her. All week he'd been thinking about her, wanting her, feeling her soft flesh beneath him, but now he realized he simply couldn't do it. The grief that had faded to the background in the past weeks now sprang to life again, as fresh and bitter as it had ever been. He had to say good-bye to Diane.

When the door closed behind them, Sarah turned into his arms, swaying against him, her arms going around his neck. He kissed her lightly, hating the stiffness of his body; then he took her arms down and put her away from him. "Let me take a look at this place," he stalled. "I haven't seen it since you put the furniture in it; it really looks great!"

He moved through the apartment, and Sarah weaved after him, confused by the way he'd turned away from her embrace. She swayed, then leaned down and took her shoes off, feeling much steadier in her bare feet than she had tottering on three-inch heels. Rome gave his approval to the decor, then seemed to run out of words. He sighed, running his hands through his hair. Finally reaching a decision, he came back to her and put his arm around her waist again, steadying her as he took her to the door of her bedroom. Despite his need to be alone, the fact that this room was off-limits to him without an invitation still angered him. He opened the door and reached in to turn on the light, then put both of his hands on her shoulders.

"I'm sorry," he said in a low, raw voice. "Things have really hit me hard tonight, and I can't... I have to be alone tonight. I'm sorry," he said again, waiting for her reaction.

There wasn't one. She simply looked up at him, seeming smaller than usual because she was barefoot, no expression at all now in the exotic eyes that had been sparkling only a few moments before. She said "good night" and stepped back, closing the door before he could say anything else, if indeed any other words would come to mind. He was left staring at the blank wood of the door, and he stood there, his broad shoulders slumping in defeat, painful memories winging through his mind for several long minutes before he turned and went to his own room.

He went to bed, but he couldn't sleep. The years he'd spent with Diane ran through his mind's eye like home movies, reacquainting him with every nuance of expression that had crossed her expressive face, the plans they'd made during her pregnancies, the bone-deep pride and adoration he'd felt when he'd taken his infant sons in his arms for the first time. Scalding tears burned the back of his eyes, but never fell. His sons. Justin. Shane.

The pain of losing them was so great that he tried never to think of them; it was something he still couldn't handle. They'd been a part of him. He'd felt each of them growing inside Diane; he'd been there when they were born, been the first to hold them. Justin's first wavering steps had been into his waiting arms. He remembered the two A.M. feedings, the lusty, grunting sounds as the infant mouths took the bottle. He remembered Justin's two-year-old perplexity when a new baby entered his world and took so much of Diane's time, but soon the toddler had become devoted to the infant Shane, and the two boys had been inseparable since then.

He remembered their laughter, their innocence, their fearless exploration of the world, and the boisterous way they'd always greeted him when he came home.

Putting them in their graves had been the hardest thing he'd ever done.

Dear God, it shouldn't have been allowed to happen. A parent should never have to bury a child.

He couldn't think of a day when the sun had shone since then.

His head was pounding with a sudden fierce headache, and he pressed his fingertips to his temples. He wanted to scream his pain aloud, but he ground his teeth and soon the torment abated. Exhausted, he closed his eyes and slept.

In her bedroom, lying in the empty expanse of her bed, Sarah didn't sleep. She lay very still, feeling the effects of the champagne in the way the room seemed to whirl slowly around her, but it wasn't because of the champagne that she lay so motionless. She was filled with such pain that she felt as if she would crystallize if she tried to move.

She should have known, should have realized, how the ceremony would affect him, but she hadn't until she'd seen the hell in his eyes. Rather than celebrating their marriage, he'd been regretting it, because she wasn't the one woman he loved.

Had she been a fool to think she could ever earn his love? Did he even have any more love to give, or had it all gone to the grave with Diane? There was no way of knowing, and she'd made her decision when she'd agreed to marry him. Whatever he could give, she wanted it.

Whatever it cost her, she had to keep him from seeing how she was hurt; she didn't want to add to his pain by making him feel guilty. She'd carry on as normal, as if this were the way every couple began their marriage. She didn't think he'd try to probe too deeply if she put on a nonchalant facade, but rather that he would accept it with relief. All she had to do was get through the weekend; then he would go back to work and she could begin seriously looking for work, or decide if she really wanted to start a small business for herself.

Her weary mind seized on the subject with relief, wanting something, anything, to prevent her from thinking about Rome. There were really no plans she could make concerning him; she'd just have to take each moment as it came. So she put him out of her mind and tried to decide what sort of business would hold her interest, because she wanted something that she liked as well as something to take up her time. She made a mental list of all her hobbies and interests, and several possibilities sprang to mind. She turned the ideas over and over, until at last sleep claimed her.

She woke early, the strangeness of her surroundings having prevented deep sleep. Her bedside clock told her it was six thirty. She got up and showered, then pulled on her nightgown again and a robe as well, as she didn't feel like dressing, and the early autumn temperature had taken a surprisingly sharp dip overnight. It had been so balmy the day before that she'd used the air-conditioning in her car, but now, with typical Texas unpredictability, the weather was distinctly chilly. She went straight to the thermostat and flipped it over to HEAT, and in a moment the comforting pop and crackle of the furnace told her she'd soon have the apartment comfortable.

Though she'd put everything away, the kitchen was still a surprise to her. She had to hunt for the coffee maker; then she couldn't find the dipper that she used to measure the coffee. She opened all the drawers and searched through them, slamming them shut in increasing temper when the search failed to turn up the missing object. She simply wasn't in the mood for anything to go wrong, and she muttered dire threats to the dipper for hiding itself.

Finally she found it in the can of coffee. She closed her eyes at her own stupidity, because now she remembered putting it in the coffee can where it wouldn't get lost.... She *hated* moving! She hated turning everything topsy-turvy, with nothing where she was accustomed to finding it. The refrigerator was on the opposite side of the stove from where it had been in her old apartment, and she turned in the wrong direction every time she wanted something from it. This kitchen was larger than her old one, and she rattled around in it. She felt small and lost, just as she'd felt as a child when she lay in her neat, colorless room and listened to the bitter arguments her parents had.

She knew that Rome was customarily an early riser, so she started breakfast, trying to force herself to relax and perform the familiar routine even though all her cooking utensils were in the wrong places. As soon as the coffee had finished brewing, she poured a cup and sipped it, closing her eyes and trying to will herself to calm down. She knew that, in time, she'd become accustomed to her new surroundings. It was just a matter of adjusting herself.

But what about Rome? He was the cause of at least half her nervousness, because she didn't know what to say to him, and she knew she'd have to face him soon. What could a woman say to a brand-new husband who'd spent the night alone? Perhaps she shouldn't have married him; perhaps he simply wasn't ready to form any sort of permanent relationship with another woman. Should she have turned down his proposal and hoped that he'd ask again when time had healed him? But what if he hadn't asked again? What if he'd simply shrugged and gone his way, then eventually found some other woman and married her? Sarah cringed inside at the thought. It had been bad enough losing him to Diane. She simply couldn't have borne the idea of him being married to someone else, some stranger.

The smell of bacon frying was a universal magnet; soon Rome entered the kitchen, sniffing appreciatively. Sarah darted a glance at him, then just as quickly looked away, before their eyes met. He'd taken a shower, because his hair was damp, and he'd dressed in jeans and a plaid shirt, which he'd left unbuttoned and hanging outside his pants. He wore socks but no shoes. She was so used to seeing him in more formal clothing that his casualness that morning caught at her heart, for it was such a homey, comfortable thing. He was dressed the way husbands usually dressed on lazy Saturday mornings.

"Why were you trying to tear the kitchen down?" he asked, smothering a yawn and covertly watching her with more than a little uneasiness, wondering what his reception would be that morning. What he'd done would be unforgivable for most women, and he felt like a heel. He should at least have talked with her about it.

Sarah was tense, and she felt ridiculously close to tears. "Did I wake you? I'm sorry; I didn't mean to."

"No, I was already awake."

Quickly she poured a cup of coffee for him, and he took it, moving to the small breakfast table and dropping into a chair, sprawling his long legs out before him. She *was* upset, though she didn't seem to be angry. He drank his coffee, not knowing what to say to her.

Sarah took up the bacon, then turned to the refrigerator to get out the eggs, but once again she turned in the wrong direction. She made a choked sound, then jammed her fists over her eyes to hold back the threatening tears. "Oh, damn," she said weakly. "I'm sorry, but I can't get organized. I can't *find* anything!" she burst out, her voice cracking with strain. "I . . . I feel so lost!"

Rome sat up, his brows drawing together at the hint of panic in her voice. She was falling to pieces because she had to cook in an unfamiliar kitchen! It wasn't artifice, and she wasn't using it as an excuse; her panic was real, and she couldn't deal with it.

Without thinking about it, just knowing that she needed comforting, he got up and went to her, wrapping her in his arms and hugging her close against him. "Hey, calm down," he advised soothingly, stroking her moonbeam hair and pressing her head to his chest. "What's all this about?"

He must think she was an absolute ninny. Sarah could feel herself trembling as he resumed his seat and pulled her onto his lap, cradling her against him as if she were a child who'd hurt herself while playing. He rubbed her back, his big hands moving slowly over her spine.

"Didn't you put everything up yourself?" he asked easily.

"Yes. That's what makes it so stupid!" She sought his warmth, her hands going inside the open shirt to clasp his ribs, and she burrowed her face against him like a cat. "It's just that everything's so turned around, and I'm not used to it. I hate for things to change!" she muttered. "You won't find me moving the furniture around every month, or even every year. I like to feel safe in my own home, not a constant stranger."

Struck by her words, he rocked her gently, wondering why he'd known her for so long without realizing that she had such a strong need for a stable base. He tried to remember if he'd ever heard anything about her home life while she'd been growing up, but he drew a blank.

She was usually so serene and competent that it was a little startling to feel her cuddle against him, seeking the safety of his arms, but he liked it. She was so delicately built, she was only a puff in his arms, soft and light, but with the warm, beguiling curves of a woman. She sighed and moved her hands up the strong muscles of his back, and he quivered in delight, and something more. Her hair spilled over his arm in a pale cascade, warm and silky, and he could smell the sweet perfume of female witchery that came from the velvet curves of her breasts. She had a scent all her own, not based on perfume but on the wondrous chemistry of her own sleek, soft skin, warmed by the coursing of her blood, and it wafted into the air with every breath that lifted her breasts like a tantalizing offering.

Desire, heavy and urgent, began tightening his body. He lifted her hair away from her neck and bent his head to trail his mouth down the slender column, taking his time, tracing the source of her female scent. "I promise not to ever move anything around," he murmured as he found the tiny betraying flutter at the base of her throat. He didn't deserve it, but she was responding to him without even commenting on his behavior of the night before; she wasn't going to reject him, or spend the day pouting and feeling hurt. She was accepting him for what he could give, and accepting him joyously, tilting her head back to allow him better access.

He took advantage of her unselfishness, his greedy mouth plundering her flesh as he bared it. Sarah clenched her fingers in his hair, gasping as he pulled open her robe and dispensed with it, then rapidly slid down the straps of her nightgown until the silk fell away from her breasts. He bent his head and closed his hot mouth over one sensitive nipple, wringing a cry of pleasure from her.

"Do you like that?" he muttered fiercely against her, filling his hands and his mouth with velvet mounds and firm jutting nipples.

"Yes...yes." Her answer was thin and faraway, and she tried to put her arms around him, but the strap of her nightgown prevented her from moving her arms.

kissed her lightly on the mouth and left the bed and the room, quietly closing the door behind him as he sought his own bed to sleep alone because, Sarah knew, in his heart his only wife was Diane.

She lay willing him to return, silently begging that there not be a repeat of the night before. But the door didn't open again, and she curled up sadly, dying a little inside. He'd told her once that when the night came, he spent it alone, and she'd never reproached him with it, had even chosen their apartment with that in mind. But in the magic of the day they'd spent together, for the most part in that very bed, she'd forgotten, and now she cried silently, not wanting him to hear.

Chapter Six

Rome put his key into the lock and opened the door, stepping inside the apartment with a deep sense of relief and anticipation. This trip had seemed to drag on unendingly, and he was deeply, utterly weary of hotel rooms and hotel food. Just stepping inside the foyer, he was instantly aware of the comfort and serenity that Sarah had brought to the apartment, a sense of being home, which was something that he'd been missing for a long time now. He couldn't say just what it was that she did, but somehow everything was more comfortable.

Even though they'd only been married two weeks, he'd looked forward to the trip, feeling an uneasy need to distance himself from the soft, unseen bonds that were pulling at him. It wasn't that Sarah demanded anything; rather, she demanded nothing. But still he found himself thinking of her at odd times during the day, wanting to talk to her about some little detail of the job, or wanting to make love to her, an urge that could have embarrassing results when he was at work. It took very little to remind him of making love to her: hearing her name mentioned, or walking by Max's office. Any small detail could plunge him into the memory of how she tasted, how she felt, how she responded. She was so astonishingly sensual, he was still astounded by the contrast of her cool, quiet image and the moaning, writhing woman in his arms.

He'd wanted time away from her, but the trip had dragged on too long; what was originally to be a three-day trip had become eight, and Sarah hadn't seemed upset at all when he'd called and told her he'd be delayed. She'd simply said "All right; just let me know when you'll be home" and gone on to other subjects. He'd felt a little deflated by her lack of interest, and suddenly the trip and the myriad details he had to deal with had become tiresome. He wanted to go home.

The need to relax and be with Sarah had become so compelling that he'd pushed himself and everyone else to the breaking point, but he'd wound everything up a day earlier than he'd told Sarah to expect him, and now he looked around the quiet apartment, the sunlight streaming in the windows, a faint, tantalizing aroma, the smell of homemade apple pie, lingering on the air. He sniffed and grinned, because apple pie was his favorite.

"Sarah?" he called, dropping his briefcase and overcoat, suddenly anxious to have her in his arms again. What would she think when he hustled her off to bed? But it had been a long, frustrating eight days, and he wasn't accustomed to celibacy. He was, however, as he'd described himself to Sarah, a faithful husband, preferring domesticity and one woman to a multitude of brief tawdry encounters. Besides, he hadn't wanted any other woman. He'd wanted Sarah, with her cool reserve and comfortable silences, and her fairy-pale hair wrapped around his arms like silken ropes.

But she didn't come running out, and a frown drew his black brows together. Impatiently he searched through the apartment, already knowing she wasn't there. Where was she? Shopping? She could be job-hunting; she'd mentioned that she had a few interesting prospects. He checked his watch. It was almost four, so she should be getting back anytime.

He unpacked, then sat down to read the newspaper. He watched the evening news. As the sun went down, the temperature dropped sharply, and he turned on the heat and sat for a long time watching the blue flicker of the fire. The October twilight was short, and soon there wasn't a hint of daylight left.

Keeping his irritation under control, Rome prepared his dinner and ate it alone, and he helped himself to a big chunk of the apple pie. As he cleaned up the kitchen a sudden black rage seized him, compounded in part by the unspeakable fear that he wouldn't name, even to himself. Diane had gone out and not returned; he wouldn't even let himself consider anything happening to Sarah.

But, damn it, *where was she?*

It was almost ten when he finally heard her unlock the door, and he got to his feet, a mixture of relief and pure fury filling him. He heard her say ''Thanks, Derek. I don't know what I'd have done without you! See you tomorrow.''

A deep, quiet voice said, "Anytime that you need help, Mrs. Matthews, just call me. Good night."

"Good night," Sarah echoed, and in a moment she walked into the kitchen, turning left instead of right into the living room where Rome was. At that moment she became aware of the puzzling fact that the lights were on, when everything should have been in darkness, and she stopped in her tracks. Standing where he was, Rome could see her slender back stiffen; then she whirled, and her face lit up like the Fourth of July.

"Rome!" she said, and launched herself at him.

Her open enthusiasm disarmed him, and he found himself forgetting about being angry; instead he was just glad to see her. He opened his arms to her, then at the last moment grabbed her shoulders and held her back, away from him.

"Whoa!" he commanded, laughing a little. "I'm not certain ... who are you? The voice is familiar, but I've never seen this dirt before."

Sarah laughed ruefully, so happy to have him home again that she wanted to whirl on her toes like a child. She wanted very much to kiss him, but she was filthy and she knew it. She looked down at her jeans, blackened down the front with grease and grime and various other stains, including one ketchup stain where she'd dropped the hotdog that she'd had for lunch in her lap. Unfortunately the grease and grime extended from her toes to her head. She'd covered her hair with a red bandana and now she carefully pulled it off; beneath it, her hair was still in a pristine knot, and the contrast was incongruous.

"I'm a mess," she admitted. "Let me take a quick shower; then I'll tell you all about it."

"I can't wait," he said dryly, wondering what catastrophe could have turned his spotless, impeccable wife into that ragamuffin. Her shirt-sleeve was torn, he noticed. Had she been in a fight? Impossible, and there were no bruises or cuts, which also ruled out an accident.

He followed her to the bathroom. "Just tell me one thing: Have you been doing anything illegal, or has something happened to you that will require police action?"

She gave the low, husky chuckle that always started a fire low in his gut. "No, nothing like that. It's good news!"

He watched as she stripped off her soiled clothing, her dainty nose wrinkled in distaste as she dropped each garment to the bathroom floor. Hungrily he gazed at her slender fluid curves, the body that was his, with the sweet honey nipples and pale gold curls, all his. He noticed the way she flexed her shoulders, as if they were stiff, and an unconscious sigh of weariness escaped her.

"Have you had anything to eat?" he asked.

"Nothing since lunch."

"I'll get something together for you while you're showering."

When she left the shower, feeling clean again, Sarah felt as if the warm water that had washed away the grime covering her had also washed away the last dregs of her energy. She was so tired, she could have fallen facedown on the bed and slept through the next day, but Rome was waiting for her, and she had to see him. He hadn't even kissed her yet, and it had been forever since she'd touched him, felt his mouth on hers. She pulled on a robe, the only garment she bothered with, and went to the kitchen.

He'd opened a can of soup and made a grilled-cheese sandwich for her, and that seemed like ambrosia. She stumbled into the chair, already reaching for the sandwich as he placed a glass of milk beside the plate.

"So, tell me your good news," he invited, turning a chair around and straddling it, propping his arms along the back.

For a long moment she simply stared at him, unable to believe how good he looked to her. His thick dark hair was tousled, and his face was tired, but he was the most beautiful man she'd ever seen.

"I've bought a store," she said.

He rubbed his cheekbone with a finger, a little surprised at how the news made him feel. He'd told her that their respective careers gave them much-needed independence from each other, but when it came down to the nitty-gritty, he wanted Sarah's undivided attention. Reminding himself yet again not to push her, that she expected, and deserved, the right to make that decision herself, he hid his reaction and instead asked "What kind of store?"

"A combination do-it-yourselfer and handicrafts store. I bought it for a song, because the building was in ratty shape," she explained blithely. "The location is great; it's only a mile from here. But the stock is included, and most of it is handmade. Just wait until you see the pottery! The pottery wheel is in a back room, and I might try my hand at it. I did some pottery in high school. I've been killing myself trying to get it ready before you saw it," she said. "We've cleaned and painted and put up new shelving, and Derek has put in new lighting fixtures—''

''Who's this Derek?'' Rome interrupted, remembering the man who'd come with her to the door.

Sarah made an exasperated sound at him. ''Derek Taliferro, Marcie's son. I've mentioned him to you. He saw me to the door.''

''*That* was Derek? I thought he was fourteen or fifteen.''

''He is. Fifteen. Just wait until you meet him! He looks twenty, at least, and he's a great kid. I don't know what I'd have done without him. It's a school night, and he should have been at home studying, but he wouldn't leave me alone down there.''

''Smart kid,'' Rome said, lifting his brows at her in a way that told her he didn't like the idea of her being alone in the store so late at night.

Ignoring that comment, Sarah devoted herself to her meal, demolishing it with well-mannered greed. Just as she finished, she looked up to find him watching her intently, an unreadable expression in his eyes. ''You're back a day early,'' she finally said.

''I tied everything up this morning and caught the first flight home. I got in about noon, dropped by the office for an hour, and got here a little before four.''

''I'm sorry I wasn't here,'' she said softly. ''I wish I'd known.''

He shrugged, and the indifferent gesture made her draw back. She'd been about to reach out for him, but now she kept her hands tightly in her lap.

''I ate half of that pie,'' he said, changing the subject. ''Do you want a slice?''

''No. No, I—'' She stopped, a wave of exhaustion sweeping over her. She tried to fight it off, but weariness overwhelmed her, and she couldn't keep going any longer. "I'm so tired," she sighed, closing her eyes for a moment.

She heard the clatter of dishes as he cleared the table, and with a supreme effort she opened her eyes to give him a sleepy little smile, one that sent a surge of electricity through him. "Let's go to bed," she invited.

Without waiting for a second invitation, he bent and lifted her into his arms, his mouth at last finding hers in a long penetrating kiss. He knew she was tired, and he'd meant to wait, but when she'd asked him to go to bed, all of his good intentions fled. After carrying her quickly to her bedroom, he pulled back the covers and placed her on the bed, leaning down to loosen the robe and pull it away from her, baring her to his gaze.

She sighed and closed her eyes, and he stripped quickly, dropping his clothes to the floor. It took him only a moment, then he slid naked between the sheets and drew her into his arms.

She snuggled against him with a little murmur, and her bare breasts pushed against his chest. With sure, hard fingers he cupped her breast, his thumb rubbing against the small tight nipple. Aching with desire, he bent his head to kiss her, and in that moment realized she was asleep.

A low growl of frustration rose to his throat, but he lay back against the pillow, cradling her to him because he needed to feel her silken flesh in his arms; he had to hold her, if just for a while. She was exhausted, and he could wait, but every fiber of his body, every masculine instinct he possessed, wanted him to bury himself in her. There would be times when his work would demand long hours of him and he'd be too tired to make love, he reminded himself, trying not to resent the unseen store that had already taken her away from him. It was just that ... hell, she was so comfortable to have around! Everything was right where it should be, and organized to the nth degree. He had the whimsical thought that, give Sarah a roomful of worms and within an hour she'd have the worms crawling in formation. The humor lightened his mood, and he lay for a long time, holding her while she slept, because he began to feel drowsy and reminded himself that if he didn't get up then, he probably wouldn't, and she'd made it plain how she felt about sleeping together. Making love with him was fine, and she obviously enjoyed it, but afterward she wanted her own bed and privacy. Easing away from her, he went to his own room.

Sarah woke several hours later, uncomfortable from the glass of milk she'd drunk at such a late hour. Automatically she reached out for Rome, but her hand encountered the empty pillow and fell back listlessly. He wasn't there, and no matter how often he left her to go to his own bed, she couldn't become accustomed to it. Her body, her mind, just couldn't accept that he wasn't where he belonged.

She got up, feeling suddenly bleak, and wondering if she had any chance at all of ever winning any emotion from him other than mild affection. And lust, she reminded herself. But that wasn't an emotion—it was a physical reaction.

There was a bad taste in her mouth from the milk, so she brushed her teeth, then yawned, and stared at herself in the bathroom mirror. Her hair was a mess. She was too tired to worry about it right then, though, so she pushed it back and stumbled her way back to bed, where she promptly fell asleep once more.

In the gray light of dawn, she came slowly awake, stretching under slow, warm caresses that roamed over her body and touched her with familiar intimacy. There was a magnetic warmth beside her and she turned to it, her head finding the hard pillow of Rome's chest, her arms wrapping around him without thought.

"Wake up," he crooned softly in her ear, nipping at the lobe with his sharp teeth, then kissing his way along her jaw to find her mouth.

"I'm awake," she murmured, sliding her palms up his naked back and feeling the hard ripple of muscle under his warm skin.

He took her immediately. She was warm and pliable from sleep, her body rosy, and she drew in a quick breath of pleasure as he moved with slow power into her. "I can't wait; I have to have you," he muttered.

The room was considerably brighter when he lifted his head from her breasts and said on a note of astonishment. "Damned if I'm not going to be late for work."

"You've been away for eight days," she murmured, snuggling against him. "You deserve to sleep late."

"But I haven't been sleeping." His wry observance brought a sleepy smile to her lips, a smile of complete physical satisfaction. During the normal course of the day, he treated her as if she were an old, comfortable house slipper: easy to have around, but nothing to get excited about. He wasn't affectionate with her, didn't often call her by endearments, and in fact often seemed to discourage any signs of deepening emo-

tional intimacy between them. But in bed there were
no barriers, no polite distances. In bed with him, she
could forget about everything else and simply savor
their closeness. The world was blotted out by the grip
of his hard, strong arms and the heavy pressure of his
body.

His hand stroked slowly down her side and found
the curve of her hip, his fingertips feathering over the
smoothness of her buttock. He'd missed more than the
startling passion of her lovemaking, he realized in astonishment; he'd missed the silences that so often fell
between them, comfortable silences that held no sense
of strain. He could talk with her, and he could also be
silent with her. There was a sense of ease that envel-
oped him when he was with her, as if she were a very
old friend who expected nothing but his company.

"If I don't get up," he announced five minutes
later, when his stroking hand had begun making
bolder forays that were already exciting him, "Max
will probably come over just to pull me out of your
bed."

"Then, I'll help you by removing temptation,"
Sarah volunteered, rolling away from his hand and
carefully sitting up on the side of the bed. She'd have
liked nothing better than to stay in bed with him all
day, but she'd sensed that at any moment he'd have
moved away from her and gotten up, and abruptly she
couldn't stand to have him leave her lying in bed one
more time. The thing to do was to call a halt to it herself, to get up first and make the decision, as if she had
other things to do. She stood up a little stiffly, her
muscles protesting both the heavy work she'd been
doing and the vigorous exercise they'd had in the last
couple of hours. As she walked across the room,

Rome frowned when he saw the jerkiness in her usually fluid movements.

He left the bed and went to her, putting his hand on her shoulder as she selected her underwear from the dresser. "Are you all right?" he asked a little gruffly, and she understood the meaning of his question. He was a big, strong, highly-sexed man, and he dwarfed her in bed, in every way. He usually handled her slender, fine-boned body with a great deal of care and patience, but there were times when his passions were too strong and he took her with shocking powerfulness. That morning had been one of those times.

"Yes, I'm fine," she said, and because he was still frowning, she added, "I'm sore all over from working in the store, which is where I need to be right now. You're not the only one who's late."

He dropped his hand, not liking the idea of her doing heavy physical work. Some women could handle it, but Sarah was too delicate, like a fragile, translucent piece of china. He wanted to see about this store himself, decide what had to be done, and hire people to do it. If Sarah wanted to supervise, she could do that, but he didn't want her to hurt herself. Only the knowledge that he didn't have the right to interfere kept him from laying down his strictures; if he used the dictatorial hand on her that he used at Spencer-Nyle, she'd merely give him one of those patented iceberg looks and remind him of their bargain.

"I'd like to see the store," he began carefully, following her into the bathroom.

She gave him a surprised look. "Of course. I'll probably still be there this afternoon when you get off work; why don't you come by? The name of it is Tools and Dyes, spelled with a *y*."

"I've seen it," he said thoughtfully. "I always thought it was a machine shop. Hell, that place *is* a dump!"

"Was a dump," she corrected cheerfully, turning on the shower. When the water was warm, she stepped in and closed the door, which opened immediately. He got into the shower with her, his big body taking up most of the room and making her feel inordinately small. She looked up at him, her green eyes questioning as he took the bar of soap and rubbed up a rich lather in his hands.

"Turn around," he ordered, and she did. He began sliding his hands over her back and shoulders, kneading her stiff, sore muscles, and she groaned aloud at the mingled pain and pleasure, her head hanging forward to allow him full access to her neck and shoulders. When she thought she couldn't stand it any longer, he knelt at her feet and gave the same thorough attention to her legs. She felt her muscles loosening as the pain eased, and she sighed in ecstasy. It was wonderful to have him pampering her, and not a day passed that she didn't pinch herself to make certain it wasn't a dream.

She wanted him to make love to her again, but he didn't. He was already late, and she knew that although she could probably entice him back to bed, he'd resent it should she interfere with his work.

Rome had already left when Sarah went down to her car; he'd hurried through breakfast and gone without even kissing her good-bye, an omission that totally destroyed the warmth left by their morning of passion. She reminded herself over and over that she had to accept the limits of their relationship; they were married, but he didn't love her, so she shouldn't expect him to act like a lover.

Marcie hailed her as she opened her car door, and she paused, her eyes narrowed against the bright morning sun as the other woman crossed the small brown strip of grass between the street and the building. The weather was still cool, but Marcie was in her shirt-sleeves, an abstracted frown on her face.

"Good morning," she said, and that was Marcie's total nod to conventional chitchat. She plunged right to the point. "Sarah, were you going to hire anyone to help you in the store?"

"Of course," Sarah said readily. She'd have to, just to give herself time enough to eat lunch. One person really couldn't handle things, and even in its ramshackle condition, the little store had had a fairly steady stream of customers.

"Would you consider Derek? He can only help you after school and on weekends, but I'd appreciate it. I don't like that grocery store where he's working now," Marcie said worriedly. "One of the cashiers is chasing him."

"I'd love to have Derek," Sarah said, and meant it. The boy was so strong and efficient, he could do whatever had to be done after school hours. She looked at Marcie and saw that her friend was really worried about her son.

"How old is the cashier?"

Marcie grunted in disgust. "She's closer to my age than she is to Derek's!"

"Does she know that he's only fifteen? He looks so much older."

"I know, I know. Sarah, girls from his school follow him home! He takes it all for granted, but it's get-

ting harder for me to handle. He was my baby!'' she
wailed. "He's still just a baby! I wasn't cut out to be
the mother of a...a Greek god! Italian god,'' she
corrected herself, with scrupulous adherence to the
facts.

"If Derek wants to work at the store, I'll thank
heaven for him every night.''

"He'd love to. He likes you, and he likes that sort
of work. You don't know how I appreciate it!''

Sarah smiled and waved away her thanks. Derek
would take a huge load off her, and she liked having
him around. Despite his spectacular looks, there was
a calm, capable air about him that made her feel more
comfortable. The only person who gave her a greater
feeling of physical security was Rome.

"Why don't you come by and see how the store's
shaping up?'' she invited Marcie.

"Thanks, I will. If you have time today, why don't
I bring in lunch?''

"I never turn down lunch!''

She was proud of the store, she thought, as she
pulled her little car into the parking area in back of the
building. It sparkled under new paint, now pristine
white, with crisp blue trim around the windows and on
the door. The windows had been cleaned with a mixture of vinegar and lemon juice, and they literally
sparkled in the morning sun. The diamond panes gave
a homey air to the crowded little store, with its raw
plank flooring and old-fashioned bins for the merchandise.

New shelves lined the walls, however, and the pottery took up one entire wall. Bright hues of red and
blue, earth brown, and a unique salmon color, were
splashed against the wall like an abstract design, be-

cause all of the pottery had been colorfully glazed. Homemade quilts were draped across a couple of ladder-back chairs, while others were neatly folded and stacked on the woven straw bottoms of the chairs. There were nails, hammers, screwdrivers, nuts and bolts, scissors, pins and needles, and scores of other small necessities, but already Sarah had ideas for expanding the selection. She would carry supplies for macramé, cross-stitching, candlewicking, and knitting, complete with patterns. Doll-making was very popular, and that could be another section; there were two more small rooms in back besides the pottery room and the tiny office, and she could turn one into a doll room, with everything necessary to make anything from a soft-sculpture doll to china dolls. Stuffed animals were another possibility. She had so many ideas, she feared she'd never have room for them all.

The small store brought her much more satisfaction than working in a large corporation ever had. She'd liked the demanding work at Spencer-Nyle, but the corporate structure really wasn't for her; it was far too impersonal. This small, homey, and homely store was very personal, uniquely hers even in the short length of time she'd owned it. The soothing colors, the comfortable display of items, all spoke of her personal touch. She hadn't hesitated at all when she'd learned by chance that the store was for sale; some intuition inside her had recognized that this was what she'd wanted. She'd looked at the building, and at the stock and hadn't haggled. The price had been very reasonable, probably because of the condition of the building. Buying it had made a considerable dent in her savings, and the renovations had further depleted her funds, but she thought it was worth it. This was *hers,* something she'd bought herself and shaped to reflect her own personality.

The old building was drafty, and she turned on the ancient furnace, thinking that here was something else needing replacing. It was only October; what would it be like during January and February? A new roof and insulation was a necessity.

The store had been closed while she'd been cleaning and painting, and Derek had been putting in the new lighting fixtures. She'd been astonished that a boy his age would know how to do electrical wiring, but he'd explained it and made it all seem very simple. It was only after he'd done it that Sarah had gleaned from Marcie that he'd never done any wiring before; he'd simply read about it and decided to try it. As she flicked on the lights she noticed how much better the merchandise looked with the brighter, better-placed lighting. What would she have done without Derek? She wouldn't be anywhere near ready to open.

But as it was... She took a deep breath and flipped the sign on the front door for the first time from CLOSED to OPEN FOR BUSINESS. Sarah's store was officially open.

The little store had its own regular customers, who were used to dropping in and puttering around whenever someone needed a pack of finishing nails or a skein of yarn. She was never overflowing with business, but the place was seldom completely empty either. There was a slow relaxed pace about it, with people comfortably looking things over, commenting on the changes. She kept a pot of coffee on the counter, which encouraged people to come up and talk to her while they drank a free cup of coffee. She especially liked talking to old people, who had fascinating tales of making almost everything by hand in days long past.

The time passed so quickly that when she looked up to see Marcie coming in the door, she was amazed to realize it was time for lunch. Past time, she thought; it was almost one o'clock.

"Sorry, I'm late," Marcie panted. "I was just leaving when I got a call from a magazine on a proposal I'd submitted."

Sarah's eyes shone warmly. "Do they like it?"

"They do," replied Marcie promptly. "Now all I have to do is think of something to write."

Marcie was so organized, she could probably put her hands on a thousand pages of research material, so Sarah didn't take the last comment seriously. "What type of article will it be?"

"It's for one of the slicks, a women's magazine. I've been doing a lot of thinking about it." Marcie began emptying the paper bag she'd brought, putting a paper plate in front of Sarah and then filling it with fried chicken and cole slaw, with hot rolls on top of it. "'Marriages of Convenience—Past and Present,' is what I think I'm going to call it. I know you've read something about them; at times they've been more the norm than the exception. You can call them arranged marriages. The fact is, people get married for a lot of reasons other than love. Convenience is one of the more common reasons, which is probably why they're called marriages of convenience. Two people combine their assets, support each other, rather like a business partnership, except it's a marriage and they sleep together."

Amusement made Sarah's eyes sparkle with a soft green. "You don't believe in marriages in name only?"

Marcie gave her a disbelieving look. "Do you honestly know a man who'd be content with a platonic marriage? I'm talking about a normal, healthy man."

"Usually, no, though I do think there are some situations—"

"*Unusual* situations," Marcie put in.

"All right, unusual situations—"

"I still don't think so," Marcie interrupted again with blithe unconcern. "And you don't either, because I can see the way you're biting your tongue."

Sarah laughed, because she had indeed been trying to get an argument out of Marcie, who loved to argue. "I give up. Let's get back to your article."

"I got the idea from a get-together I had with six of my old high school chums. We'd been having a good time, and the martinis had been flowing freely, you might say. Now, these aren't unusual women, just your normal, everyday sort of female. Of the seven of us, two had gotten married because of a pregnancy, one because she'd never had many dates and thought his proposal might be the only chance she'd ever have, one admitted that she just sort of drifted into marriage because she'd gone with him for so long that everyone took it for granted that they'd get married, and one was very open about marrying her husband because of his money. She liked him, but his money was the main attraction. That's five out of seven."

"And the other two?"

"One was married because they were in love, and they still are. They're almost embarrassing, even after all these years. The other one...well, I'm the other one. I got married because I *thought* I was in love. If you could see Derek's father, you'd know why. But instead of love, it turned out to be sex, which was very good and remained good, but that just wasn't enough to hold the marriage together.'' For a rare pensive moment, Marcie rested her chin on her hand, thinking of her ex-husband. ''Dominic and I had some good times, but in the end, we simply didn't care enough about each other. But I think I'd do it all over again, even if I knew we'd eventually divorce, because I'd want Derek.''

''So, out of the seven, only one married for love?''

''Ummm. I haven't done any real deep research yet, but I've talked to some men, and I'd almost believe that even more men marry for convenience than women. Men are very straightforward in their needs, and they still have a lot of the cavemen instincts.''

''Me Tarzan, you Jane?''

''In a way. They still want a fire and someone to cook the meat they bring home, bandage their wounds, do their laundry—which probably translates from curing the animal hides and making clothing—and a warm body when they need one. Simple, basic needs that haven't changed all that much in substance; only the ritual is different. They marry to fulfill those needs.''

''You don't paint a very romantic picture,'' Sarah commented, beginning to feel chilled by Marcie's precise descriptions. The conversation was reminding her too painfully of her own marriage. Rome had married her for all those reasons, and he'd been very open with her about them. He wanted a home, a stable relationship, convenient sex. In return, he'd be a faithful, dependable husband. A marriage of convenience for him. For her, a marriage of love.

"There's romance in it," Marcie continued thoughtfully, nibbling on a chicken leg. "Some people learn to love each other after they're married. Most care for each other to some degree, even if it never becomes love. Some marriages don't last. But I'm convinced that convenience is the basis for more marriages than most of us would like to admit."

"I wonder how many people do fall in love after they're married?" Sarah wondered aloud, unaware of the hint of wistfulness in her tone.

Marcie gave her a piercing look full of awareness, and a hint of pity. Sarah caught the look and knew immediately that Marcie had guessed how lukewarm Rome was in his feelings for his wife. She went pale and looked down, and Marcie put her hand on Sarah's.

"I'm being such a pessimist," Marcie said with false cheerfulness. "Probably men fall in love as readily as women, but they're just too contrary to admit it."

No, Rome admitted to loving. The trouble was, it was Diane he loved.

But again Sarah reminded herself that she'd take what she could. She couldn't afford to be proud and turn him away because she demanded his complete devotion or nothing. The passing years had taught her that there'd be no other love for her, no other man to push Rome out of her heart.

Marcie tried to break the moment by looking around and exclaiming at the changes that had been made in the store since the last time she'd seen it. "Have you had many customers today?"

"More than I'd expected," Sarah said, gratefully accepting the change of subject and wrenching her mind away from Rome. She looked around the small cozy store and had the painful thought that, in years to come, the store might be all she had. Age and familiarity would dilute Rome's desire for her, and she could predict that his business trips would come more frequently and last longer. They'd achieved an easy physical intimacy and talked comfortably on a lot of subjects that never, never probed too deeply. Rome had set a limit on how close he would let her come, and he never allowed her to pass that boundary. He held her at an emotional distance, and Sarah shivered, feeling cold all over again.

Chapter Seven

The small bell above the crafts shop door rang at ten minutes after five, signaling the arrival of someone else. The bell jangled all day long, surprising Sarah with its frequency, and she looked up automatically. Just as automatically, her heartbeat increased and her skin flushed as she met Rome's dark eyes across the width of the store.

She was waiting on a customer, so he didn't approach her. He lifted a straight black brow at her and began to wander through the aisles, examining the merchandise, his hands shoved into his pants pockets, his suit jacket open. He'd loosened his tie; the silk noose now allowed a good two inches of freedom about his neck. Sarah tried to help her customer, but at the same time she wanted to watch Rome; she felt nervous, and anxious for his approval, like a mother whose child was debuting in a school play. What if he made some comment of unenthusiastic praise? She didn't know how she'd take it.

The middle-aged woman finally bought several skeins of yarn and a book of afghan patterns. As she left, Derek came out of the back and approached Sarah. "I've put that dead-bolt lock on the back door and cleaned up in back. Are you closing at five thirty? If you are, I won't start painting that other room until tomorrow."

Rome was slowly approaching, still looking over the merchandise, and Sarah eyed him over Derek's shoulder. "Yes, five thirty's closing time."

"I'll follow you home, Mrs. Matthews," Derek offered, but somehow it was firmer than an offer.

"That's all right," Rome said easily, coming up behind the boy. "I'll stay with her until closing, if you want to go on home."

Derek turned, his golden brown eyes meeting Rome's darker ones. He'd seen Rome at a distance, so he knew immediately who the older man was, but they'd never been introduced. Sarah took care of that. "Rome, this is Derek Taliferro. Derek, my husband, Rome."

Rome held out his hand, man-to-man, and Derek took it with complete ease, as if he'd expected nothing else. "Sir," he said with his unshakable good manners.

"I'm glad to finally meet you," said Rome. "Sarah raves about you. From what I hear, she wouldn't have been able to open so soon without your help."

"Thank you, sir. I was happy to help, and I like working with my hands."

Evidently feeling that he'd said all that needed saying, Derek turned to Sarah. "I'll go home, then. I called Mom after I got out of school, and she told me that she's working on an article, so that probably means she's forgotten about food. I'd better stuff a sandwich down her before she gets too weak to type. I'll see you tomorrow, Mrs. Matthews.''

"Fine. Be careful," she admonished.

He flashed her a brilliant smile, so bright, it was startling. "I'm always careful. I can't afford to get stopped."

When Derek had gone, Rome said suspiciously, "How is he getting home?"

"Driving," Sarah said, grinning.

"And he's just fifteen?"

She nodded. "But he never gets stopped, because he *looks* old enough to have a license. He's an extremely good driver, of course. I can't imagine him being anything else." Then she couldn't stand it any longer, and she burst out, "Well, what do you think?"

Again he lifted a sardonic eyebrow, leaning against the checkout counter. "About the store, or Derek?"

"Well . . . both."

"I'm surprised as hell," he said bluntly. "By both Derek and the store. I was expecting a lot of bare space, not this permanent, been-here-for-centuries feeling. The handmade stuff is really something; where do you find it?"

"People bring it here. I sell it on commission. People will pay dearly for handmade quilts and pottery."

"So I saw from the prices on those quilts," he murmured. "Derek is something else too, isn't he? Are you *sure* he's only fifteen?"

"Marcie swears he is, and she should know. He'll have a birthday next month."

"Sixteen doesn't sound that much better. The kid's a rock."

"I've hired him to help me in the afternoons and on weekends. He was working in a grocery store, but one of the cashiers was chasing him, so Marcie asked me if I'd hire him. I snapped him up."

"He's young to be working like that."

"He's saving for college. If he wasn't working here, he'd be working somewhere else, whether Marcie liked it or not. I get the feeling that once he's decided on his course of action, a stick of dynamite couldn't blow him off it."

Their conversation was interrupted when the bell jangled again, as a young mother entered with a toddler in her arms and a boy of about five right on her heels. Rome glanced at her; then he saw the two children and something congealed in his eyes. He went still, a blank mask taking all the life from his face. He moved back, and Sarah gave him a helpless glance as she walked over to offer her assistance to her new customer. The young woman smiled and expressed interest in a collection of clowns with stuffed bodies and china heads and limbs. Her mother collected clowns and was having a birthday soon. As the woman examined the selection, she put the toddler on the floor; the older boy hung over the counter, staring wide-eyed at the clowns.

It was a moment before either Sarah or the young mother noticed that the baby had strayed. "Justin, come back here!"

The baby giggled and toddled around the end of the counter, heading straight for Rome. A spear of pain had gone through Sarah at the mention of the baby's name, and she almost cried out when she saw the chalky look on Rome's face. He stepped aside, avoiding the baby, not even looking down at it. "I'll wait in the car," he said in a harsh, strained voice that didn't sound like his, and he walked out, his back stiff. The young woman hadn't noticed Rome's reaction; she scooped up her errant offspring, tickling his stomach and making him laugh. "I guess I'll just have to hold you, you big lug!"

She bought two of the clowns, and as soon as she'd left, Sarah flipped the sign to CLOSED and began locking up. Her heart was pounding heavily, and she wanted to go to Rome. Peering out the window, she saw him sitting in his car, parked just a few parking spaces down the street, staring straight ahead.

Deciding it was better to give him a few minutes alone, she finished securing the store for the night, then went out back to her own car. When she drove out of the back alley onto the street, Rome's car nosed in behind her.

He was completely silent on the elevator going up to the apartment, his jaw set, his eyes bleak. Sarah said "Rome?" hesitantly, but he didn't look at her or indicate that he heard her.

She waited until the door was closed behind them in the apartment; then she put her hand on his arm. "I'm sorry. I know how you feel—"

"You damned well don't know how I feel," he said harshly, throwing off her touch. "Let me know when dinner's ready."

Sarah stood in the foyer for a moment after he'd turned his back and walked off, feeling as if he'd slapped her. Moving as if in shock, she took off her coat and hung it up, then went into her bedroom to change into older clothes before starting their dinner.

Her face in the mirror was pale and taut, her eyes darkened with hurt. She set her mouth and deliberately blanked her expression. She'd overstepped his boundaries and been coldly rebuffed for it. He wanted a distinct emotional distance between them, and she had to remember that.

She didn't allow herself to hide in her bedroom, though she felt a need to lick her own wounds. She went out to the kitchen and began calmly preparing the meal she'd already planned, not letting herself think about his absence from the kitchen. He usually helped, and she was accustomed to having his tall form taking up a lot of space, to talking to him while they worked.

She called him to the table, her manner carefully free of reproach or hurt. He didn't initiate any conversation, so she didn't either. When they were finished, he lingered for a moment at the table, as if searching for something to say. Not wanting him to feel uncomfortable, Sarah kept herself busy clearing the table and cleaning up the kitchen, even humming quietly to herself as she worked, though she couldn't have identified what tune she was humming. Then she said casually, "I'm going to take a shower and make an early night of it, since this is a chance to catch up on my sleep."

He didn't reply but watched her narrowly as she went to her room.

She didn't tell him good night after she'd taken her shower and put on a nightgown; there was a limit to her self-control. She simply turned out the light and went to bed, then lay curled on her side, staring at the wall, unable to fill the emptiness inside her.

Much later she was still awake, listening to him in his own room, hearing his shower running. The water stopped, and she heard no other sounds. When her door was opened, she jumped, startled, and rolled over onto her back.

He was a darker outline against the night. He pulled the covers back and bent over her, pulling the nightgown over her head and dropping it to the floor. Sarah felt his hands on her breasts and thighs; then his heavy weight came down on her and his mouth closed fiercely over hers. A shudder of relief shook her, and she put her arms around his neck, letting him part her legs and take her.

"All of me," he demanded harshly, as she lifted her hips up to him. "Take all of me. More. More! Yes, like that. Just like that!"

He was silent then, taking her with barely controlled violence. Sarah gave herself up without a struggle to the tumultuous responses he demanded of her, knowing that the comfort of her body was the only comfort he'd accept from her. She quickly reached her pleasure, and he slowed then, forcibly bringing himself to an easier rhythm and a lighter touch. When she began to move under him again, telling him without words that the tension was building in her once more, he unleashed his strength and drove into her with a power that took her breath and shattered her senses, sending her spiraling over the edge of pleasure again. Never before had he taken her like that, with such raw, unbridled need, holding her so tightly that she felt crushed. But when it was over, he began moving away from her, and panic seized her.

Before she could stop herself, she reached out for him. "Please," she whispered tightly. "Hold me, just for a little while."

He hesitated, then stretched out on the bed and pulled her up against him, settling her head on his shoulder. Sarah clenched her fingers in the hair on his chest, as if she could hold him in place during the night. She melted against him, her soft body flowing to meet the contours of his, adjusting and fitting. Suddenly she felt herself going to sleep, as her body relaxed and a sigh of contentment escaped her.

Several minutes later she was almost asleep when she was awakened by the feel of him moving away from her, cautiously disengaging their limbs. He eased himself out of the bed, obviously trying not to awaken her, and she forced herself to lie still, her eyes closed until she heard him leave the room and close the door behind him. Then her eyes flared open, hot and bright with unshed tears. She curled into a tight little ball and thrust her hand against her mouth to stifle the sound of the sobs that couldn't be controlled.

Over breakfast the next morning he said abruptly, "I'm sorry if I hurt your feelings last night."

Reminding herself not to overreact and blunder past his boundaries again, Sarah gave him a smile that was friendly **but** faintly aloof. "That's all right," she said, shrugging it away, then changed the subject by asking if he had any suits that needed to be cleaned.

He regarded her thoughtfully, and there was a hint of iron in the set of his jaw. Sarah braced herself for one of his patented interrogations that were the terror of Spencer-Nyle, but she reminded herself that she was no longer an employee of the company and didn't have to let him delve into her emotions. Perhaps he sensed how remote she was, for after a moment he accepted the change of subject.

As he left he said, "I have a business dinner tonight, so I'll be late getting home."

"All right," she replied calmly, not asking him where he'd be or what time she could expect him.

A frown touched his brow, and he paused. "Would you like to come along? You know him, Leland Vascoe, with Aames and Vascoe. I can call him and have him invite his wife too."

"Thanks, but I'll pass. Derek and I will be painting this afternoon, so we'll probably be working late anyway." The smile she gave him was casual, as was the kiss he leaned down and took. She sensed that he would have made the kiss deeper and longer, but she moved back, still smiling. "I'll see you tonight."

The hint of iron was stronger in his expression as he left.

Determined not to fall into the mopes, Sarah didn't let her thoughts linger on him during the day. She kept busy, and whenever the store was empty of customers she went back to the other rooms and worked on them. Derek came in as soon as school was out, with a hamburger in one hand and a large soft drink in the other.

When no one else was in the store, Derek was warmer and friendlier. He grinned at her and held up the burger. "Mom's really into that article. I'll probably have to live off these things until she gets it finished."

Sarah smiled in return. "I tell you what, Rome's working late tonight, so when we get finished here, why don't we pick up a super pizza and take it home for dinner? Maybe we can entice your mom away from the typewriter.''

"Put pepperoni on the pizza, and I'll guarantee it," he said placidly.

He painted by himself until Sarah closed the store; then she put on a pair of coveralls and helped. With both of them working, it was finished by seven, and Derek went home while Sarah drove to a pizza parlor and ordered the largest pizza they made. When she drove up to the condo, Derek came out to get the pizza, and she knew he'd been standing in the entrance, watching for her.

As they entered the ground floor apartment he and Marcie lived in, he whispered, "Watch this. Ten seconds at the most." He walked over to the closed door from behind which came the staccato clattering of typewriter keys, and he gently waved the pizza box back and forth. In a few seconds, the clattering faltered, then stopped altogether.

"Derek, you *fiend!*" Marcie shrieked, and the door was wrenched open. "Give me that pizza!"

Laughing at her, he held it out of her reach. "Come on, sit at the table and eat it like it should be eaten; then you can go back to the typewriter and I swear I won't say a word to you about eating until sometime tomorrow."

"Like breakfast, tomorrow?" asked Marcie whimsically. Then she saw Sarah. "Are you in on this plot too?"

Sarah nodded, admitting everything. "We're calling it the Pepperoni Plan."

"It works, damn it," sighed Marcie. "All right, let's pig out on pizza."

The family warmth, the unquestioning love between Marcie and her son, lured Sarah like a magnet, and she lingered in their apartment long after the pizza was gone. Her own apartment, which she'd tried so hard to make into a warm, secure haven, was painfully empty because it wasn't filled with the one thing that was most important to security: love. Marcie filled her in on how the article was developing, then excused herself and locked herself in her study again. Derek invited her to play a game of gin, but halfway through the game they began talking about blackjack, and the game was abandoned while Derek began teaching her how to be a card counter, employing the one system most likely to get a gambler invited *out* of any casino in the world. From there he went on to the different types of poker, and Sarah decided that Derek was a cardsharp as well as a wonder kid. He was sharp in reading people too, because she sensed that he knew she was at loose ends, and was devoting himself to keeping her entertained until she felt she could go to her own apartment. He was a kind boy, wise beyond his years.

At ten o'clock she said good night to Derek and went home, opening the door to rooms that were dark and chilled. Hurriedly she turned on the lights, then the heat. She hadn't been home five minutes when the door slammed shut, signaling Rome's arrival. She was in her bedroom, preparing to take a shower, and she went to the door to greet him. They almost ran into each other, and she stepped back hastily.

"Where the hell have you been?" he barked, coming into her bedroom and standing over her like an infuriated angel of vengeance. "I've been ringing the phone off the hook since seven thirty, and don't tell me you were at the damned store, because I tried there too."

Sarah looked at him, stunned, unable to think why he was so angry. And he was angry, blazingly so. His eyes were black with fury. And he'd said "damned store." Did that mean anything? She'd thought he approved of the idea of her having another job, but there had been disparagement in his voice and words. She wasn't good at arguing, at countering a display of his temper with her own, as Diane would have done. Instead she withdrew into herself, erecting a mental shield against any hurt he might deal her.

"Derek and I painted until seven; then I bought a pizza and shared it with Marcie and Derek, rather than eating alone. Derek and I have been playing cards since then. Why were you trying to call me?"

Her calm, cool, remote voice seemed to inflame him even further. "Because," he ground out from between his clenched teeth, "Leland Vascoe brought his wife and they wanted you to join us. You didn't have to eat with the Taliferros, if eating alone was your only problem. I'd already invited you to have dinner with me, but you had to paint some grim little back room instead. Now you tell me that you were finished by seven, and you could've had dinner with me anyway. Your support is overwhelming," he said with biting sarcasm.

Sarah was very still, her delicate shoulders erect. "I didn't know what time we'd finish painting," she said quietly.

"Damn it, Sarah, you worked for years for the corporation, and you know the routine. I expect you to be available for these mixed business and social meetings, not puttering around in that—"

"Grim little store," she finished for him, not flinching or looking away from him. She was beginning to feel sick inside, a cold feeling spreading through her chest. "Before we married, you said that we'd respect each other's business responsibilities. I'm willing to attend whatever business dinners you want me to attend, and after the repairs are finished at the store, I shouldn't have to stay late. But that isn't the real issue, is it? You don't want your wife to work outside the home at all, do you?"

"There's no need for you to work," he rapped out.

"I won't sit here all day and twiddle my thumbs. What else is there for me to do? I can only dust so many times in one day before even that fascinating occupation becomes boring."

"Diane wasn't bored."

The lethal jab was right on target, and Sarah's eyes widened, but that was the only clue she gave as to how much that hurt. Staring bleakly at him, she said, "I'm not Diane."

That was the whole problem, she thought, turning away from him. She couldn't stand there and let him cut her to ribbons. Diane would have been jaw to jaw with him, and their argument by now would have deviated far from the original subject. In another two minutes they'd have been kissing and falling on the bed, which was how Diane had told her they always ended their arguments. Sarah couldn't do that. She wasn't Diane, but herself, lacking Diane's fire and strength. That was the one thing Rome could never forgive her for: not being Diane.

At the bathroom door, she turned to face him again, her expression a pale mask. "I'm going to take a shower and go to bed," she said without inflection. "Good night."

Rome's eyes narrowed, and suddenly, chillingly, she knew she'd made a mistake by retreating. It was his aggressive male nature, as a hunter, to pursue his fleeting prey. Sarah froze, expecting him to spring across the room and capture her; it was in his eyes, in the tension in his stance. Then he visibly controlled the urge, dampening it down, though his eyes were like black marble as he stared at her. "I'll be in later," he finally said, his voice a deep purring threat.

Sarah took a deep breath. "No. Not tonight."

The primitive male rose up in him again, and like a great stalking cat he crossed the floor to her, cupping her chin in his hand. "Are you refusing to go to bed with me? Be careful, babe," he warned, still in that dangerous purr. "Don't start a war that you can't win. We both know I can make you beg for it."

Sarah went even whiter, and the force of his hard fingers left reddened imprints on her jaw. "Yes," she admitted in a stifled tone. "You can make me do anything you want, if that's really the way you want it to be."

He looked down at her, at her colorless face and closed expression, and something savage moved in his eyes. Then he dropped his hand to his side, releasing her jaw. "Have it your way," he snapped, striding out of the room and closing the door behind him.

Shaking, Sarah took a shower and went to bed, lying awake for a long time and waiting to see if he'd come to her in the later hours, as he'd done the night before, but she heard him go to his own room and this time her door remained closed. Her eyes burned rawly as she stared into the darkness. How ironic that she should have to defend her outside work, when her dream had always been of a typical, traditional family life. It should have been Diane passionately defending a woman's right to a career: she'd never been short of arguments or opinions. Their plans had been derailed, and they had each taken the route meant for the other one. Diane was to have been the career woman, while Sarah was the housewife. Now, even more ironically, Sarah had the chance to devote herself to her husband, only to find that she had to cling to her career in order to keep some stability in her life. Rome wasn't offering her anything more than convenience and sex, and she needed more. She needed a place where she belonged, and that belonged to her, where she felt safe. If she had Rome's love, she knew she'd feel safe anywhere, but she didn't have his love. She was still on the outside, wistfully peering through the window.

Rome lay awake too, his gut twisting with anger and frustration. It made him see red when she froze up on him like that! He'd wanted to apologize for the night before, when he'd hurt her by rejecting her offer of sympathy, but she'd put up that damned blank wall and refused to respond or let him make it up to her. She'd been *humming,* as if it didn't matter to her what he did. It probably *didn't* matter, he thought savagely. But when he'd gone to her room and made love to her, she'd taken down the barrier and turned as hot and sweet in his arms as she always did. He'd wanted to grind his flesh into hers, to make her forget about keeping him at a distance, and he'd thought he'd succeeded; then that morning, she'd been as cool and remote as ever, as if she hadn't gone wild beneath him.

That damned store was more important to her than anything else, including him. He'd asked her to go with him, but the store came first. He'd known how devoted she was to working, and he'd proposed to her, knowing that she'd expect the same priority for her work as he expected for his. He'd agreed to give her the room she needed, and now he found it was driving him insane. Whenever she put up those frosty barriers of hers, he wanted to smash them down and take her in the most primitive way, until she couldn't build them again. She didn't even care enough to argue; she simply stated her position, then turned away. The disdainful lift of that little chin had almost broken his control, but she'd made it plain that if he'd taken her to bed, it would have been rape, and he'd forced himself to leave before he sank to that. He didn't want to hurt her—he wanted to possess her, totally and irrevocably. He wanted never to see that reserved, distant expression on her face again. And he wanted that shining eagerness that she reserved for that damned store to be for him. The challenge she represented was becoming an obsession for him, until even at work he found himself thinking of ways to break through her defenses. So far, the only way he'd found had been through sex, but that was only temporary.

He wanted her now. He was burning with need, and he moved restlessly on the bed. He waited, knowing that if he went in to her now, she'd fight, and he didn't want to put her through that sort of experience; he wasn't certain of his ability to control himself. He didn't want her unwilling body; he wanted her all soft and melted beneath him, clinging to him with all the silky strength of her arms and legs, her cool image shattered by the earthiness of the act. For that, he'd wait.

When Sarah got up at her usual time the next morning, she was surprised to find Rome already up, with the preparations for breakfast almost finished. She looked at him warily, but the hard-edged anger had left him, though she still sensed an indefinable tension in him that made her keep her greeting merely polite.

"Sit down," he said, and the words were a command, not an invitation.

Sarah sat down at the small table, and he served the meal, then took his place across from her.

They were almost finished eating when he spoke. "Are you going to keep the store open all day today?"

Cautiously, Sarah placed her coffee cup on the table. "Yes. Mr. Marsh, the previous owner, said that Saturday was always his biggest day. He closed for half a day on Wednesdays, and I think I'll keep doing that too. People like a familiar schedule."

She'd expected him to object, but instead he gave a curt nod. "I'll go with you today. I'd like to look things over more carefully than I did before. Have you got your bookkeeping system set up yet?"

"Not completely." Grateful that he wasn't going to pick another argument, Sarah relaxed her guard and unconsciously leaned toward him a little, the unusual deep green of her eyes beginning to warm. "I've kept a record of everything I've spent, and of what I've sold, but I haven't had time to begin organizing it yet."

"If you don't have any objections, I'll set the books up for you," he offered. "Have you thought about buying a personal computer and putting your inventory on it? For that matter, you need your bookkeeping system on computer too. It would be a lot easier to work with."

"I'd thought about it, but a computer will have to wait. The store needs a new roof, and I've got several ideas for expanding the merchandise selection. Then there's a burglar alarm system that I want installed too. I've just about used up all my savings, and I need to build a little working capital."

"You used your savings?" he snapped, his heavy dark brows drawing down, and Sarah automatically withdrew from him again, the barrier springing into place to protect her. His jaw set as he saw her change of expression, and grim determination rose in him. He wasn't going to let her lock him out this time; he was going to go over that damned wall as if it weren't even there, ignoring its existence.

He reached out and snared her wrist, wrapping his hard fingers around the fragile bones. "That was the wrong way to do it," he said, releasing all the irritation he felt. "You don't spend your capital; you use it as collateral. Borrow the money, and let your own money collect interest while you use someone else's. The interest you pay on the loan is tax-deductible, and believe me, babe, you'll need every tax break you can get. Don't wait for a profit to make those improvements; borrow the money and do it *now*. If I'd been here when you bought the store, I'd have marched you down to a bank to set up a business loan."

Sarah relaxed, her eyes widening. She could handle his criticism and advice on business matters; she even welcomed it. She'd have to be a fool not to trust his business sense.

"You'll also need a good accountant," he continued. "I'd volunteer to do your taxes, but I have to spend too much time away from home. If you're going to do this, do it right."

"All right," she agreed mildly. "I didn't know all that. My instinct is to pay for everything outright, so it's legally mine and can't be taken away from me. I've never been interested in the ins and outs of business finance, but if that's the way you say it should be done, I'll take your word for it."

His dark eyes sharpened, and like a hawk he swooped down on the most significant thing she'd said. The morning after their wedding, when she'd come unglued because the apartment was unfamiliar to her, he'd realized that she liked everything in its place. She was, in fact, almost fanatic about it. But now this second statement alerted him to a deep-seated insecurity in her that he hadn't realized before. "Taken away from you?" he asked casually, though there was nothing casual in the way he watched her. He felt as if he were on the verge of finally getting around that barrier inside her, of knowing what went on in that reserved mind of hers. "Do you really think I'd let you go belly up if you enjoyed the store that much? You don't have to worry about bankruptcy, ever."

Sarah shivered, a movement that he felt immediately, as he was still holding her wrist. She stared at him across the cold, empty wasteland of her childhood; then her lashes dropped as she tried to push the emptiness away. "It isn't that," she vaguely explained. "I just needed to feel that it was *mine*, that I belonged . . . I mean, that it belonged to me."

"Do you realize I don't know anything about your family?" he asked conversationally, and she flinched, telling him without words that he was on the right track. "Where are your parents? Did you have a deprived childhood?"

Abruptly Sarah looked at him, awareness dawning in her eyes. "Are you psychoanalyzing me?" she asked in an attempt at lightness. "Don't bother. I can clear it up for you; it's no big mystery, though I really don't like to talk about it. No, I didn't have a deprived childhood, not in material things anyway. My father is a successful lawyer, and we were definitely upper-middle-class. But my parents weren't happy together, and they stayed married only because of me; when I started college and was officially launched, they promptly divorced. I've never been close to my parents. Everything was so . . . so *cold* at home, so polite. I guess I grew up knowing how shaky everything was and expecting it to fall apart without notice. I intended to make my own little nest, where I'd feel safe," she confessed.

"And you're still doing it."

"I'm still doing it. I pull things in around me and pretend that nothing will ever change." She darted a look at him and shifted uncomfortably, aware that she'd bared a large part of herself to him. He was watching her with a look in his eyes that she took for pity, and she didn't want that. She forced herself to shrug and say lightly, "Old habits die hard, if they die at all. I don't easily accept any changes in my life; I have to think about things for a while and become accustomed to them, then gradually move things around. Except for the store," she added thoughtfully. "I wanted the store immediately. It has such a permanent, homey feel to it."

So that was what those barriers were all about, he thought. The wonder was that she'd married him at all, if she disliked changes so much. Probably she'd taken the step only because he'd assured her he wouldn't interfere with her life, and since their marriage, he'd been trying to force himself past her reserve, while she'd been frantically trying to keep it in place. If he eased up, she'd gradually relax with him and accept his place in her life. She wasn't cold and aloof at all, something he should have known immediately from the passionate way she responded to him in bed. She was more like a shy, wary doe, and she'd have to trust him and accept his presence before she'd let him venture close to her. Physical closeness and mental closeness were two very different things for her, and he'd have to remember that.

She wasn't Diane. Diane's personality had been firmly based on a loving, secure tightly knit family, and she'd had the inner self-confidence to handle his temper and dominant personality, while Sarah felt threatened by it. She was far softer, far more vulnerable, than he'd ever imagined.

She shifted, freeing her wrist from his grip and rising to her feet, smiling a bright smile that didn't fool him in the least. "I have to hurry, or I'll be late opening the store."

"Go on and get ready; I'll clean up in here." He stood too, but halted her departure with a hard hand on her waist. "Sarah, understand one thing: An argument doesn't mean your life is going to be torn apart. I was worried last night when I couldn't find you, and I blew up. That's all there was to it."

Her eyes were bottomless pools of green, and she stood motionless under his hand. If he wanted to think that was why she'd been so upset, let him. Better that than his knowing that he could hurt her deeply just because she loved him.

Chapter Eight

Their life together settled into a routine, defined by the mundane details that gave things a sense of continuity; no matter what else, there was always laundry, and cooking, and cleaning. He did as much as she did in the housework department, when he was there, but he was often gone, and when he wasn't there, she threw herself into work, trying to fill the emptiness that came from his absence. He didn't call her every night when he was on a business trip; he always gave her the number where he could be reached if she needed him, and he invariably called her if he was delayed, or to tell her when he'd be home, but other than that she had no contact with him. She understood, though she missed hearing his voice, if nothing else. What could they say to each other every night? She couldn't tell him how much she missed him, how the time dragged while he was gone, how much she loved him, because he didn't want to know that. It was much safer not to talk to him except when necessary; she'd simply wait until he came home, and his initial sexual urgency would give her the chance to hold him, to silently give him the love that had been building up in her. She always knew what to expect from Rome when he returned from a trip; he walked through the door ready to fall on her like a starving man falling on a feast.

When she let herself think about it, she admitted to herself that, while he did like her and to some extent care for her, she still hadn't replaced Diane in his heart. Their love life was fantastic: He was an experienced, virile lover, and she could never say that sex with him was routine. He often took her wherever they were at the time, not bothering to take her to the bedroom, and that more than anything told her that he still grieved for Diane. He preferred that their lovemaking be *out* of the bed. When the demands of his work forced him to come home late, after she was already in bed, then he'd come to her there, but when the act was finished, he always left. He'd hold her and pet her, waiting for her to go to sleep before he went, but she always sensed his uneasiness and had begun to feign sleep so he'd feel free to slip from her bed. When the door had closed behind him, she'd open her eyes and lie there, feeling the desolation of knowing herself unloved. Sometimes she couldn't prevent herself from crying, but for the most part she kept the tears at bay; they solved nothing, and she had a terror of him hearing her weeping in the night.

Still, there was a lot of contentment in their life together. Cool autumn became winter, and there were cozy nights in front of the fire, watching television;

other times, she read while he worked. There were shared lazy breakfasts, and cold, sunny Sundays when they watched the Cowboys play football. If he was at home, he went with her to the store every Saturday, and he and Derek became good friends.

Shortly before Christmas Sarah broached the subject of Derek's future with him. Derek was brilliant; it would be a shame if his potential was limited by lack of money. They'd become close enough that Rome caught her drift immediately.

"Do you want me to put him through college?"

"That would be nice," she admitted, giving him a sparkling smile. "But I don't think Derek would stand for it. He's very proud," she said thoughtfully. "But if you could arrange for a full scholarship from some foundation that won't limit his choice of college, I think he'd jump at that."

"You don't ask for much, do you?" Rome observed wryly. "I'll see what I can do. I think Max will have to be brought in on it; he's got some connections through his family that could be helpful."

Max had become a fairly frequent visitor, and though he never stopped teasing Rome about taking Sarah away from him, their marriage had made all the difference in the world in the way Rome reacted. He'd won, and he knew it. Max's heart wasn't broken; nor would he try in any way to undermine his friend's marriage. He frankly admired Sarah and saw no harm in letting her husband know it, and that was the extent of it.

When Rome decided to get something accomplished, he didn't wait around. The next day Max just happened to show up at the store with Rome; Sarah saw the stunned look in Max's vivid eyes when he was introduced to Derek. Derek had that effect on people. In a few moments, Max wandered over to Sarah and whispered, "Rome's lying, isn't he? Derek's twenty-five if he's a day."

"He was sixteen last month," Sarah whispered in return, smiling in amusement. "Isn't he something?"

"He's bloody impressive, is what he is. Give him wings and a sword, and he's my image of the archangel Michael. Tell him to decide which college he wants, and when the time comes, Rome and I will see to it that he gets a full scholarship."

Sarah told Marcie what Rome and Max were planning, and to her surprise, the other woman burst into tears. "You don't know what it means to both of us," she sobbed. "He's such a special kid, and it's been breaking my heart for him to have to work to save the money for college, instead of having a good time the way he should be doing. This is the best Christmas present you could have given me!"

With the approaching Christmas season, Sarah's business was booming—so much so that she had to hire someone full-time just to help her wait on customers. Rome was all for the idea; he hadn't liked Sarah being there alone during the day until Derek got out of school. She hired a young neighborhood woman whose youngest child had started school that term, and who wanted out of the house. It worked out nicely. Erica would leave shortly before her children were due in from school, and Derek usually arrived within the half-hour. Having Erica there during the day also gave Sarah an opportunity to have lunch, which had been limited to grabbing a bite from a sandwich between waiting on customers, when she'd been by herself.

Three days before Christmas she arrived home to find that Rome was already there; when she reached his bedroom door, she stopped, staring at the open suitcase on his bed.

He turned from the dresser where he'd been taking out a selection of underwear and shirts. He looked at her wryly. "Emergency. We have a hell of a mess in Chicago."

She wanted to protest, to make the traditional wife's lament of "Why can't someone else go?" but she bit the words back, knowing he wouldn't appreciate the hassle. "When will you be back?" she asked, going into the room and dropping down to sit on his bed, sighing in resignation.

"I'm not hanging around up there; I've already booked the red-eye flight back. I should be getting in about four A.M. on the twenty-fourth."

"Well, all right," she grumbled, and for the first time in their marriage she pouted. He dropped a stack of shirts into the suitcase and looked at her sulky face. Her pouting lower lip gave her face an unexpected sensuality, as if she were begging to be kissed, and more. He grinned suddenly, and shoved the suitcase to one side.

Sarah was unprepared, and she gasped in surprise when he tumbled her back across the bed. He gave her a slow wicked smile as he bent over her and pushed her skirt to her waist, then calmly stripped away her underwear. She gasped again, this time with the instantaneous excitement that rose in her whenever he touched her. "Is this to tide you over?" she murmured teasingly, her eyes bright.

"Something like that." He unzipped his pants and shoved them down, then knelt on the bed, between her relaxed thighs. "You're my credit card; I don't leave home without this."

She laughed, twining her arms around his neck as he lowered his weight to her. The laughter caught in her throat at the slow delicious shock of his entry, and he heard the little intake of breath she always gave when he took her. It was music to him, and he buried his face against her neck in sudden need, pulling her legs up around his waist. "I miss you like hell when I'm gone," he said roughly, and with his confession he began thrusting deeply into her, reconfirming their partnership with the bond of their flesh.

Sarah didn't drive him to the airport; he preferred leaving his car there, so he'd always have ready transportation home or to the office without taking a taxi. Despite herself, tears glittered in her eyes as she kissed him good-bye at the door, and he swore softly, dropping the suitcase to take her in his arms again.

"I'll be back for Christmas, I promise," he said, giving her a hard kiss. "You won't have to spend the holiday alone."

As if she cared about the holiday! She hated for him to leave regardless of the time of year, or what holiday was coming up. She blinked back the tears and managed a shaky smile for him. "It's all right. I'm just being silly."

It had to happen: he called at midnight on the twenty-third. "Chicago is having a blizzard," he said with grim sarcasm. "All flights are grounded until this mess clears."

Sarah sat up in bed, clutching the telephone so hard that her fingers were white. "Any weather predictions?" she made herself ask with a fair amount of calm, though she'd been counting the hours until he'd be home again.

"Early afternoon. I'll call you when I have a definite flight."

She spent Christmas Eve moving restlessly around the apartment, adjusting ornaments on the small fragrant evergreen she'd put up for a Christmas tree, fluffing pillows and moving articles of furniture that seemed a fraction of an inch out of place. She'd worried about how Rome might feel about celebrating Christmas, when the holiday must bring painful memories for him of his two small sons and their wide-eyed excitement, their toys underfoot, the complete chaos they'd created every Christmas Day in their ecstasy over the presents they'd received. So far, she hadn't detected any sign that he might be dreading the day, and she was keeping her fingers crossed that this would be a good holiday for him.

She couldn't wait for him to get home; she felt more on edge than she'd ever been before while he was gone, and she knew it was because of what he'd said while he'd been making love to her that last time. "I miss you like hell when I'm gone...." It was the only indication he'd ever given her that he might dislike leaving her while he went on a business trip. She'd always assumed that he even looked forward to the trips to give himself a break away from her. But if he missed her...

She tried to caution herself against hoping too much. Rome was so virile, he could have meant merely that he missed making love to her. But what if he was missing *her,* her companionship, the things they shared? Her heart was thumping crazily in her chest at the thought. Christmas was the season of miracles, after all.

The waiting made her restless, and she thought of going down to visit Marcie, but she didn't want to intrude during the holiday, and she was afraid she'd miss Rome's call. She baked an apple pie for him and put clean sheets on their beds.

The phone rang, and she nearly broke her neck getting to it, tripping over her own feet. Snatching up the receiver, she said breathlessly, "Hello."

"My flight is supposed to be leaving within the hour," he said, his deep voice making her knees go weak even over the telephone lines. "But everything's stacked up, so it'll probably be later than that. I estimate I'll be home close to midnight. Don't wait up for me, baby. Go on to bed."

"I . . . maybe," she stammered, knowing that she'd still be awake even if he didn't get in until midnight the next night.

He laughed, a low promising sound that made her swallow. "All right, then, stay awake. I'll be home as soon as I can."

It was just after eleven that night when she heard his key in the lock. She jumped up from the table, where she'd been sitting nursing a cup of hot chocolate, and ran to meet him. He dropped his suitcase with a thud and caught her as she launched herself into his arms; then he kissed her, so long and hard and thoroughly that she shuddered and pressed herself against him.

His eyes glinting, he released her and rubbed his shadowed jaw with his hand. "I need a shower and a shave, in that order. I spent the night at the airport, so I'm pretty grimy. Go to bed; I'll be there in fifteen minutes, tops."

Sarah poured out the rest of the hot chocolate and turned out the lights, then went to her bedroom. She sat down on her bed and clasped her hands tightly together when she noticed how they were trembling. He was home. In only a few more minutes, he'd be in here, in the bed with her, and he'd make love to her as if he'd like to devour her. Then . . . then what? Would he make another tantalizing confession, another small indication that his feelings for her were deepening? Or would he silently hold her until she pretended to fall asleep, then go to his own solitary bed?

She sucked in a painful breath at the thought, and suddenly she knew that she couldn't bear for him to walk away from her again after making love to her. She was on her feet before she realized what she was doing; if anyone left afterward, it would be her. That way she wouldn't have to watch his back as he left. If, when the loving was finished, he didn't make any indication that he wanted more, then she could kiss him good night and calmly leave his bed without looking back. She couldn't lie there any longer, waiting for him to break her heart by leaving.

He came out of his bathroom just as she opened his door and walked in, and he lifted a black brow at her in astonishment. "In a hurry?" he drawled, dropping the towel that he held to the floor.

Sarah looked at him, at his tall hard body, and her mouth went dry. "Yes," she whispered, pulling her nightgown over her head and dropping it to the floor also.

He walked past her and threw the covers to the foot of his bed, then extended his hand to her in silent invitation. She walked into his arms.

He told her a lot of things: he told her how much he wanted her, what he wanted to do to her, what he liked for her to do to him. His whispers were raw, elemental with need. He told her how sleek and pretty her body was, how he wanted to bury himself in her, how it felt when he took her. But he didn't tell her the one thing she needed most to hear.

When his tumultuous passion had been satisfied, he lay sprawled on the bed, stroking her back with lazy possessiveness. Quivering inside, she knew that she had to leave now, while he was still content and drowsy, before the familiar impatience began eating at him. Lifting herself to her elbow, she kissed him quickly and whispered "Good night," then left the bed before he could react.

Rome's eyes snapped open, and he watched her scoop up her nightgown, then practically run out the door. Grim lines of tension settled around his mouth. As much as he wanted her, as crazy as he went when he was making love to her, he always dreaded when it was over because he knew she would withdraw from him, curling away from him and pretending to go to sleep so he would leave. But at least she usually wanted to cuddle, and he could hold her in his arms a little longer; tonight, despite the wild response of her slim body when he'd made love to her, she hadn't even lingered for a moment of gentle caresses. Sometimes, when her eyes lit up at the sight of him, when she clung desperately to him in the heat of passion, he'd think that he was making progress, slowly beating down her defenses and getting to the soft, warm woman behind them. But then she'd withdraw from him again, as if she had to compensate for any gains he might have made.

Sex with her was fantastic...more than fantastic.
The physical awareness, the passion between them,
was so intense, it overshadowed every sensual experience he'd had before her—but it wasn't enough. It just
wasn't enough. He wanted it all, everything she had to
give, her body and mind and, yes, her heart.

For Christmas, she gave him a hideously expensive
designer briefcase. She'd outraged the clerk at the
hideously expensive department store by having the
designer's insignia removed and substituting Rome's
initials in its place. He laughed when she told him the
tale, then casually gave her a tiny box wrapped in gold
paper. Her mouth fell open when she saw the diamond stud earrings; she tried to thank him, but no
words would come. Each brilliant diamond glittered
with icy fire; those stones had to be a carat each, and
she was stunned by the magnitude of the gift.

Smiling at her reaction, he pushed back her heavy
veil of white-gold hair and removed the earrings she
was wearing, then slipped the studs into her ears himself. She lifted her hand to touch them. "How do they
look?" she asked nervously, finding her voice at last.

"You look fantastic," he said deeply. "I want to see
you naked, with your hair loose, and the diamonds in
your ears."

She watched his face, watched his eyes grow heavy-
lidded with desire, and her body began to warm. A
delicate tint rose to her cheeks. She knew, even as he
reached for her, that he was about to get what he
wanted.

He surprised her by swinging her up in his arms.
"Where are we going?" she asked breathlessly, hav-

ing expected him to make love to her on the sofa, as he'd done several times before.

"To bed," he answered briefly, and her eyes widened.

In the quiet aftermath, he kept her beneath him in his bed, settling himself on her and keeping their bodies together. There was no way she could get up and leave. He turned his face into the warm fragrance of her neck, feeling the heavy satisfaction of his body. He dozed, then came awake sometime later when she wiggled beneath him, seeking a more comfortable position.

"Am I too heavy for you?" he murmured, pressing his lips into the warm hollow below her ear.

"No." Deep pleasure was in her voice, and her arms tightened around his back. He was crushing her, and she could barely breathe, but that didn't matter. All that mattered was the warm, heavy feel of him against her, the almost tangible contentment that radiated from him. This was how she'd always wanted it to be.

Outside, the short winter twilight was deepening into dusk, bringing a growing chill to the room because he kept the heat vents in his bedroom almost closed. He reached down for the sheet and pulled it over them, settling himself on top of her again, with his head on her breasts.

Lazily he kissed her nipples and the sensitive undersides of her breasts before finding a comfortable place for his head. He covered one breast with his hand, then sighed softly and went to sleep. Sarah put her hand on his dark hair, then moved it slowly down to his strong neck and wide, powerful shoulders, feeling the hard muscles beneath his smooth, warm skin.

Feeling safe and protected, wrapped in the cocoon of his body warmth, she too slept.

He woke her for a late dinner, his eyes sleepy and satisfied as he watched her try to sort out the jumbled mess he'd made of her clothes when he'd taken them off. With her wild pale tangle of hair streaming down her back and the glitter of diamonds in her ears, she looked like some primitive queen in her glorious nudity. In more barbaric times, she'd have been worshipped for the color of her hair, the incredible pale gold with streaks of almost pure white running through it. He'd often suspected her of bleaching her hair, until he'd seen her naked for the first time. His wife. The thought filled him with possessiveness, and satisfaction.

In the middle of February she caught a cold that lingered for an unreasonable length of time, her stuffy nose robbing her of sleep and making her cranky. Rome tried to get her to stay home from work and give herself a chance to get over it, but Erica had both children at home with the flu and Sarah had no one to open the store, so she had to work, though she felt listless and achy. Rome had to take another trip, one that could stretch into two weeks, and he frowned at her pale face as he kissed her good-bye.

"Take care of yourself, and stay warm. I'll call you tonight to see how you're feeling."

"I'll be fine," she reassured him, hating the congested sound of her voice. "Don't kiss me; you'll get germs!"

"I'm immune to your germs," he said, kissing her anyway. He folded her in his arms, gently rubbing her back. "Poor baby. I'd like to stay with you."

"I'd like for you to stay with me too," she grumbled, something she'd never have said if she hadn't had a cold. "Actually I feel a little better today. I'm not as tired."

"Maybe you're finally getting over it." He surveyed her critically. "It's about time. If you aren't better tomorrow, see a doctor, and that's an order."

"Yes, sir," she said smartly, earning herself a slap on the bottom.

He called that night as he'd promised. She'd closed the store early when a cold rain turned into sleet, as she hadn't wanted to get trapped by bad weather, so she'd been home long enough to spend an hour lolling in a hot tub, with the steam clearing her stuffy nose, and consequently she felt much better. Her voice was almost normal when she talked to him.

The next morning, however, she woke with a terrible pounding headache, and every joint in her body felt as if someone were beating her with a hammer. Her throat was on fire, and nausea roiled in her stomach at the very thought of food. "Great," she told her bleary reflection in the mirror. "I've got the flu."

Having the flu was the very devil. She ached all over from the fever that accompanied it, but every time she tried to take anything for her temperature, her stomach revolted. She tried drinking hot tea, but that didn't work. She tried drinking a cold soft drink, but that didn't work. She tried drinking milk, and that was awful. She made Jell-O and tried to eat that, but she was gagging after the second bite. Giving up, she made an ice pack for her head and took a lukewarm bath, lying in water that felt cool to her feverish body, with the ice pack reposing on her head.

When a sudden chill swept over her, making her shake so hard that she could barely climb from the tub, she gave up trying to deal with it and simply went to bed, pulling the covers over her while she was having a chill, and throwing them back when she was feverish. Her head was aching so badly, she'd have sworn she'd never rest, but she fell into a deep sleep and woke only when her telephone rang.

"Sarah?" demanded Marcie anxiously. "Thank God! Derek just called me from a pay phone because the store wasn't open. He thought something must have happened to you."

"It has," Sarah croaked morosely. "I've got the flu. I'm sorry, I should've thought to call Derek this morning before he left for school."

"Don't worry about that. Let me call Derek back at the pay phone to let him know you're all right, then I'll be up to see about you."

"I'll be okay, and you might catch—" Sarah began, but Marcie had already hung up.

"I'm not going to die," she grumbled, as the knowledge that Marcie was coming up forced her to drag her weak, aching body out of bed to unlock the door. "Why does she have to see about me today? Why can't she wait until tomorrow? Maybe I'll be ready to die by then."

She walked like someone with a hangover, holding her pounding head with both hands, as if she were afraid it would fall off. The truth was the exact opposite: The way it was hurting, she *wished* her head would fall off. Every step she took was torture, with her body aching and her head throbbing. Even her eyes hurt.

She unlocked the door and crept into the kitchen, thinking about trying another bite or two of Jell-O. She opened the refrigerator door, looked at the green mass quivering wildly at her, and slammed the door again. No way could she eat something that was moving.

The door opened, and Marcie called, "Where are you?"

"I'm in here," Sarah croaked. "Honest, Marcie, you don't want this. For your own sake, leave."

"I've had my flu shot this year," replied Marcie, entering the kitchen. "Ye gods, you look awful!"

"Then, I look exactly the way I feel. I'm starving! I want something to eat, but all I have to do is look at food and I start upchucking."

"Crackers," said Marcie. "Saltines. Do you have any?"

"I don't know," Sarah moaned.

"Where would they be?"

"Up there," she replied, waving her hand at the highest cabinet.

"They would be," Marcie muttered, dragging over a chair she could stand on. She got down the box of saltines and took out a sealed pack, then replaced the rest of them.

"We're going to try the routine doctors give pregnant women: weak tea and soda crackers. Think you can manage it?"

"I doubt it, but I'll try."

Marcie hustled Sarah back to bed, dampened a washcloth in cool water and placed it over her forehead, then stuck a thermometer in her mouth. She came back several minutes later bearing a cup of tea and one lone soda cracker on a napkin. After plucking the thermometer from Sarah's mouth, she looked at it and lifted an eyebrow. "**You** definitely have a fever."

Sarah sat up and nibbled at the cracker, almost afraid to swallow even a crumb. The tea tasted good as it wet her parched throat, and for a moment she felt better. Then her stomach began to twist, and she hauled herself out of the bed. "No good," she reported, then had to bolt.

Derek came up to see her, and she groaned aloud. "What is it with everybody? Why do you want to catch the flu? I'm contagious!"

Derek gave her a serene look. "I don't get sick."

Of course not. What germ or virus would dare even sit on that perfect body?

The second day Marcie wanted to call Rome, but Sarah refused to consider it. What could he do from a distance of a thousand miles? All the call would accomplish would be to distract him. Marcie was concerned because Sarah's fever had climbed even higher and she had a wracking cough. She couldn't eat anything the second day either. Marcie kept her sponged off with cool water, trying to keep the fever down, but Sarah grew even more listless and pale. Marcie spent the night on the floor beside Sarah's bed, listening to the deep hollow-sounding cough, prepared to haul Sarah off to a hospital at any time.

The third night Rome called. Marcie snatched up the telephone on the first ring, because the noise hurt Sarah's head so much.

"It's about time you called, Rome Matthews!" she fumed, breathing fire. "Your wife is almost dead, and it's three days before you check in!"

Rome was silent for three full seconds, then barked, "What? What's wrong with Sarah?"

"She says it's just the flu, but I'm afraid it's turning into pneumonia. Her fever is high, it's been three days since she's had anything to eat, and she sounds like a hollow drum when she coughs. I can't talk her into going to the doctor; she just lies there and says to give it time. Damn you, Rome, you get back here!"

"I'll be there on the earliest flight I can catch."

"I heard all that," Sarah said weakly when Marcie entered her bedroom. "I do not have pneumonia. I have a dry cough."

"Protest all you want; when Rome gets home, then you'll do what you should, instead of lying here getting worse."

"He's coming back?" she asked, and even as badly as she felt, her eyes got brighter.

"Of course he's coming back. He said he'd take the next flight out."

Sarah felt conscience-stricken. "Oh, no! He can't be half through all he had scheduled."

"It'll wait," Marcie said grimly.

Rome wasn't going to like being called back from a business trip, Sarah thought glumly. She was sick, but she wasn't that sick. Still, it was more Rome's place to tend to her than it was Marcie's, and she knew that Marcie had other duties, as well as her free-lance work to be done.

"Marcie, if you have work you need to be doing, I'll be all right by myself," she offered.

Marcie gave her an incredulous look. "Sure you will; you're so weak, you can't even get to the bathroom by yourself. Look, will you stop worrying about imposing on someone and just let yourself be taken care of? You're not being a nuisance, and you're really sick. No one's going to think any less of you because you caught the flu."

Sarah didn't feel like listening to any logic. Her fever was rising again, making her bones and muscles ache, and she twisted restlessly on the sheets. Recognizing the signs, Marcie began to sponge her down again.

The fever made Sarah feel disoriented. Time became elastic, making a few minutes drag by like molasses in January; then all of a sudden several hours would telescope into nothing. She woke once to find Derek sitting by her bed reading, and she said, "Why aren't you in school?"

He looked up. "Because it's three o'clock on Saturday morning. I've made some tea; would you like to try drinking some?"

She groaned aloud, because for three days she'd been trying to drink tea, and for three days it had been coming back up. But she was so thirsty, she felt parched, and she said "Please."

He brought what looked like an ounce of tea in a cup, and Sarah drank it. "Is that all I'm allowed?"

"For right now. If that stays down for half an hour, I'll give you another swallow. I've been reading up on influenza," he said.

Well, that explained it. Because Derek tried it, it worked, even though Marcie had been unsuccessfully pouring tea down her for three days. Sarah's stomach rolled several times but remained under control, and she drifted off to sleep again before Derek could dole out her second ounce of tea.

She woke again several hours later to find Rome sitting on the side of her bed, his hand on her forehead and his dark face taut with worry. "You're going to catch it too," she said, feeling obliged to give her standard warning, though everyone else had ignored it and she didn't see why Rome should pay any attention to it either.

"I don't get sick," he murmured absently, and she made a disgusted sound.

"Not you too! All you healthy people make me sick. Derek doesn't get sick either. Marcie had her flu shot. I suppose I'm the only person in Dallas who gets sick!"

"Actually there's a flu epidemic," he said, noting how fretful she was. Her skin was dry and hot, her hair dull and lifeless, and dark bruised-looking shadows lay under her dulled eyes. He lifted a cup to her lips. "Drink this."

She drank it, and the cool, fresh taste was delicious. "What is it?"

"Peppermint tea. Derek made it."

Her back was hurting so badly, she turned on her side, wincing as she searched for a comfortable position. "I'm sorry Marcie told you to come home. It's really just the flu, instead of pneumonia like she said, and I think I'm getting over it."

"You're still pretty sick, and I'd rather be here." He rubbed her back, knowing without being told that she was aching. She was soon asleep again.

She slept a great deal, and she was listless and cranky when she was awake. Her fever yo-yoed up and down, and when it was at its highest point, she sank into a stupor. Rome stripped her and bathed her in cool water, and when she'd roused a little, he risked giving her aspirin to bring the fever down. For an hour or so she seemed to feel better, and she sat in a chair while he put fresh sheets on the bed. He fed her a soda cracker and more peppermint tea, and she went to sleep.

He sat up until he felt he couldn't keep his eyes open a moment longer. He didn't dare leave her, but he was afraid that if he slept on the floor, he might not awaken when she became restless with fever again. Without hesitating, he took off his clothes and got into bed beside her, lying on his side with one hand touching her, so he'd know if she started tossing around.

She woke him up twice during the night, twisting around trying to ease the aching of her body. Once she went into a paroxysm of coughing, and he winced at the deep, harsh sound. No wonder Marcie had been alarmed!

"I'm all right!" she said aggressively, her thin colorless face set in mutinous lines. He put his hand on her cheek, feeling for a rise in fever, because he'd said nothing to set her off. She glared at him. "I hate being sick."

"I know," he soothed.

"You're sleeping in my bed," she accused. "You lied. You told me you couldn't sleep with a woman. I've always wanted you to sleep with me, but you never would. Why are you here now, when I don't feel like fooling around?"

Despite himself, he grinned. Lifting the cup of tea to her lips, he held it while she gulped thirstily. "Just a case of bad timing, I guess. Boy, are you going to regret talking like this when you're feeling better."

"I know," she agreed, and pouted. "But it's the truth anyway. Rome, when am I going to be well? I'm so tired of hurting all over. My legs hurt, my back hurts, my neck hurts, my head hurts, my throat hurts, my stomach hurts, my eyes hurt, and even my skin hurts! Enough is enough!''

"I don't know, honey. Maybe tomorrow. Do you want me to rub your back?''

"Yes,'' she agreed instantly. "And my legs. That makes me feel better.''

He pulled off her nightgown and helped her to roll over on her stomach. Gently he kneaded her aching muscles, and even though she'd lost weight she hadn't needed to lose, he still found himself admiring the clean, delicate lines of her body. Her long legs were fantastic, so slim and straight and well-rounded. Her bottom was a feminine work of art, shaped just right to drive a man mad. He placed his hand on one satiny buttock, and even in her illness, she smiled a little.

"I like that. I like it when you touch me. When I'm better, will you make love to me again?''

"You can bet on it,'' he said under his breath. He moved up to massage her back, feeling the fragility of her ribs just under her skin.

"I've wanted you for years,'' she said, the words a little muffled by the pillow, but he understood them and his hands paused for a moment. "I had to be a little unfriendly to you to keep Diane from guessing.''

"You did even better than that,'' he said ruefully. "You kept me from guessing too. How many years have you wanted me?''

"Since I've known you.'' She yawned, and her eyes closed.

"That makes us about even, then.''

She smiled and drifted to sleep. Rather than wake her to put her back in her nightgown, he simply pulled the covers up over them, turned off the lamp, and settled down beside her. He smiled into the darkness.

He'd hate for her to be this sick very often, but she carried on some very interesting conversations when she was ill. She admitted to things that wild horses wouldn't have been able to drag out of her if she'd been thinking clearly. He knew he wouldn't forget them, and he hoped she wouldn't either.

Chapter Nine

She was much better the next day, with no nausea at all, and only a light fever. She slept most of the day, and when she awoke, Rome fed her chicken broth. She wrinkled her nose at him. "This is invalid food. When do I get something really hearty, like Jell-O? Or maybe a mashed-up banana?"

He shuddered at the idea. "I draw the line at mashing up bananas."

"Okay," she agreed easily, a smile lighting her wan face. "I'll forget about the bananas if you let me have a bath and wash my hair."

He started to refuse, but she'd already divined his answer and the light had faded from her face. He sighed, relenting. She was too weak to do it by herself, but he could understand how she felt. "I'll help you after you finish this broth," he gave in, and immediately she was smiling again.

If he'd expected any sign of discomfort from her over the things she'd said, he was disappointed. He thought she might not remember the night very clearly, because she'd been feverish and disoriented, but he wanted her to remember. To find out for certain, he murmured, "Do you remember talking to me last night?"

For the first time in days, color was in her face, but she didn't look away from him. She lay back on the pillows and met his gaze evenly. "Yes, I remember."

"Good" was all he said.

He ran a tubful of warm water, then carried her into the bathroom and carefully placed her in the tub. Leaning against the wall, he watched her carefully as she soaped and rinsed herself, ready to pluck her out if she showed signs of fainting. She finished her bath without incident and raised her arms to him. "I'm finished." The natural way she reached out for him took his breath—that and the way the movement had lifted her high, rounded breasts. Taking her bodily from the water, he stood her before him and wrapped a big fluffy towel around her.

"Now my hair," she said determinedly.

She bent over the basin and he washed her hair, but it was so long that rinsing it was difficult, and he solved the problem by stripping his clothes and getting in the shower with her. "We should have washed your hair first," he grumbled.

"I'm sorry; I didn't think about it," she apologized. She looked so fragile standing there before him that he gently pulled her to him, cradling her against his naked body. She put her arms around his waist and sighed in contentment.

"I'm glad you came home."

"Ummm. I think you need a spanking for not calling me when you first got sick," he muttered. "Why didn't you?"

"I didn't think you'd appreciate being interrupted while you were working. I knew I wasn't dying, though Marcie was a little hard to convince."

He hesitated, then lifted her on tiptoe so he could crush his mouth hungrily against hers, with water running in both of their faces. "You're more important to me than work," he growled. "You're my wife, and I want you healthy. If you don't call me the next time you need me, I really will spank you."

"I'm shaking in my boots," she teased him, and he cast a significant glance at her bare feet.

"So I see."

He turned off the shower and quickly dried her again, before she could become chilled. Then he patiently dried her hair with a brush and a blow-dryer, turning it into living silk.

But when he tried to put her in a nightgown and return her to bed, she rebelled. "I want to wear regular clothes, and sit in a chair in the living room like a human being, and I want to read a newspaper!"

She was weaving on her feet, and she looked like a ghost, but her soft mouth was set in stubborn lines. Rome sighed, wondering why a woman who was normally unargumentative and even rather docile would turn so willful just because she had the flu. He wanted to firmly place her back in bed and make her stay there, but he also wanted to make her happy.

"We'll compromise," he suggested, trying to keep his voice soothing. "Put on your nightgown and a robe, because you probably won't feel like sitting up for very long. Deal?"

Sarah was heartily tired of nightgowns, but though he was trying very hard to be reasonable, she could tell that if she refused his compromise, she was going to find herself bundled back into bed. She didn't want that, so she gave in. His mouth was set in a grim line as he pulled a clean nightgown over her head, then helped her into her robe. He found her bedroom slippers and put them on her feet.

"I can walk," she protested when he lifted her.

He gave her a steady look that told her not to push it. "You can walk the next time."

She gave in and looped her arm around his neck, cuddling her face into the warmth of his neck, and she smiled a little. Being in his arms wasn't any hardship at all.

She found that she couldn't concentrate on a newspaper; it seemed like too much of an effort, and her hands kept shaking, so she gave up. But it was nice to be in a different room, and to sit up. Rome turned on the fireplace, and the cheerful flickering of the fire made her feel much better. He settled beside her on the sofa, quietly reading the newspaper.

After fifteen minutes, she began to feel tired and sleepy, but she didn't want to go back to bed. She curled on her side and put her head in Rome's lap, rubbing her cheek against him. He put his hand on her head, sliding her long hair through his fingers. "Do you want to go back to bed?"

"No, not yet. This is nice."

It was more than nice, he thought, swallowing. He looked down at the bright head in his lap and thought of what he'd like her to be doing. He tried to control his thoughts, but with her cheek pressed against him like that, he was fighting a losing battle.

She knew it too, the little witch. She put her hand under her cheek, and he shuddered as her fingers rubbed him delicately. He caught the tiny smile that broke through her control, though she quickly straightened her lips again, and he found himself grinning.

He tossed the newspaper aside and pulled her up onto his lap. "Sarah Matthews, you're a tease. You know damned well I'm not going to do anything until you're a lot better, so cut it out, okay?"

"But I've missed you," she said, as if that explained everything. With his arms around her, she knew everything was going to be all right. She had no worries at all when he held her. She found a comfortable place on his shoulder for her head and went to sleep.

He held her for a while, admitting to himself how much he'd missed the feel of her in his arms. Getting married had been a damned good idea. Coming home to her warmth was enough to lure any man.

She barely stirred when he finally carried her back to bed but she was awake and hungry when Marcie and Derek came to visit two hours later. They all sat in the kitchen, grouped around the tiny breakfast table, while Sarah drank a cup of broth. She demanded and got a slice of plain toast, and her stomach delightedly embraced the first solid food she'd had in almost a week. She looked up from eating to find everyone staring at her, and she self-consciously dropped the toast. "Why is everyone looking at me?"

"I'm just glad to see you eating," Marcie said bluntly. "I thought you were dying on me!"

"I just had the flu," Sarah chided. "Haven't you ever seen anyone with flu before?"

Marcie thought, then shrugged. "No. Derek's never sick."

Sarah cast a disgusted look at Derek, who smiled gently. Derek was always gentle, as if he felt obliged to be kind to mere mortals. No, it wasn't an obligation to him—he was simply a kind person.

They didn't visit long, as Sarah tired easily. After they left, she resisted going back to bed. She went into the living room and that time managed to read the newspaper. She sat up, by sheer willpower, until the time she normally went to bed, then gratefully let Rome support her as she walked to her bedroom.

He left to turn out all the lights and check that everything was locked; she was drowsy when he came back to her room and began undressing, but she opened her eyes when he turned out the light and got into bed beside her. She was suddenly wide awake, and her heart was pounding. She was much better; she knew she didn't need anyone with her that night, and he had to know it too. He pulled her into his arms and settled her against him, with her head on his shoulder. His lips brushed her forehead in the lightest of kisses. "Good night," he murmured.

He was sleeping with her!

She was almost afraid to let herself think about it. There had been signs that he was beginning to care for her; when she tried to think back, she realized it had been some time since she'd seen the bleak moodiness on his face that had always told her he was thinking about Diane and the boys. Was time working its healing miracle? If he was finally recovering from his grief, then he would be able to start loving again, and she had the inside track!

"What's wrong?" he asked sleepily, sliding his hand up her arm. "Your heart's racing like a runaway engine. I can feel it."

"I've tired myself too much," she managed to say, pressing even closer to him. The security of his big warm body began to calm her, and she eased into sleep.

The next morning, despite her reassurances that she was much better and could safely be left by herself, he called his secretary to let her know he wouldn't be working that day. "I'm staying," he told Sarah firmly after he'd hung up the telephone. "Now, what about breakfast?"

"Anything! I'm starved!"

She ate an almost normal breakfast, and decided that food was the answer to everything. She was much stronger, able to walk without weaving, and except for a lingering headache and a cough that occasionally seized her, she felt fine.

Rome worked in the living room, spreading papers out around him, instead of working in the small study, as he usually did. Sarah knew he wanted to keep an eye on her, and the thought made her feel pleasantly warm. Being spoiled had its good points.

Around noon, she became sleepy and dozed off in the chair where she'd been reading. Rome glanced up, saw her closed eyes, and got up to carry her to bed. She woke when he began undressing her but didn't protest when he made her put on a nightgown. She was asleep again before he could pull the covers up over her.

She slept for almost four hours. She woke to use the bathroom and drink several glasses of water; she felt as if she couldn't get enough water. Still feeling drowsy, she went back to bed and had just pulled the sheet up when the door opened and Rome came in.

"I thought I heard you moving around," he said, seeing that she was awake. He came over and sat on the side of the bed, gently touching her face. There was no fever at all. She was warm, but it was the rosy warmth of sleep.

She stretched lazily, then sat up to put her arms around his shoulders, hugging him. The way she'd stretched had pulled the thin fabric of the nightgown tight across her breasts, and now he felt the soft mounds pressing against him. He caught her to him and cupped her chin, lifting her mouth for his kiss. Sarah melted against him, her lips parting to accept the play of his tongue. He kissed her several times, and each time his kiss was harder, more demanding. Gently he lowered her back to her pillow, and he went with her, his mouth still on hers. She felt his hand close warmly around her breast, and she arched to his touch. It seemed as if it had been forever since he'd made love to her; the cold she'd had prior to the flu had made her feel miserable too, and he'd left her alone. "Yes," she said against his mouth, pulling at his shirt. "Please, don't stop now."

"I wasn't going to," he said huskily, sitting up and removing the offending shirt. He dropped it to the floor, then stood to unfasten his pants and step out of them. Sarah watched him with wide dreamy eyes, her body already tingling in anticipation of his touch. Leaning over her, he removed her nightgown, enjoying the sight of the soft, slim body that belonged to him. He put his hands on her and stroked her silky flesh, finally cupping both her breasts and leaning down to kiss them, then sucking both nipples to hardness. Drowning in pleasure, Sarah reached for him, pulling him down to her.

When they got up later, she felt satisfied in every pore of her body, and the satisfaction was plain on her face. She was radiant, her skin glowing with the warmth generated by his caresses. As they sat across from each other at dinner, Rome felt his gaze returning again and again to her face. He'd put that look on her face, and he knew it. When Sarah looked at him like that, something moved inside him. He'd wanted to break down the barriers of her reserve, to find the heat of her passion, but he'd found much more than that. The ice-queen was gone, and in her place was a woman who glowed from his touch. Was she falling in love with him? He liked the idea of that; having the devotion of a woman like her was nothing to be taken lightly. Her love would warm the years, provide a tender, safe haven for him to come home to, a cushion against the painful memories of his past.

As she showered and got ready for bed Sarah wondered if he'd sleep with her that night. She was actually trembling, wanting him so much, wondering if the past two nights had been due to unusual circumstances. If he went back to his bedroom that night, she didn't think she'd be able to bear it, not after having the two best nights of her life. He'd acted as if he really cared, giving her a glimpse of paradise. If the gates closed again and left her on the outside, it would be a blow she'd never recover from.

A brisk knock on the door made her jump. "Are you going to spend the night in there?" Rome asked, impatience in his voice.

She opened the door, gasping as she found him leaning against the facing, totally naked. He was awe-

some, so tall and muscular, with that virile field of
dark curls on his chest. Her breath coming quickly, she
dropped the towel that she'd wrapped around herself
and reached for her nightgown, then dropped it too.
''I don't think I need a nightgown,'' she said breathlessly.

''I don't think so either.'' Dark amusement lit his
eyes for a moment as he held his hand out to her, but
the amusement faded into something far more intense when she walked into his arms.

They made love, then slept, and he made no move
to seek his own bed. He woke after midnight and took
her again, sliding deeply into her before she was really
awake, enjoying the spontaneous response she gave
him. He lingered over her that time, using his expertise to prolong the experience and carefully raise her
to shattering heights. Sarah was totally lost in the intensifying physical sensations as he fondled her breasts
and sucked them in just the way she liked, as he
stroked her and touched her in ways that made her cry
out. His slow, steady thrusts were driving her mad,
carrying her just to the brink of satisfaction but not
putting her over.

She clutched at him with damp, frantic hands, begging for release. He held her hips, not letting her speed
the pace, holding her to his rhythm. He kissed her
deeply, then lifted his mouth just enough to command deeply, ''Tell me you love me.''

Her response was automatic, plucked from a deep
reservoir of primitive need that she couldn't control.
Without thinking about it, without even realizing the
significance of what he asked and what she answered,
she moaned, ''Yes. I love you.''

He shuddered, the soft words setting off small explosions deep inside him that signaled the swift approach of his own satisfaction. He slid his hands beneath her and lifted her to receive his deep thrusts. "Tell me again!"

"I love you.... I do...love..." Her voice trailed off, and a choked cry came from her throat. Feeling the exciting gut-wrenching sensual inner convulsions that signaled her release, he groaned aloud, ground his teeth, then was totally lost in his own response.

Lying under his heavy body, Sarah came to slow awareness of what she'd said to him, and cold dread filled her. "I...about what I said..."

He lifted his head from her breasts, primal satisfaction etched on his face and in his eyes. "I wanted to know. I thought you might, but I wanted to hear you say it."

She sucked in her breath at the possessiveness of his manner. "You don't mind?" she whispered.

He stroked a bright strand of hair back from her face and lingered to trace the soft outline of her lips with his finger. "It's more than I expected when I asked you to marry me," he admitted deeply. "But I'd have to be a fool not to like it. You're a warm, loving, fantastic lady, Mrs. Matthews, and I want everything you have to give."

Hot blinding tears gathered in her eyes and slipped down her cheeks. He gently wiped them away, a little shaken by the trust and devotion she offered to him. In swiftly rising passion, and in an effort to comfort away her tears, he made love to her again.

Rome had already left for the office the next morning, and Sarah was rushing around trying to get ready so she could open the store on time, but memories of the night before kept distracting her. She'd find herself standing in the middle of the floor, staring dreamily at nothing, instead of putting on her makeup or dressing, as she should have been doing. He hadn't said that he loved her, hadn't returned the words, but a deep feminine understanding told Sarah that the wish she'd made in the deepest recesses of her heart, in the darkness of countless nights, was coming true. He cared for her, and he was growing to love her. A man didn't treat a woman with the solicitous, tender concern he'd shown if he didn't feel far more for her than a lukewarm respect and liking. The intimacy of their married life had spun a web that had drawn him to her, binding them together. She was so happy, she felt almost blinded by the sheer brilliant glory of it.

Shaking herself back to awareness once again, she dashed to the dresser to get out a bra, and happened to see her small packet of pills. "Whoa! I almost forgot," she said and took out the pack.

Abruptly she realized and dropped the pills from her suddenly nerveless hand. She'd taken the last pill the first day she'd been so sick, though she doubted it had stayed down. She'd missed six pills. Frantically she searched through the dresser drawer for the instructions she knew were in there, finally locating the folded sheet way in the back.

If more than three pills were missed, don't resume taking them. Wait until the fourth day of the next cycle, then begin taking as normal. Pregnancy was unlikely, but not impossible, so normal precautions should be taken during intercourse. Sarah read the words over again, trying to calm the wild galloping of her heart. Unlikely, but not impossible. She tried to forget the last three words, and just concentrate on the reassuring "unlikely."

She thought of how Rome would look when she told him and knew immediately that, wrong or not, this was something she couldn't tell him. She couldn't even worry him with it. The way he'd looked when that young mother had called the name Justin had broken her heart, and she still remembered the pain of the way he'd rejected her comfort. She couldn't face that again.

But she'd have to tell him. She realized with a sinking heart that there was no other way she could explain having to take other precautions. When she thought of the closeness they'd shared, the possibility that it would be shattered made her clench her fists in pain. Not now. Please, not now.

She pulled herself together, dressed, and managed to make it to the store just as Erica did, right at opening time. She didn't have time to worry about anything—soon the store was busier than it had ever been, with regular customers who'd gotten to know her over the months coming in to see how she was, as they'd heard she'd been ill. People needed yarn and patterns, odd buttons, supplies from the doll room, finishing nails and picture frames. It seemed as if all her customers had simply waited until Tools and Dyes was open again, instead of going to another store, and the thought filled Sarah with a special warmth. A small but energetic woman of at least eighty brought in an afghan made from the softest yarn, in varying shades of green, and insisted on giving it to Sarah as a gift. "To keep the chill away from you," the old woman said, her faded blue eyes twinkling.

Sarah almost cried, and hugged the old woman. She'd been making afghans and bringing them to the store to be sold on commission, and Sarah knew that the money they brought did a great deal to supplement the woman's fixed income. It said a lot that she'd spend her time and supplies on a gift.

Just before lunch Rome came in. Sarah glanced up at the bell, her eyes widening as she recognized him.

"Let's go in the office for a minute," he said gently, and Sarah called Erica to run the cash register for her.

When the door closed behind them in the tiny cubicle that she used for an office, she looked at him worriedly. "What's wrong?"

"I have to leave, to finish up everything I left in the lurch when I came home to see about you." A crooked smile touched his mouth. "I could've told you out there, but I want to kiss you too, and the way I'm going to kiss you shouldn't be done in public."

She went weak and leaned back against her desk. "Oh? How is that?" Her voice was husky, almost a purr.

An almost predatory expression crossed his face, and he reached out to lock the door. "Naked," he said.

That night, lying alone in bed and missing the warmth of him beside her more than she would have thought possible, she knew. Even then, with an almost telepathic insight, she knew, and her hand strayed to her stomach. "Rome, I'm so sorry," she whispered to the empty darkness. .

"It's not unheard of," Dr. Easterwood said quietly. Her own examination had told her all she needed to know, even without the confirmation of the tests that lay before her on her desk. "Those pills were the lowest effective dosage available; given the right timing, a pregnancy is very possible when the dosage is interrupted as yours was. In your case, pregnancy is a reality."

Sarah was very composed. She'd had weeks to accustom herself to the idea. She didn't know what she'd do, but she'd already accepted the reality of the small life inside her, and already she loved it. She'd loved it from the moment of its conception; how else could she feel about Rome's child?

"You'll be thirty-four when the child is born," Dr. Easterwood continued. "That's late, for a first child, but you're healthy, and I don't expect any complications, though of course I want to keep a very close watch on you, and I want to run certain tests on the child at various stages of its development. I'm going to set you up for a biweekly checkup, rather than once a month. The only possibility of a problem that I can foresee at this stage is that, if the child is large, you'll probably have to have a cesarean section. Your pelvis is very narrow."

Sarah listened, too full of other concerns now to worry about the circumstances of the child's birth. That was months in the future, and she had a very big problem to handle in the present. How was she going to tell Rome? More important, how would he react?

Dr. Easterwood gave her enough vitamins to put a corpse well on the road to good health, then did an odd thing. She hugged Sarah and kissed her gravely on the cheek. "Good luck," she said. "I know you've wanted this baby for a long time."

Forever. She'd wanted it forever. How cruel it would be if she had to choose between Rome and this baby!

She told Rome that night. The temptation had been strong to keep it a secret for as long as she could, to put off the confrontation and steal every moment she could with him, but she knew he had a right to know. If she kept it from him, he'd rightly resent that as much or more than he'd resent her pregnancy. Telling him wasn't easy; she tried all through dinner to say the words, only to find them sticking in her throat. After dinner he went to the study to work on some papers he'd brought home with him, and finally Sarah went into the study. Very simply, she told him.

Every vestige of color washed out of his face. ''What?'' he whispered.

''I'm pregnant.'' She kept her voice steady, and her icy fingers were laced together in front of her to keep them from shaking.

He dropped his pen, his eyes closing. After a moment he opened them, and they were black, full of bitterness. ''How could you do this to me?'' he asked rawly, shoving himself away from the desk to stand with his back to her, his head bent while he rubbed his neck.

The accusation lashed her with pain, robbing her of speech. She'd known it would be a shock to him, but somehow she had never dreamed he might think she'd become pregnant deliberately, in spite of his wishes.

His wide shoulders were tense. ''You knew how I felt. You knew...and you did it anyway. Is that all you married me for? To use me as a stud?'' He turned, revealing a face full of pain and rage. ''Damn it to hell! Sarah, I trusted you to *take the damned pills!* Why didn't you?''

Very thinly, she said, ''I had the flu. I couldn't take anything.''

He froze. Swallowing, he looked at her paper-white face and the hell in her eyes. As he realized what he'd said and how it must have hurt her, remorse hit him with a force that almost doubled him over. She loved him. If he knew anything, he knew that, and he also knew she would never have purposely betrayed him.

He moved, reaching for her, but she stepped back, her hand coming up to ward him off. "I saw Dr. Easterwood today," she said, her voice still thin and expressionless. "When I had the flu and couldn't take the pills, the break in the schedule allowed for ovulation . . . and conception."

She'd seen the doctor that very day, and had had the courage to tell him immediately, had loved him enough to tell him. He'd reacted by lashing out at her for something that was more his fault than hers. If he'd thought, he'd have known that she hadn't been able to take the pills; the first day she'd felt better he'd tumbled her into bed. Had it been then, he wondered, or the other times he'd made love to her that night? Or the next day, in her tiny cramped office, with her perched on the desk, her lovely face ecstatic from his rough, hasty, and wonderfully satisfying possession? "I'm sorry," he said gently, wishing more than anything in the world that he hadn't hurt her. He saw the stiff way she was holding herself, as if braced against further pain, and an odd pain squeezed his own heart. In that moment, despite his own pain and desperation, he knew he loved her, and the realization made it vital that he ease her hurt. Slowly he reached out for her again, and this time she allowed him to take her in his arms.

He folded her against him, rubbing his hands up her slender back, trying to take away the hurt that he'd dealt her. She wasn't crying, and that worried him more than violent tears would have; if she'd been crying, she'd have had an outlet for the emotions she was holding inside. Her body was stiff in his arms, and she hadn't put her arms around him. He kept holding her, stroking her back and murmuring gently to her, until she began to relax against him. Slowly her arms crept up to his shoulders.

It took some time before he could coax her completely out of her shocked, silent condition, before he felt that she would be able to discuss the best solution to the problem. Still holding her, reassuring her with his touch, he asked, "Did you make an appointment?"

Sarah was confused, not quite understanding. "Dr. Easterwood wants me to see her twice a month."

He shook his head. "I meant an appointment for an...an abortion." Even the way he felt, it was hard to say, and he shuddered with the effort it took.

She jerked and looked at him wildly. "What?"

In that moment, he knew that she hadn't thought of the solution to the problem, hadn't even considered it, and something cold touched him. He moved away from her, his eyes black with his inner hell. "I don't want you to have this baby," he said rawly. "I don't want it. I don't want any baby, ever."

Sarah felt as if she'd received a huge blow to the chest; she tried to suck in air, and couldn't. Blindly she stared at him, afraid she'd faint; then she finally managed to pull some oxygen into her constricted chest. "Rome, it's *your* baby too! How can you want—"

"No," he interrupted, his voice harsh with pain. "I buried my children. I stood by their graves and watched the dirt cover them up. I can't go through that again. I can't accept another child, so don't . . . don't ask me to try. I've learned to live without them, without my boys, but no other child can ever—ever!—replace them.'' His face twisted with agony, and he was gasping for breath too, as if it were almost impossible for him to continue. He fought for control and gained it, though sweat had broken out on his brow from the effort. ''I love you,'' he said, more quietly. ''Sarah, I love you. That's more than I ever thought I'd have again. Loving you, having you, has given me a reason to live again, something to look forward to every day. But another baby . . . no. I can't do it. Don't have the baby. If you love me, don't . . . don't have the baby.''

She staggered, then brought herself upright only by sheer bone-crunching determination. No woman should ever have to hear this, she thought dimly. No woman should ever be faced with this decision. She loved him, and because she loved him, she had to love his child. She understood the strain he was under; she'd seen his face when he'd stood by the graves of his sons, and known that he would have lain down and died with them, if he could. But knowing, and understanding, didn't make it any easier for her.

He looked at her with pure screaming hell in his eyes, and suddenly his eyes and his cheeks were wet. ''Please,'' he begged shakily.

Sarah bit her lip until her teeth went through flesh and brought blood. ''I can't,'' she said.

Chapter Ten

She faced him across the study, her slender body braced under a burden she wasn't certain she could carry. "I'd do anything for you that you asked," she said in a slow, careful voice. "Except that. I love you so much that I could never harm any part of you, and this baby is a part of you. I've loved you for years, not just for the past few months, since we've been married. I loved you before you married or even met Diane, and after. I loved Justin and Shane because they were yours." She shook her head a little blindly. "I don't expect I'll stop loving you, no matter what you do. If you can't, absolutely can't, accept this baby, that's your decision. But I can't destroy it."

Rome turned away, his movements slow, like an old man carrying too many years. "What now?" he asked in a leaden voice.

"It's your decision," she repeated. She couldn't believe her voice was so calm, but her back was to the wall and she knew it. "If you want to go, rather than live with me, I'll understand, and I won't stop loving you, ever. If you stay, I'll try—" Her voice broke suddenly and she stopped, breathing heavily for a moment before she could trust herself to speak again. "I'll try to keep the baby away from you, out of your way. I'll never ask you to care for it, or hold it. I swear, Rome, you'll never even have to know its name if you don't want to! For all intents and purposes, you *won't* be a father!"

"I don't know," he said lifelessly. "I'm sorry, but I just don't know."

He walked past her, and after a moment Sarah managed to control her legs enough to follow him. He paused on his way out of the apartment, his dark head bent. Without looking at her, he said, "I do love you. More than you know. I wish I'd told you before now, but..." He made a helpless motion with his hand. "Something died in me when they died. They were so little, and they always looked to me for protection. I was their daddy, and there wasn't anything I couldn't do, in their eyes. But when they really needed me, I couldn't do anything to help them. All I could do...was hold them...when it was too damned late!" His mouth twisted with pain, and he rubbed his eyes, rubbed away the tears for his two little boys. "I have to go. I have to be alone for a while. I'll be in touch, one way or the other. Take care of yourself." At last he looked at her, and what she saw in his eyes made her clench her fists to keep from crying out.

Even after the door had closed and minutes had ticked past, Sarah stood there, staring at the blank expanse of wood, because she could do nothing else. She'd known it would be difficult, but never had she guessed his reaction would be so strong, or his pain so raw. She felt his agony like a knife cutting into her own flesh.

He'd said he loved her. How awful to have heaven offered to her with one hand and taken away with the other!

She groped her way into the living room and sat down, her entire body numb with shock, but slowly she began to come alive again. If he loved her, perhaps he'd stay. One miracle had already happened; was it so unreasonable to ask for another one? And if he stayed, perhaps in time the wound left by the loss of his sons would heal enough for him to love another child, her child. She'd keep her word though. If he stayed, she wouldn't try to force the child on him.

Rome didn't come home that night. Sarah lay in the bed she'd shared with him every night he'd been home since she'd had the flu, and she cried until she couldn't cry any longer.

She got up the next morning without having slept and went to the store as usual. Erica noticed her pale face and tear-swollen eyes but discreetly didn't mention them. Tactfully, she waited on most of the customers, while Sarah remained in the office and brought all the books up-to-date. Even that was painful, because everything reminded her of Rome. He'd set up the books, helped her choose her computer system, worked in here every Saturday, and possibly gotten her pregnant on the very desk she sat at.

Erica wouldn't ask, but when Derek came in that afternoon and saw her, he reached out to help if he could. "What is it?" he asked. "Can I help?"

Sarah felt a surge of love for him. How any sixteen-year-old boy could be so wonderful was beyond her. For Derek, she could smile, and she did. "I'm pregnant," she said.

He drew up the one other chair in the tiny office and folded his muscular body into it. "Is that bad?"

"I think it's wonderful," she said shakily. "The problem is that Rome doesn't want it. He was married before, and he had two beautiful little boys. They were killed in a car accident almost three years ago, and he can't bear being around children since then. It's still too painful for him."

Derek's beautiful eyes were sober, and endlessly kind. "Don't give up. He won't really know how he feels until the baby is born and he can see it. Babies are pretty special, you know."

"Yes, I know. So are you," she said.

He smiled his lovely, utterly peaceful smile, and got up to do his chores.

Another night came and went without word from Rome, but that night Sarah slept, exhausted from the lack of sleep the night before and the demands pregnancy was making on her body. Fatalistically, she realized that there was nothing more she could do, that they were both bound by the people they were and the circumstances of their lives. All her life she'd wanted a stable home, a husband and children to love, and she simply couldn't give up. As long as there was a chance, she had to hope, and she had to try.

As she drove home the next night she became abruptly aware that spring had arrived. It was still brisk, but not really cold, and trees were putting out tender, budding leaves. Late last summer she'd sat in her office, seeing the passing of summer as the passing of her life, fading into autumn and then winter, with no future and no love, only an empty road spiraling down for the rest of her years. Now she knew that after winter came spring. The winter had brought love into her life; with this spring, there was new life, inside her as well as springing forth from the earth. She felt suddenly more peaceful; the sense of continuity in life itself calmed her.

Rome's car was in his parking slot.

On shaking legs, she went up to the apartment. Was he back to stay, or was he inside packing to leave? Knowing that the next few minutes were crucial to her happiness for the rest of her life, she opened the door.

A delicious, spicy odor greeted her.

Rome appeared in the kitchen doorway. He looked oddly thinner, though it had been only two days since she'd seen him, and his face was lined with strain. But he was cleanly shaven and still dressed in the trousers from one of his suits, as well as a pale blue dress shirt, and she knew he'd been going to the office as usual. "Spaghetti," he said quietly, indicating the kitchen. "If you can't eat it, I'll dump it out and we'll go somewhere for dinner."

"I can eat it," she said, her voice as quiet as his. "I haven't been sick yet."

He nodded, then leaned his shoulder against the door frame as if he were very tired. "I don't want to leave you, babe. I want to be with you, sleep with you, and look at that pretty face across the breakfast table from me. But I don't want to know about the baby," he said deliberately. "Don't talk to me about it, and don't involve me in it. I don't want anything to do with it."

Sarah nodded, too shaken to say anything other than "all right." Then she went to her bedroom to change clothes, leaving him leaning in the doorway.

Dinner was quiet, strained. She didn't ask him where he'd been, or why he'd made the decision he'd made, nor did he volunteer the information. He'd said he wanted to sleep with her, but when they went to bed, Sarah realized he'd probably meant in the rawer sense of the word, because he went to his own bedroom for the first time in a long while. She tried not to be disappointed, knowing what a shock he'd had, but she still missed him. Without him, she felt lost; the bed was far too big and cold. Moreover, pregnancy was having the curious side effect of intensifying her physical needs, as one of the booklets Dr. Easterwood had given her mentioned. She wanted Rome as her lover, not just her sleeping partner.

Two days later Max came to see her at the store. "Have lunch with me," he invited.

Sarah glanced quickly at him, in time to see the concern in his eyes before he masked it. She nodded and called to Erica that she was going to lunch.

Max took her to a small, quiet restaurant; as it was an early lunch, they were the only customers, except for a man in the back corner who was absorbed in his newspaper. They ordered their lunch; then when the waitress had left, Max gave Sarah a searching look. "Are you all right?"

"Yes, of course," she replied, startled.

"I wanted to reassure myself. You see, Rome spent two nights in my apartment, and he was the closest thing to a basket case I've ever seen."

So that was where he'd been. Sarah said "thank you" with deep open gratitude.

Max's crooked smile would have melted stones. "Dear girl, you know I'd slay dragons for you, if only there were any left to slay. Tell me what I can do."

"I suppose you know the entire story?"

He nodded. "As I said, Rome was in shock. I tried pouring tea down him, but he wouldn't have any, so I switched to Scotch. I couldn't get him drunk," he reflected, "not even on my favorite Scotch, but he stopped looking like walking death and finally began to talk. No one had ever mentioned his background; when he told me about his first wife, and his sons, it was almost more than I could bear in a civilized manner, and I'm not known as a particularly emotional man." For once, there was no devilish gleam in his turquoise eyes. "That was all he'd tell me the first night. He worked the next day, as normal, though *he* wasn't normal. On my solemn oath, it was a danger to even speak to the man. The second night he told me that you're pregnant."

Sarah twisted her water glass around, her eyes sad. "Did he tell you—"

"Yes." He reached out and covered her hand. "I thought he was mad, or a fool, or both. If it were my child you were carrying, I'd be intolerable with pride. But then, I haven't had his experiences."

"Diane was my best friend," Sarah whispered. "I knew his babies. It was...awful."

"He told me of your ultimatum. Love, you have to be the most courageous woman I've ever met. You gambled everything, didn't you? And you won."

"I haven't won yet, not completely. I have a second chance, that's all."

"He told me that he won't have anything to do with the child, that he isn't interested in it. If it works out

like that, and you ever need anything, call me. I'd be
honored to be a surrogate father. I'll drive you to the
hospital, hold your hand during labor, whatever you
want. Do you realize," he said thoughtfully, "what
I've just committed myself to? Rome isn't the only
fool. I suppose I can always comfort myself with the
thought that he's too bloody sharp to let any other
man stand in with his wife like that."

Sarah began to laugh, touched by his concern. "You
poor dear. You were doing so well until you thought
of childbirth, weren't you?"

He grinned. "I've always been extremely gallant, as
far as my squeamishness will allow."

Their lunch arrived, and Sarah ate hers with a good
appetite, the best she'd had in days. Max waved his
fork at her. "I realize now why Rome was so determined to have exclusive rights to you. After the
trauma of his past, he must have been desperate to
make certain of you, to put some sort of stability back
into his life. He didn't know that you loved him, did
he?"

"No, not then. He does now."

"He loves you too. I realize that he didn't when you
got married, but he's not an idiot, so he promptly
recognized what a treasure he had. He's still a barbarian, of course, but he's bloody smart, and stupidity is really the only thing I can't abide. It galls me,
sometimes, to find that I like him as well as I do."

Max was priceless, using his casual, caustic wit to
cheer her up and reassure her at the same time. He was
sincere in his offer of help too. She was lucky in being
surrounded by friends who cared for both her and
Rome. Rome might feel as if his back were to the wall
and he had to fight for his marriage, but in truth peo-

ple cared about him and would do anything to help. Max had reassured Sarah of Rome's whereabouts the two nights he'd been away from her, as much to help Rome as to relieve Sarah's mind. He didn't want Rome's marriage in jeopardy over an erroneous conclusion.

"You're a marvelous man," she told him, then had to tease, "What you need is a marvelous Texas girl to shake you out of your British reserve."

He gave her a long mocking look. "My British reserve is tossed out the window on certain occasions, love, and for your information, I've found a marvelous Texas woman. I would take her home to meet the family, but she wants taming first. I'm breaking her to the saddle, I believe is how you Texans would say it."

The idea of sophisticated Max with a fiery drawling woman was fascinating. She leaned forward, a multitude of questions bubbling to her lips, but he lifted a brow at her. "No, I do not kiss and tell," he said gently. "Have you finished with your lunch?"

Rome came to her bed that night and made love to her very gently. She clung to him, responding to him eagerly. Afterward, when he started to leave, she put her hand on his arm. "Please, not yet. Stay with me a while longer."

He hesitated, then lay back down and took her in his arms. "I don't want to hurt you," he said into the darkness, his voice rough velvet. "I want you too much; if I stay, we'll be making love again."

The way he'd thought of it had changed, she noticed. When they first married, he'd always avoided the phrase "making love." She rubbed her cheek against the crisp curls on his chest, then tenderly bit his nipple. "I hope so," she said, and there was a smile in her voice. "I'd like you to sleep with me again, for as long as you feel comfortable with me."

He tangled his fingers in her hair and tilted her head back. "Comfortable? This is how I feel with you," he said, taking her hand and sliding it down his body. He was as eager for her as if they hadn't already made love. "It's not very comfortable, but that's the way you affect me. If you're not physically able to spend the night the way I'd like to, then you'd better let me go."

"I'm able," she breathed, wiggling atop him. "I'm perfectly healthy."

He was careful with her, restraining his power and not letting her do too much. She knew his concern was solely for her, not for the baby, but still it warmed her. In the darkness he told her he loved her, and when they finally slept, he held her clasped to his side. Pregnancy forced her to get up several times during the night; every time she returned to bed, it was to find him awake. Without a word he'd draw her back into his arms.

When she went in for her biweekly examination, Dr. Easterwood checked her thoroughly, then gave her the thumbs-up sign. "Perfect," she pronounced. "Any morning sickness, or spotting?"

"Nothing," Sarah reported happily.

"Good. Let's keep it that way."

"Why are you seeing me every two weeks?"

"Your age, and the fact that it's your first child. I'm being overly cautious, I'm certain, but I want to deliver that baby in November. Take your vitamins, and every two hours, I want you to take a thirty-minute break, with your feet up. No exceptions."

Taking a thirty-minute break at the store was an iffy thing, until the customers found out that she was pregnant. She told Erica what Dr. Easterwood had said, and soon, promptly at eleven o'clock in the morning, Erica or someone in the store would say, "It's time for your rest." The baby was becoming a community project. Marcie got in the habit of dropping by at least once a day, Max came by at unexpected times, Erica and the customers rigidly supervised her rest, and Derek oversaw the entire operation. If she lifted anything, Derek somehow found out about it, and a gentle scolding from him had the power to make her feel as if lightning could strike her at any moment.

She was in her fourth month when Rome came home unexpectedly early one Wednesday, the day when the store was closed after lunch. She was putting new shelf paper in the cabinets, and she was working on the bottom shelves, down on her hands and knees, with her entire torso inside the cabinet. Rome looked at her, bent down to grasp her hips, and firmly drew her out. "I'm hiring someone to do the housework," he said calmly. "Tomorrow."

The idea amused her. "Millions of women all over the world do housework while they're pregnant until the very day they give birth."

"You aren't millions of women," he said. "If I didn't travel so much, it would be different. I can help you while I'm here, but when I'm gone, I want to know that you aren't climbing around on cabinets, or in them."

She'd done it before, when she wasn't pregnant, but she didn't point that out to him. Having his concern based on her pregnancy was a very good sign. It wasn't because she was awkward or clumsy, because even though she was four months pregnant, she had gained only one pound and was still wearing her normal clothes. The only visible sign of her pregnancy was the increased plumpness of her breasts, and their added sensitivity, both of which seemed to fascinate Rome.

He leaned down and kissed her. "Promise me," he said, and she did.

He was quieter than he had been before, at the same time both closer and more remote. She couldn't tell what he was thinking, but whenever he went on a trip, he called more often to check on her. When he was home and had a business dinner, he more often than not arranged for wives to attend, so she wouldn't be spending the evening alone. His hand was always on the small of her back when they walked, and he always held her hand while she was getting into or out of his car. But he never asked about the baby, how her latest checkup had gone, or even when it was due, though if he could count, he should have been able to figure that out.

She knew she wouldn't have the joy of picking out baby names with him, or speculating on the fascinating subject of whether it was a boy or a girl. On the other hand, a lot of fathers exhibited little or no interest in their offspring, then went to pieces when labor began. She still hoped. She had to hope, though she knew she had to face a lot of heartbreak in the future, not the least of which would be trying to explain to a small child that Daddy wasn't to be bothered— ever.

But she had a baby to prepare for, with or without Rome, so she quietly began preparing the third bedroom as a nursery. To make room for baby furniture she had Derek help her move several items of furniture she'd brought from her old apartment, and those she took down to the store and sold them. Marcie took her shopping, calling on her half-forgotten experiences as a new mother in helping Sarah select what she'd need. A baby bed was bought and installed, with a merry crib-mobile attached to it, ready to be wound up to fascinate the infant who would occupy the bed. A cradle and a rocking chair took up residence. A teddy bear appeared one afternoon, sitting smugly in the passenger seat of her car, but when Sarah looked around for Derek he'd already disappeared from sight. The teddy bear was placed in the rocking chair and promptly named Boo-Boo.

One night, searching for some papers he'd misplaced, Rome opened the door of the third bedroom and turned on the light. He froze momentarily, then quickly turned out the light and backed out of the room, closing the door behind him. His face was white. He didn't open the door again.

Sarah asked Marcie to attend natural childbirth classes with her, to be her coach and partner. Marcie drew a quick breath. "Are you certain?" she asked, pleased but uneasy at the same time. "I really don't know anything about having babies. I mean, I had Derek, but he had it all organized." She blushed like a young girl. "That sounds stupid, but I swear, that's the way it seemed. I went into labor at eight o'clock in the morning, just as the doctor was making his rounds at the hospital. Derek has always been considerate. He was born at nine thirty, with no trouble and very little effort on my part, just a few pushes. He cried by himself, before the doctor could make him, then began sucking on his fist and went to sleep. That was it."

They looked at each other; then Marcie rolled her eyes and they began laughing.

Sarah did all the exercises Dr. Easterwood recommended to strengthen her back and abdominal muscles, and took her vitamins faithfully. When she was five months pregnant, Dr. Easterwood performed a relatively simple test, drawing a small amount of amniotic fluid from Sarah's womb. The baby was pronounced perfectly normal, and the doctor then confessed that that had been her foremost concern, but everything was going along great guns.

Soon after that, Rome settled her into place one night to sleep, with her head on his shoulder and her body curved against him. He'd just made love to her, and Sarah was sleepy, her body replete. At that moment, the baby kicked, hard, the first time it had moved so vigorously. Sarah had felt small, discrete flutters for several weeks but never before an honest kick. The tiny foot thudded against her abdomen where she was pressed into Rome's side. He went rigid, then shot out of bed, stifling a curse.

He turned on the light, and Sarah stared at him, uncontrollable tears stinging her eyes. He was sweating. "I'm sorry," he said hoarsely. He leaned down and kissed her, stroking her hair. "I love you, but I can't take it. I'll sleep in my bedroom until after it's born."

She tried to smile, despite the tears in her eyes. "I understand. I'm sorry too."

Two days later he left on an extended trip. Sarah suspected that he'd volunteered for it, but if that were so, she supposed she couldn't blame him. Things were out of his control, and despite his efforts to ignore it, her pregnancy kept making itself obvious to him. Her figure was rounding out now, and she had to wear maternity clothes. The baby had changed his sleeping habits and his love life; no wonder he felt the need to get away.

While Rome was gone Max called her every day. She'd never been so cosseted in her life, all because of a perfectly normal pregnancy. Derek ruled her like a gentle despot at the store, and since school was out for the summer, there was no break from him. He was there when she arrived and left only when she did. The only privacy she had was when she went home at night to the perfectly clean apartment. Rome had indeed hired a housekeeper, a nice comfortable middle-aged woman who didn't at all mind receiving a nice salary for cleaning an apartment that was never really mussed anyway. Mrs. Melton knew a good deal when she saw it, and the apartment was always spotless, the laundry always done. If it hadn't been for the interest and distraction of the store, Sarah would have gone crazy.

Rome was gone for three weeks, three of the longest weeks of her life, but everyone made a herculean effort to keep her cheered up. Not everyone knew all of the circumstances—only Marcie, Derek, and Max—but all her customers fussed over her as well. If only Rome had looked forward to his child's birth with even a fraction of the eagerness that relative strangers revealed, she'd have been delirious with joy.

He called her at work one day to tell her briefly that he was in a meeting but would be home the next day. Sarah hung up the phone and began crying.

Derek took her in his arms and led her to the office, closing the door behind them. She cried on his strong young shoulder, while he rocked her soothingly back and forth. Then he dried her eyes and seated her in her chair, pulling up the other chair to sit before her.

"Was that Rome?"

"Yes. He'll be home tomorrow." She gave a watery sniffle. "I was just so glad to hear his voice and know he'll be home soon that I couldn't handle it."

He smiled and patted her knee. "I received the final confirmation on my scholarship yesterday," he said, taking her mind away from Rome. "Rome and Mr. Conroy really went to bat for me, didn't they? And all because of you."

"I'm glad for you. You deserve the best."

He was watching her steadily. "I've been reading about pregnancy and childbirth, just in case something happens and you need me, before you can get to a hospital. I think I could deliver a baby."

There was no doubt in Sarah's mind, if Derek had been reading up on something, he could do it. Some people would have thought he'd changed the subject, but knowing Derek, she simply waited for him to tie delivering a baby in with his scholarship.

"I've decided that I'm going to be a doctor," he said, with great dignity. "An obstetrician. Watching you grow, with the baby inside you, is the greatest thing I've ever seen. I want to help a lot of babies into the world."

"I can't think of a better start a child could have," Sarah said, touched almost to tears. No man would be a better doctor than Derek Taliferro.

"I love you, you know." His calm golden brown eyes drifted over her face. "You've given me a chance I wouldn't have had otherwise, and helped Mom too. I'm not talking man-woman love, because I'm not ready for that, but it's still love." He leaned over and put his palm on the swell of her stomach, a touch of love. "But if this baby is a girl, I just might wait for her. I figure your daughter would have to be something really special."

A tender smile touched her lips, and she stroked a black curl away from his forehead. "She couldn't have a better man waiting for her," she whispered and kissed his cheek.

She went home early the next night, leaving Erica and Derek to close up because she wanted to see Rome. Feeling that she'd burst into tears if he wasn't home, she almost cried anyway when she saw his car. She ran inside and fretted as the elevator made its way upward. "Rome!" she called as she unlocked the door and thrust it open. "Rome! Where are you?"

"In here," he called from his bedroom.

She ran to his room, her heart thumping wildly. He came out of the bathroom just as she skidded through the doorway, looking lean and gorgeous with his hair damp and a white towel slung around his neck. She caught a quick breath and fairly leapt across the room, only to falter midway. She gave him a helpless, confused look, then fainted for the first time not only in her pregnancy, but in her entire life.

Rome gave a startled cry and leapt for her but wasn't able to catch her before she hit the floor. Swearing beneath his breath, he lifted her in his arms and placed her on the bed, a cold sweat breaking out on him at the limpness of her body. He wet a washcloth in cold water and washed her face and hands with it, then placed it across her forehead. Her eyelids fluttered open, and she stared at him in confusion. "I fainted," she said in tones of pure astonishment.

He couldn't think of her doctor's name. "Who's your doctor?" he asked fiercely, leaning over her.

"Easterwood. But why—"

He grabbed the phone book and flipped to the E's, then began running his finger down the column. "Rome," she began patiently, trying to sit up. "There's nothing wrong with me. I just fainted."

He put his hand on her chest and pushed her back onto the bed. "Don't get up again," he warned flatly, punching out the numbers on the phone.

"She's not at her office; you'll get an answering service."

"Dr. Easterwood, please," he said into the phone, all the authority of a senior vice president in his tone. "This is Roman Matthews, Sarah Matthews's husband."

Against all the laws of nature as well as those governing doctors' offices, Dr. Easterwood came on the line. Sarah lay on the bed and glared at Rome, wondering if, somehow, he and Derek were related. It was disgusting.

He briefly told the doctor what had happened, then Dr. Easterwood asked a few questions, and he gave Sarah a grim look. "Yes, she made an abrupt movement. She was *running*."

He listened for a while longer, and his expression became even grimmer. "I see. What are the dangers if she goes into premature labor and the baby is in the birth canal before a cesarean can be performed?"

Sarah groaned aloud, knowing now that she'd had it. All the signs were that she'd have a perfectly normal labor and birth, as the child didn't seem to be a large one, but she knew that it wouldn't make any difference to Rome. He was giving her a look that would have scorched grass.

He hung up the phone and turned to face her. "You're in a certain amount of danger by having your first child at your age," he said with scathing control. "You're at an even greater risk because of the narrowness of your pelvis. And you were *running,* damn it!" His face contorted, and he clenched his fist. "I don't want this baby at all, and certainly not at any risk to you. Why didn't you tell me? What do you think it would do to me if something happened to you because of a baby I'd—" He broke off, his chest heaving as he fought for control again.

Sarah sat up and went into his arms, holding him and trying to comfort him. "Rome, darling, I'm fine. Honestly. And don't worry, because the only possibility of my needing a C-section is if the baby is a large one, and so far, it isn't."

He shook his head, his arms closing around her. "Don't you remember how big Justin and Shane were? They both weighed over nine pounds! Shane only lacked one ounce of hitting ten pounds. The very thought of you even carrying a baby that big is . . . it's scary," he finished.

"Don't borrow trouble before it happens. Please. I haven't had any difficulty at all; no nausea, no swelling in my feet, no back pain. I'm in perfect health!"

He tilted her head back, hungrily examining her face, seeing the love and concern there, concern for him instead of for herself. He kissed her, then held her head to his chest. "I love you," he said shakily. "Don't let my miracle slip away from me now."

"I'm not going anywhere," she assured him. "I've waited too long for you; I'm not about to let anything happen now. Years and years and years," she said softly. "That's how long I waited for you. That's why I never married, and why everyone thought I was so devoted to my job. I wasn't interested in any other man except you."

He rubbed his chin against her temple, his eyes closing.

"I love you so much, it scares me," he finally said, very quietly. "I loved Diane, but the pain of losing her is gone, because of you. It's as if Diane prepared me for you, gave me the base to stand on so I could reach you. I always knew you were there, and I think I always knew that someday, when I knew how to love enough, I'd have you. If I forget to say it sometimes, remind me, because I don't ever want *you* to forget how I feel. I can't want this baby, but that doesn't change the way I feel about you, and I want you to always remember that. There's just something in me that broke when the boys died, and I don't think it will ever heal. Another baby won't replace them."

No, nothing would ever replace the little boys he'd loved, and he couldn't yet see that this new child wasn't a replacement, but a person in its own right. That was the other miracle she prayed for, the day when he would look at his child and feel his heart mend.

If that day never came, eventually her own heart would break.

Chapter Eleven

"Give me your car keys," he said the next morning as he was leaving for work. Frowning, she got the keys from her purse and gave them to him. He took his own keys from his pocket and put them in her hand. "Drive my car for the duration. It's bigger, more comfortable, and will give you more protection, as well as being an automatic. You don't need to be changing gears."

"Well, if you insist." She took the keys and lifted an elegant eyebrow at him. "What's this going to do to your corporate image?"

"Send it right down the old tubes," he said and grinned.

The Mercedes felt huge around her, and she drove with ponderous care, fearful of putting the slightest scratch on its unblemished surface. She was used to wheeling her dashing little ZX into the narrowest of parking spaces, to darting through holes in traffic that looked limited to bicycles, but there would be none of that with Rome's car, which was precisely what he'd intended.

The summer days ended. Derek went back to school, and time seemed to slow. Sarah felt her pregnancy weighing heavily on her now, though she was still in good health and Dr. Easterwood was well satisfied with her condition. She hadn't gained all that much weight, only ten pounds, but it was amazing how heavy ten pounds could be when they were concentrated in one spot. When Dr. Easterwood told her she'd probably gain another ten pounds before she delivered, Sarah groaned in disbelief. "I won't be able to get out of bed!" she protested. "I have to roll out on my hands and knees now! I won't be able to buckle my shoes!"

"I've heard it all before," Dr. Easterwood said, unimpressed. "Wear slip-on flats, and get your husband to help you get up."

Since Rome was sleeping in his bedroom, he was never around to see her struggles to get out of bed, and she was always careful to sit on the edge of a chair now, so she'd be able to get up without making a spectacle of herself. Relaxing tub baths were a thing of the past, and showers were the order of the day. Shaving her legs or putting on panty hose involved some incredible contortions. She sighed, looking at the tight little mound of her stomach. Ten more pounds was out of the question.

Forgetting her promise not to tell him anything about the baby, that night she groaned to Rome, "Can

you believe it? Dr. Easterwood said I'd gain *ten* more
pounds! I'm huge already! I won't be able to walk."

He looked at her, startled by the real distress in her
voice. She was seven months pregnant, and Diane had
been that big at four months. But Sarah had never
been pregnant before, and he realized with amaze-
ment that he had far more experience with this than
she had. He also knew of a woman's fears and dis-
comforts as her time came nearer and her waistline
kept expanding. The one thing he couldn't do was
laugh, though when he looked at her swollen little
stomach he wanted to absolutely roar with laughter. It
was a small baby, he realized with relief, and a weight
lifted from his shoulders.

She looked so forlorn, he was reminded of when
she'd had the flu and she'd been disgusted with being
ill. She couldn't take being in anything but tip-top
shape, capable of handling whatever came her way.
She needed comforting; she needed him, just as she
had when she'd been ill.

He pulled her onto his lap and kissed her, careful
not to let his arm touch her stomach; instead, he put
his hand on her knees. "I think you're beautiful," he
said, and she was. She was glowing, her hair lustrous,
her skin radiant. He kissed her again, his hand going
automatically to her full breasts.

She sighed with pleasure, her lips parting for his.
Shaken by her nearness and by the softness of her in
his lap, he kept kissing her while he unbuttoned her
top and sought the warm satin of her flesh. Her
breasts were rounded, growing to fulfill the needs of
his child, filling his palm. Her nipples strained to the

touch, and she clenched her hands in his hair, kissing him wildly.

"I'm going to explode," he groaned, pulling his mouth away.

Dr. Easterwood hadn't told Sarah that she had to abstain yet, but she didn't try to push Rome into making love to her. That was his decision, and she felt a little shy at the thought anyway. She was no longer slender; she'd feel awkward and not sexy enough for him.

He rebuttoned her blouse, and Sarah knew he'd made his decision. She accepted it without argument, sliding from his lap. "I'm sorry for being such a crybaby," she apologized, then suddenly realized what she'd said, and that she'd broken her promise.

He gave her an unreadable look, one that made her flinch inside. No matter how she felt, she never mentioned her problems to him again. When the baby began kicking so energetically that she couldn't sleep at night, she tolerated it in silence. She endured the growing aches and pains in her overburdened muscles, the total discomfort; though it seemed like forever, she knew that in a matter of weeks it would all be over.

On the first of October Dr. Easterwood told her to stop driving at all, and to get more rest. That was something she had to tell Rome, as that effectively put a stop to working at the store. So instead of being fussed over by Erica and Derek and a steady stream of customers, there was only Mrs. Melton to fuss over her, though Marcie did run up to see about her several times a day. Rome began spending all his evenings at home, though Sarah knew he would normally have at least a few business dinners to attend. Max was covering for him, was all he said when she asked him about it.

Sarah found that she was too lethargic to even miss the store. She read a great deal and tried to decide on baby names, but she really couldn't concentrate on anything. She slept a lot in the afternoons, because that was when the baby seemed to sleep. At night, it did aerobic exercises.

During the nights, lying awake with only her unborn child for company, Sarah tormented herself, trying to decide if she'd made the right decision. Just the very thought of *not* having the baby was insupportable; it was Rome's child, conceived in an act of love, and even before its birth she loved it with a deep devotion that startled her, for somehow she hadn't expected to feel such a sense of physical ownership. The child was part of her too, an extension of herself. As such, she felt it keenly when Rome rejected the child.

But the decision she'd made, even if it had been the only decision she *could* make, could blight the child's life. She knew that Rome's aversion to it wasn't one to be taken lightly, that it had been formed in the blackest days of his life. She could still feel his anguish, his deep and utter despair, and even now she cried for him when she remembered the emptiness of his eyes. She had backed him into a corner, forced him to choose between accepting the physical presence of a child he didn't want, or losing the warmth of his wife's love, which still seemed so new and fragile to him. He'd never even hoped to find love again, not after the tragedy that had left his life a wasteland; when he did love, he was both astonished and frightened by it. But when faced with a choice, he'd chosen Sarah, even at the cost of considerable emotional pain to himself.

Adoption was an alternative that kept springing to Sarah's mind, only to make everything in her writhe in rejection. There was no easy answer; no matter what she did, someone would be hurt. If she gave up her child, its loss would haunt her for the rest of her life. If the love Rome felt for her eventually died under the weight of a burden he couldn't carry, would *she* come to resent her own baby?

Ever since she'd made the decision to keep the baby, she hadn't let herself think of all those things. She'd taken each day as it came, not planning too far into the future, ignoring the problems she knew were waiting for her, because she simply couldn't handle them. All she had been able to do was live in the present, her mind and body preoccupied with the processes of life going on inside her. She'd been kept busy by the store, distracted by the constant company of other people. But now she was spending her days mostly alone, with nothing to do but think, and she was afraid.

If she lost Rome now, what would she do? She'd reached for a miracle when she married him, and found it. To have him walk away from her now would shatter her. Yet she'd risked destroying her marriage, and done it deliberately. Already he was more remote from her, and growing farther apart every day. He was kind, and solicitous of her comfort and health, but the baby prevented any real intimacy with him, and she was beginning to fear that they were merely polite strangers.

The Rome she knew was an impatient, dynamic man; he made things and people *move*. He'd overcome a horror so great that many men would have buckled under it, broken forever. That Rome wasn't the polite, carefully controlled man who came home from the office every night, asked if she felt all right, and ignored her for the rest of the evening. What if his distance was the result of indifference, and he wouldn't approach her even without the bulk of pregnancy as a barrier? Was he simply doing the polite thing and lending her his name until after the baby was born?

Sarah was thankful that the first natural childbirth class that she and Marcie attended came on a night when Rome was on an overnight business trip, so she didn't have to explain to him where she'd gone. Sarah had put off the classes, hoping against hope that Rome would decide to attend them with her, but at last, time forced her to make a decision. If she didn't attend the classes soon, the baby would come anyway. She felt shy and awkward about attending the classes so close to term, and she keenly felt Rome's absence. Marcie was a dear friend, but every other woman in the class was accompanied by her husband, and Sarah intercepted several pitying glances that came her way.

The class made her feel better in one respect: She was near term, but there were a lot of women so swollen with pregnancy that they made her little pumpkin of a stomach look hardly respectable. She patted her unborn child fondly, thinking that she liked it just the way it was.

Rome came home early the next afternoon; he came into the living room where she was sitting with her feet propped on the coffee table while she industriously tried to complete every puzzle in a crossword puzzle book. Placing his briefcase down with controlled movements, he said, "I called you last night, but you weren't here. Where were you?"

Startled, Sarah looked up at him; then her glance slid away. She'd been wishing that he weren't so remote, but somehow she'd forgotten just how disconcerting he could be when he pierced someone with those fierce dark eyes. He wasn't remote now; he was angry.

He unbuttoned his suit jacket and shrugged out of it, tossing it across the back of the sofa. Sitting down across from her, he raked his fingers through his wind-tossed dark hair. "I'm waiting," he said softly.

Sarah closed the crossword book and laid it aside. "I'm sorry that I didn't tell you before, but I didn't know how to bring it up," she admitted. "Marcie took me to the natural childbirth classes that hospitals give now; she's going to be my coach. Last night was the first class."

His mouth tightened, and again she caught the flicker of something deep in his eyes, the same unreadable something that had been there several times before. "I suppose I'm lucky you didn't ask Max," he said.

"Rome!" Shocked, a little hurt, she stared at him.

He made an abrupt movement with his hand. "Sorry. I didn't mean that. Damn!" he swore softly, sliding his hand to the back of his neck and rubbing the tense muscles there. "I'll be glad when this is over."

"A few more weeks," she whispered, watching him with her heart in her eyes. "What then?"

He breathed deeply, his powerful chest stretching the fabric of his shirt. There were grim lines in his face, bracketing his mouth. "Then I'll have my wife back," he said bluntly.

"I know it's been difficult for you—"

"No, you don't know. You don't have any idea." His voice grew sharp. "You made it pretty plain when you gave me your ultimatum: Put up with it, or get out. You want that baby more than you want me. I thought about it, harder than I've ever thought about anything before in my life, and I came close to leaving, but in the end I decided to take what I could get. I may come in second with you for now, but that state of affairs won't last. When that baby is out of the way, when I can touch you again, you're going to be my wife, first and foremost, before anything else. If you can't live with that, tell me now."

She sat very still, a little pale, but meeting his gaze unwaveringly. "Your wife is all I've ever wanted to be."

"I don't want the baby between us. Take care of it, yes, but when I come home at night, your time becomes mine. I want your attention, all of it, without you jumping and running every time it whimpers."

"Even if it's sick, or hurt?" Couldn't he hear his own words? Did he really expect her to ignore her own child?

He winced, as if he suddenly realized what he was asking. "No, of course not." Shaken, he looked at her. "I don't know if I can handle it. I want you, only you, the way it was before. I don't want anyone else intruding.''

"We'll manage," she said softly, wanting to put her arms around him and reassure him of her love, but she knew he'd recoil from the pressure of her stomach. But something of what she was thinking must have been in her eyes, because he got to his feet and leaned over her. For the first time in weeks he kissed her, not just a brief touch of his lips to her cheek or forehead, but a deep, intimate kiss. She met it shyly, almost afraid to respond, but he cupped her chin and kissed her again, demanding and receiving the passion that he knew she could give.

"How much longer?" he murmured, lifting his head.

"About three weeks until it's born, then...six more weeks after that."

He sighed. "It'll be the longest nine weeks of my life."

The next week another trip came up unexpectedly. He'd been curtailing his traveling, with Max often going in his place, but Max was on the East Coast already when the emergency cropped up in Los Angeles. Like a general directing his troops, Anson Edwards sent Rome to California.

When he told her, Rome saw the disappointment on her face. "It won't be a long trip," he tried to comfort her. "Three days, at the most. The baby isn't due for another two weeks, and I'll call you every night."

"I'm not worried about the baby," she said honestly. "I'll *miss* you!"

"Not for long. I'll drive everyone into the ground getting this mess cleared up," he said grimly, then

stunned her by taking her in his arms, the first time
he'd done that in months. Ignoring the bulk of her
stomach, he kissed her with growing desire, his hand
going to her full straining breasts. "I didn't know," he
said in astonishment, lifting his head and staring at the
ripe curves that filled his hand. "You've grown more
than I'd realized."

A warm blush was on Sarah's cheeks as she leaned
against him. He laughed and kissed her again, still
fondling her. "I'll be back before you know it," he
promised.

Late that night an ache low in her back woke Sarah,
and she lay awake for a long time, but the ache faded
and she sighed in relief. The baby was still, for a
change, and she'd been sleeping deeply. She didn't
want the baby to come while Rome was so far away;
even though he wouldn't be in the labor room with
her, or helping her with the delivery, she wanted to
know that he was close at hand. As her time approached, she began to fret about the trauma of birth;
she'd have clung to him like a frightened child if they
were closer, if circumstances hadn't put a wedge between them.

The next afternoon the ache began again and laced
around to her lower abdomen. It wasn't really pain,
just an achy, heavy tightened feeling, but she knew.
She alerted Marcie, then called Dr. Easterwood, who
instructed her to check into the hospital then, rather
than waiting until the contractions were close together. Sarah's next call was to Rome's hotel in Los
Angeles; he wasn't in, but she hadn't expected him to
be at that time of day. She left a message that she was
beginning labor and told him which hospital she would

be in. As she hung up a tear rolled down her cheek. She so wanted Rome there! But she wiped it away and touched her stomach. "We're on our way," she told her baby.

Marcie came up to collect the suitcase, and Mrs. Melton hugged Sarah; then they went to the hospital. Sarah was checked in and checked over. She was in the preliminary stages of labor, and everything looked normal. All she had to do was wait.

Rome sat in the office he'd commandeered from the West Coast district manager, an array of numbers and statistics before him, but he couldn't concentrate on paperwork. He tapped his pen thoughtfully on the blotter, wishing he were at home with Sarah, rather than having to patiently sort out a mess that never should have developed in the first place.

Sarah. She was more on his mind lately than she'd ever been before, and he'd spent a lot of time over the years thinking about her. She was so determined to have that baby, and she'd dug in her heels with a stubbornness that belied her delicate, elegant appearance. He'd somehow never thought that Sarah would be the motherly type, though Justin and Shane had adored their "aunt" Sarah.

He winced as he thought their names, and their images swam before his eyes, coming between him and the papers spread out on the desk. Laughing, rowdy little boys, with Diane's bright blue eyes and golden brown hair. How he missed them! How he'd loved them, through every stage of their development from the moment he knew of Diane's pregnancies. Diane had gotten as big as a barrel with both of them, unable to struggle out of bed or even out of a chair without his help. Many times during the night when advanced pregnancy would force her to the bathroom every hour, he'd pulled guard duty, always ready to give her a supporting hand. He'd rubbed her back for her, tied her shoes for her, held her hand during labor, and supported and comforted her during delivery.

He'd done none of those things for Sarah.

He went rigid with the thought. She wasn't as big as Diane had been, of course, but he'd seen her carefully edging her weight forward on a chair so she could get up, and he hadn't helped her. He'd left her alone in her bed to cope with backaches and midnight visits to the bathroom. She hadn't asked for help in anything, and he realized with a spear of pain that took his breath, that she hadn't asked because he'd made it plain she couldn't rely on his aid. She'd needed help, every day, but she'd never asked. She'd borne the burden of pregnancy alone, with the knowledge in her eyes that he didn't want her child.

Beads of sweat broke out on his forehead. Regardless of how he felt about the baby, he should have been with Sarah, helping her through the months. In a detached way, he could even understand why she was so determined to have the baby: Because she loved him, she also loved his child. Sarah didn't throw screaming fits, didn't demand anything from him; she simply waited, and loved him, never giving up on that love. There was a gentle strength in her that had enabled her to wait for him for years, loving him, yet still being a good friend, the best of friends, to Diane. She'd loved his sons and been silently at his side when he stood by their graves, thinking that there was no reason left for him to live.

She had many graces, but the sweetest grace of all was the bottomless, unending love she gave, its gentle glow bathing everyone in her acquaintance, and he was at the center of that glow. How could he have discounted its worth?

Without thinking, obeying an impulse that was undeniable for all that it remained nameless, he picked up the phone and called her. Mrs. Melton answered the phone, and a moment later he dropped the receiver back onto its cradle, his face pale.

He opened the door and barked at the secretary sitting at her desk outside, "Get me a flight to Dallas, right now. I don't care what airline, as long as it's the next one out. My wife has gone into labor."

Galvanized by both his tone of voice and the priority every woman gave to birth, the secretary got on the phone and in only a moment was demanding that a seat be found for Mr. Matthews.

Rome piled the reports into his briefcase and slammed it shut. He should have been there, damn it! She was two weeks early; was something wrong?

Dr. Easterwood had warned him of the possibility of complications. He knew, personally, how narrow Sarah's pelvis was; how often had he held her hips in his hands as he made love to her, marveling at how slim and delicate she was? The baby wasn't a large one, but was it too large? If anything happened to her—

He couldn't complete the thought.

He never knew what strings the secretary pulled, or whose name she invoked, but someone was bumped off a flight leaving within the hour for Dallas, and he was on it. He didn't have time to return to his hotel and check out, or get his clothing. He gave terse instructions to the secretary to have that done, and get his suitcase shipped to him. He said "thank you" roughly, then left.

Let Anson Edwards and Spencer-Nyle wait. Sarah was more important.

Four and a half hours later, after a ground delay in Los Angeles that had seemed interminable, an inordinately slow flight, and battling the traffic from the airport to the hospital where Mrs. Melton had told him Sarah had gone, he strode up to the desk nurse on the maternity floor.

Sarah was dozing, while Marcie quietly read a magazine. Both Sarah and the baby were being closely monitored, but time was dragging and nothing was really happening, though the twinges were getting closer together. They were in a private labor room; a television was mounted on the wall, and they'd watched the evening news, then a situation comedy. She'd thought Rome would have called before then, but perhaps he was being held up at the office. After all, there was a time difference of two hours.

He came into the room and Marcie looked up, her eyes widening. She got to her feet. "Where did you come from?"

"Los Angeles," he replied, his strong mouth quirking in momentary amusement. "I caught the first flight out when Mrs. Melton told me Sarah had gone into labor."

Sarah's eyes fluttered open, and she looked at him drowsily; then abruptly she was wide awake. "Rome! You're here!"

"I'm here," he said gently, taking her hand.

"I called your hotel and left a message for you."

"I know; Mrs. Melton told me. I've also talked with Dr. Easterwood. I was in a panic, afraid something was wrong because it's two weeks too soon, but she said everything's all right."

"I'm really not in labor yet, just trying to be, but she wanted me here so she could keep an eye on me."

She was beautiful, he thought. Her white-gold hair was pulled up, away from her face, and twisted into a single long braid. Her eyes were bright and clear, a soft Nile green, and her cheeks were flushed. She wore one of the plain nightgowns she'd been wearing at home, and she looked about fourteen, certainly not old enough to be having the infant who made a mound against the fabric. He kissed her gently.

"Since you're here, I'm going to go down to the cafeteria and get something to eat," Marcie said cheerfully, with the obvious intention of giving them some time alone and not being abashed about it.

But when they were alone, it was difficult to say anything. He held her hand, wishing that it was already over with, that she didn't have to face labor and birth. He didn't want her to be in any pain, not even the natural pain of having a child.

Finally he drew a deep breath. "I won't go in the delivery room with you, but I'll be waiting."

"Just knowing that you're here is all I need," she said, and it was.

Her daughter was born twelve hours later, after a relatively easy labor and birth. "Oh, she's a tiny sweetheart," Dr. Easterwood cooed as she placed the baby in Sarah's arms. "Look at that black hair!"

"She looks like Rome," Marcie pronounced flatly, only her laughing, tear-filled eyes visible above the surgical mask she wore. "I swear, she's even got black eyes."

Sarah examined the tiny infant, who'd already stopped her outraged squalling and was lying as if tired from her ordeal, ready to go to sleep. Rome's daughter. She couldn't believe it. Somehow, she'd thought it would be a boy. Tears filled her eyes as she touched the damp black curls with a shaking finger. This was the most precious thing she'd ever seen.

Several hours later she woke to find Rome sitting quietly beside her bed; she'd been so sleepy when she was placed in her bed, she'd only been able to give him a smile before drifting off. She didn't say anything but watched him as he read the newspaper. He was tired; he'd been up all night, and dark circles lay under his eyes. He needed a shave too, but he was gorgeous. With the enthusiasm of a new mother, she wanted to ask him if he'd seen the baby, but she knew he hadn't. By even coming to the hospital, he'd given her more than she'd expected.

"Hi," she said softly.

He looked up, relaxing as a deep relief spread through him. Somehow, until she spoke to him, he'd been afraid to believe she was all right. He took her hand and carried it to his lips, tenderly kissing her soft palm. "Hi, yourself. How do you feel?"

She considered her state of being, moving gingerly. "Not too bad. Better than I'd expected. How do *you* feel?"

"Dead on my tail," he said, making her laugh.

"Why don't you go home and get some sleep? I'm not going anywhere."

"You'd better not." He let her convince him to go home, because he really needed to get some sleep before he fell on his face.

When the baby was brought to her to nurse, Sarah cried when the tiny rosebud mouth automatically rooted for her nipple. Her very own baby! She was thirty-four years old and had long ago given up the thought of being a mother, but now she had this minute living, breathing miracle in her arms. She stroked the downy hair that covered the small round head, then examined the incredibly small fingers, the shell of her ear. How very much like Rome she was! There was even a smooth olive tint to her skin, a hint of her father's darkness, and her eyebrows mimicked Rome's bold slant.

The baby opened her eyes, looked around vaguely, then closed them again, evidently content that everything was right in her world. Marcie had been right; she had Rome's eyes too.

She named the baby Melissa Kay, and by the time she went home three days later, the name had already evolved into Missy. Rome had spent a lot of time with Sarah at the hospital, but he always stepped out when it was time for the baby to be brought in to her, and as far as she knew, he hadn't seen it. He didn't drive them home from the hospital—she hadn't expected him to—and she understood that she'd have been asking too

much of him if she'd tried to introduce him to his child
by that method. He would have to decide for himself
if he wanted to know his own daughter. Marcie drove
them home, and together they placed the baby in her
crib for the first time, both of them leaning over to
admire the way she squirmed around until she was
comfortable.

Missy was beautiful; Sarah knew that, if given the
chance, she was capable of working the second miracle.

Chapter Twelve

Rome took Sarah to bed and held her against him for the first time in months, his arms tender. He kissed her over and over, as if he couldn't get enough of having her in bed with him again. He was careful not to jostle her, but he felt an almost desperate need to hold her. Sarah curled against him, wishing that the six weeks were over instead of having barely begun. Her hands sought his hard, muscular body, traveling lightly over him as she reacquainted herself with the various textures of his flesh. "I love you," she said against his throat.

"I love you. Never again," he said deeply. "I'll never let you sleep away from me again."

Sarah slept contentedly but woke at the first small cry Missy gave that signaled her hunger. Gingerly she slipped from the bed and tiptoed down to the nursery to cuddle her daughter and reassure her that she wasn't in danger of starving. She changed the baby's diaper, then sat down in the rocker and hummed as she nursed Missy, slowly rocking back and forth. Missy wasn't a fussy baby, and she went to sleep immediately after her stomach was filled. Gently Sarah placed her back in the cradle, then returned to her own bed, snuggling against the warmth of Rome's back.

He didn't move, but his eyes were open, and he stared stonily at the wall.

Sarah had worked hard before, but she'd never worked as hard or been under as much strain as she was in the following weeks. If Missy hadn't been a good baby, it would have been impossible. During the day, after Rome left for work, Sarah spent as much time as she could with her daughter, playing with her, doing all of the things that a baby required. Mrs. Melton took care of the mounds of laundry and the cleaning, which freed Sarah for all her other duties. She tried to give Missy bottles as a supplementary feeding, but the formula made her spit up, and the pediatrician advised Sarah to feed the baby solely by breast until she was a little older; then they'd try the formula again. That meant she couldn't leave Missy alone for any length of time, as she demanded regular feedings.

She always had Missy bathed and in bed for the night before Rome came home from work and kept her fingers crossed that the baby wouldn't wake before it was time for her usual feeding. The door to the nursery was always closed when Rome was home, and he never glanced at it, never asked about the baby. He'd told her how it would be, but until she lived the reality of it, Sarah hadn't realized just how difficult she'd find it. She was so proud of Missy, she wanted to take her to Rome, hold her out, and say, "See what I've given you." How could he fail to be as enchanted with the baby as she was? But she always reminded herself that the next step was his, that she couldn't force him.

Other people weren't so reticent. Max came to dinner one night and insisted on going in to see the baby. Sarah cast a helpless glance at Rome's set face, then got to her feet to take Max to the nursery. Marcie and Derek were frequent visitors, and they weren't shy about talking about Missy in front of Rome. Because he couldn't close his ears, he heard in enthusiastic detail from Marcie just how beautiful his daughter was. He knew that she was growing like wildfire and that already she recognized people.

A haunted look came into his eyes. He tried not to think about the nursery or its occupant, but a painful curiosity seized him every time Sarah got up in the middle of the night and went in there. He sometimes thought of standing in the doorway and looking in, but a cold sweat would break out on him. A baby...no, he couldn't handle another baby. She wasn't Justin or Shane; she couldn't replace his sons. He couldn't take the risk.

The thought of a daughter was alien to him. He'd known only husky rough-playing little boys. He thought often of his boys, as Christmas approached, another Christmas spent without them. It was his second Christmas with Sarah, and he found that the pain was almost gone because he had her. There was still, and would always be, a haunting sense of loss, but it was bearable now. He could think of Justin and Shane, and remember the good times, the hilarious things they'd done. Diane was farther from him; there was still love for her, but it was more of a remembered love. Sarah was his present, and he was stunned anew by the fierce passion he felt for her, eclipsing the relationship he'd had with Diane, because his capacity for love had increased so much under Sarah's gentle glow.

One night during the second week of December Sarah went into his arms as usual, her head finding its customary place on his shoulder. "I'll be going back to the store tomorrow," she said casually, her voice soft in the darkness.

Moving swiftly, he reached out and turned on the lamp, then propped himself up on one elbow and loomed over her, his brows drawn together. "Dr. Easterwood released you?" he asked sharply.

"Yes. I had my checkup today. She said I'm in perfect health." She gave him a slow, bewitching smile.

It was fascinating to watch the way desire changed his face, made it harder and more intent. "Then, why did you wear that nightgown to bed?"

"So you could take it off."

He did. He was very careful with her, slowly building her to a state of readiness before bracing himself atop her and easing himself into her body. Sarah gasped, but not with pain. It had been so long! She clung tightly to him, quivering with almost unbearable pleasure. His hands were everywhere on her newly lush figure, discovering and delighting in the fullness of her breasts, stroking her intimately. She lost her grasp on reality, carried away by delight to a different realm of consciousness where only he existed.

Wrapped warmly against the weather, Missy was taken to the store the next morning, and Sarah had to fight to get to hold her own child. She was careful not to overdo it, and they went home early, but the excursion had tired both of them. She put Missy down for her nap, then crawled sleepily into her own bed. She'd just take a short nap, she told herself.

Missy's fretful cry woke her and she started up; the growing twilight told her that she'd slept much later than she'd intended and Rome would soon be home. Missy was ravenous; there was a lot to be done, but Missy wouldn't wait. Sarah sat down in the rocking chair and put the baby to her breast.

She didn't hear Rome come in, but suddenly she felt his presence, and she looked anxiously at the door. She felt weak when she saw him standing just beyond the door, not stepping inside, but his eyes were on her and the baby in her arms. He couldn't see anything but the top of Missy's head and one tiny hand as it kneaded Sarah's breast, but a spasm of pain crossed his face. Without a word, he turned and walked away.

Sarah stared down at the baby, shaking. She'd messed up her schedule, she realized. She should have bathed her before nursing her, because now Missy was going to sleep, and she wouldn't take kindly to being roused by her bath. What would she do if Missy decided to throw a howling temper tantrum? As she grew older she was showing definite signs of her father's temper, as well as a comic determination to have everything just the way she wanted it, if an infant that young could be said to be that discriminating. But there was a certain way she liked to be held, and other small things that had to be just right to satisfy her. She would fuss indefinitely until circumstances were righted. To keep things quiet, Sarah decided to skip the bath for one night, and she changed Missy's clothes, then put her to bed, hoping she'd sleep after that long nap.

"I took a nap this afternoon and overslept," she explained a little nervously to Rome when she came out of the nursery.

His shoulders were tense, but he didn't say anything about Missy. Instead he picked up on the way Sarah had given herself away. "Going to the store tired you out, didn't it?"

"Yes, and it's so silly, because I didn't *do* anything," she said in exasperation, glad that the tense moment had passed.

"You'll have to get used to it all over again, and I want you to do it gradually. Take it easy," he ordered, and kissed her hello.

But of course, for Sarah, there was no taking it easy. She threw herself back into the routine of the store with joy, for she'd missed it more than she'd ever imagined. She was always careful to leave early enough to get Missy taken care of before Rome came home, but the infant was becoming so active that Sarah could already foresee the day when there wouldn't be any of this putting her to bed and watching her go promptly off to sleep. Every day she was awake longer, her legs and arms waving around energetically.

After a particularly exhausting day, Sarah fell deeply asleep as soon as her head hit the pillow. Rome lay beside her, slowly relaxing, and was almost asleep himself when he heard the baby cry. He went stiff, waiting for Sarah to wake and go to the child. He couldn't stand hearing that cry. But Sarah was still asleep beside him; she'd worn herself out.

He knew she'd eventually hear the baby's cry and get up to tend it, but he didn't know if he could stand it that long. A moment later he knew that he couldn't. He reached out to shake Sarah awake; then something stopped him. Perhaps it was her face, so peaceful as she slept; perhaps it was the nights in years past when he'd gotten up in the middle of the night to answer a sleepy cry for daddy. For whatever reason, he got out of bed and found himself standing out in the hallway.

He realized with surprise that he was shaking, and sweat was running down his spine. It's just a baby, he told himself. Just a baby.

He stretched his hand out and opened the door, scarcely able to breathe from the band that was constricting his chest. There was a small yellow night-light plugged into an outlet close to the crib, enabling Sarah to see when she got up in the middle of the night. It also enabled Rome to see the child, who'd worked herself into a furious tantrum. Her tiny fists were clenched and jerking spasmodically, her legs were drawn up, and she was squalling for all she was worth. She was used to having her wants catered to immediately; this unreasonable delay wasn't something she intended to tolerate.

He swallowed, slowly walking closer to the crib. She was so small, the temper she exhibited was ludicrous. A girl . . . what did he know about girl babies?

Shaking, he slid his big hands under the infant and lifted her, surprised at how light she was. Missy squalled a few more times, but the touch of those big hands told her she wasn't alone, and after a few hiccuping sobs she quieted.

Old skills came back to him automatically. Hurrying, without looking at her face, he changed her diaper and was about to settle her back into the crib when she made a cooing noise, and he jerked, almost dropping her. He looked at her and froze, mesmerized, as the baby looked at him with such innocent trust and acceptance that he almost screamed aloud with pain.

It wasn't fair. Sweet heaven, it wasn't fair. He'd avoided her, hadn't even held her, hadn't looked at her; he'd rejected his own child, but none of that made any difference to her. She didn't scream in fear at being in unfamiliar hands. She simply looked at her father with automatic acceptance, then began trying diligently to control a waving fist long enough to stuff it into her open, avid mouth.

Looking at her was like looking at himself, immortalized. He stared in fascination at the dark hair, the almost-black eyes. Her mouth was Sarah's, he realized, a soft, tender mouth, but the rest of her was a feminine version of himself. She'd been born from the sweet, loving times in Sarah's arms, a part of Sarah, a part of himself. He'd wanted her life destroyed before it even began.

A low, raw cry came from his lips. He lifted her again, cradling her in his arms, and he sank to his knees. Bending over his child, he cried.

Sarah jerked awake, knowing that something was different. Her hand sought Rome but found only the empty pillow, and she sat up. An odd, strangled noise came to her ears, but it didn't sound like Missy. She whispered ''Rome?'' but there was no answer.

Quickly getting out of bed, she reached for her robe, pulling it around her. Going to the door, she looked for any light to indicate where he might be, but there was none. Then she heard the choking noise again, and she went cold. It came from the nursery. Missy was choking!

Her hand at her throat, she flew on silent bare feet down the hall, but only a split second had passed before she realized that it wasn't Missy. She stopped, her breath ragged. Rome?

The nursery door was open, and she moved silently so she could see into the room.

Rome was on his knees on the floor, Missy in his arms. He held her cuddled to his chest, and the raw, strangled sounds came from him.

Sarah almost moaned aloud. She wanted to go to him, to wrap her arms around him and comfort him in his grief, grief for the children he'd lost, grief for the child he hadn't wanted. But this was his private moment of recognition with his daughter, and Sarah silently made her way back to bed.

She lay quietly, wiping away the tears as they wet her face. It was a long time before Rome came back to bed, sliding under the covers in a careful manner. She could tell that he was simply lying there, unable to sleep, but she didn't reach out for him. He was fighting a terrible inner war, and she couldn't help him.

He didn't mention it the next day, but there was a quietness about him, a sense of peace that hadn't been there before. He left for the office, and Sarah dressed Missy for her day at the store. There was nothing she could do but carry on exactly as she had before.

Derek only had a half-day of school, and he came in after lunch. Deftly he lifted Missy from her carrier, kissing her downy cheek. With the incredible sense of timing he had, he looked at Sarah as he jiggled the baby. "Is everything going to be all right for you?" he asked.

"Yes, I really think it will be," she replied. "How did you know?"

"The way you look." He smiled at her with deep tenderness. "I knew he wouldn't be able to resist her for long."

Perhaps Derek had inside information, Sarah thought, watching him as he walked around the store with Missy in his strong young arms, talking to her as if she understood every word he said, and showing her all the brightly colored items that would interest her. And perhaps she did understand him; Max had compared Derek to an archangel. He might not be an angel, but he walked with them.

Sarah didn't deviate from her routine; Missy was sound asleep when Rome came in from the office. They ate dinner as usual, talked casually; she read while he read a few reports. Then she got ready for bed, checked on Missy, and crawled gratefully into bed, yawning.

Rome came out of the bathroom, drying his broad shoulders. ''Here,'' he said, tossing the towel to her. ''Dry my back.''

He sat on the bed and she rubbed the towel over his back, then pressed a quick kiss on his spine. Tossing the towel to the floor, he turned to push her onto the pillows. ''I can't tell you how much I love you,'' he said quietly.

''Try,'' she urged.

He laughed, bending down to kiss her with growing hunger. His lovemaking was incredibly sweet and intense that night; he held back, satisfying her time and again before letting himself go, then holding her tightly until she slept.

Missy woke in the early hours, wanting to be fed. Before Sarah could get out of bed, Rome threw the covers back and got to his feet. ''Stay there,'' he said. ''I'll bring her in here.''

In a moment he was back, with a fussing infant in his arms. As he gave her to Sarah he said, ''You know, don't you? You were awake last night.''

''Yes, I know.'' All the love in the world shone out of her eyes as she looked at him.

''You should hate me,'' he said roughly. ''For what I wanted to do.''

''No, never. You were hurting, and you wanted to protect yourself. I understood.''

He looked at the baby as she nursed, and his hard dark face took on such a tender expression that Sarah came apart inside. Very gently he touched Missy's cheek with one forefinger. ''She's more than I deserve. I got a second chance all the way around, didn't I?''

No, not a second chance, a second miracle. He'd been a man dead inside, and love had brought life back to him. He'd always carry the scars that marked the people he'd loved and lost, but he could go on living now. He could laugh again, and enjoy the passing of the seasons. He could watch his child grow, delight in her shrieks of laughter, her innocence and enthusiasm, and give his love wholeheartedly to his second miracle.

He leaned over and kissed Sarah with slow deliberation, with love and passion. When Missy had been fed and was in her crib, he wanted to make love to his wife again, to show her how much he loved her. She was his first miracle, bringing him back into the sunlight.

*　*　*　*　*

FOUR UNIQUE SERIES
FOR EVERY WOMAN YOU ARE...

Silhouette Romance ®

Tender, delightful, provocative—stories that capture the laughter, the tears, the *joy* of falling in love. Pure romance...straight from the heart!

SILHOUETTE *Desire* ®

Go wild with Desire! Passionate, emotional, sensuous stories of fiery romance. With heroines you'll like and heroes you'll *love*, Silhouette Desire never fails to deliver.

Silhouette Special Edition ®

Stories of love and life, these powerful novels are tales that you can identify with—romances with "something special" added in! Silhouette Special Edition is entertainment for the heart.

SILHOUETTE·INTIMATE·MOMENTS™

Enter a world where passions run hot and excitement is the rule. Dramatic, larger-than-life and always compelling—Silhouette Intimate Moments will never let you down.

SGENERIC

SILHOUETTE®
OFFICIAL SWEEPSTAKES
RULES

NO PURCHASE NECESSARY

1. To enter, complete an Official Entry Form or 3"× 5" index card by hand-printing, in plain block letters, your complete name, address, phone number and age, and mailing it to: Silhouette Fashion A Whole New You Sweepstakes, P.O. Box 9056, Buffalo, NY 14269-9056.

   No responsibility is assumed for lost, late or misdirected mail. Entries must be sent separately with first class postage affixed, and be received no later than December 31, 1991 for eligibility.

2. Winners will be selected by D.L. Blair, Inc., an independent judging organization whose decisions are final, in random drawings to be held on January 30, 1992 in Blair, NE at 10:00 a.m. from among all eligible entries received.

3. The prizes to be awarded and their approximate retail values are as follows: Grand Prize — A brand-new Ford Explorer 4×4 plus a trip for two (2) to Hawaii, including round-trip air transportation, six (6) nights hotel accommodation, a $1,400 meal/spending money stipend and $2,000 cash toward a new fashion wardrobe (approximate value: $28,000) or $15,000 cash; two (2) Second Prizes — A trip to Hawaii, including round-trip air transportation, six (6) nights hotel accommodation, a $1,400 meal/spending money stipend and $2,000 cash toward a new fashion wardrobe (approximate value: $11,000) or $5,000 cash; three (3) Third Prizes — $2,000 cash toward a new fashion wardrobe. All prizes are valued in U.S. currency. Travel award air transportation is from the commercial airport nearest winner's home. Travel is subject to space and accommodation availability, and must be completed by June 30, 1993. Sweepstakes offer is open to residents of the U.S. and Canada who are 21 years of age or older as of December 31, 1991, except residents of Puerto Rico, employees and immediate family members of Torstar Corp., its affiliates, subsidiaries, and all agencies, entities and persons connected with the use, marketing, or conduct of this sweepstakes. All federal, state, provincial, municipal and local laws apply. Offer void wherever prohibited by law. Taxes and/or duties, applicable registration and licensing fees, are the sole responsibility of the winners. Any litigation within the province of Quebec respecting the conduct and awarding of a prize may be submitted to the Régie des loteries et courses du Québec. All prizes will be awarded; winners will be notified by mail. No substitution of prizes is permitted.

4. Potential winners must sign and return any required Affidavit of Eligibility/Release of Liability within 30 days of notification. In the event of noncompliance within this time period, the prize may be awarded to an alternate winner. Any prize or prize notification returned as undeliverable may result in the awarding of that prize to an alternate winner. By acceptance of their prize, winners consent to use of their names, photographs or their likenesses for purposes of advertising, trade and promotion on behalf of Torstar Corp. without further compensation. Canadian winners must correctly answer a time-limited arithmetical question in order to be awarded a prize.

5. For a list of winners (available after 3/31/92), send a separate stamped, self-addressed envelope to: Silhouette Fashion A Whole New You Sweepstakes, P.O. Box 4665, Blair, NE 68009.

PREMIUM OFFER TERMS

To receive your gift, complete the Offer Certificate according to directions. Be certain to enclose the required number of "Fashion A Whole New You" proofs of product purchase (which are found on the last page of every specially marked "Fashion A Whole New You" Silhouette or Harlequin romance novel). Requests must be received no later than December 31, 1991. Limit: four (4) gifts per name, family, group, organization or address. Items depicted are for illustrative purposes only and may not be exactly as shown. Please allow 6 to 8 weeks for receipt of order. Offer good while quantities of gifts last. In the event an ordered gift is no longer available, you will receive a free, previously unpublished Silhouette or Harlequin book for every proof of purchase you have submitted with your request, plus a refund of the postage and handling charge you have included. Offer good in the U.S. and Canada only.

SLFW-SWPR

SILHOUETTE® OFFICIAL SWEEPSTAKES ENTRY FORM

4-FWSES-1

Complete and return this Entry Form immediately – the more entries you submit, the better your chances of winning!

- Entries must be received by **December 31, 1991**.
- A Random draw will take place on **January 30, 1992**.
- No purchase necessary.

Yes, I want to win a FASHION A WHOLE NEW YOU Sensuous and Adventurous prize from Silhouette:

Name _____ Telephone _____ Age _____

Address _____

City _____ State _____ Zip _____

Return Entries to: **Silhouette FASHION A WHOLE NEW YOU,**
P.O. Box 9056, Buffalo, NY 14269-9056   © 1991 Harlequin Enterprises Limited

PREMIUM OFFER

To receive your free gift, send us the required number of proofs-of-purchase from any specially marked FASHION A WHOLE NEW YOU Silhouette or Harlequin Book with the Offer Certificate properly completed, plus a check or money order (do not send cash) to cover postage and handling payable to Silhouette FASHION A WHOLE NEW YOU Offer. We will send you the specified gift.

OFFER CERTIFICATE

Item	A. SENSUAL DESIGNER VANITY BOX COLLECTION (set of 4) (Suggested Retail Price $60.00)	B. ADVENTUROUS TRAVEL COSMETIC CASE SET (set of 3) (Suggested Retail Price $25.00)
# of proofs-of-purchase	18	12
Postage and Handling	$3.50	$2.95
Check one	☐	☐

Name _____

Address _____

City _____ State _____ Zip _____

Mail this certificate, designated number of proofs-of-purchase and check or money order for postage and handling to: **Silhouette FASHION A WHOLE NEW YOU Gift Offer,** P.O. Box 9057, Buffalo, NY 14269-9057. Requests must be received by December 31, 1991.

ONE PROOF-OF-PURCHASE

4-FWSEP-1

To collect your fabulous free gift you must include the necessary number of proofs-of-purchase with a properly completed Offer Certificate.

© 1991 Harlequin Enterprises Limited

See previous page for details.